Kaiki:
Uncanny Tales from Japan

Volume 1 – Tales of Old Edo

Kaiki: Uncanny Tales from Japan
Volume 1: Tales of Old Edo

Book design and layout by j-views, Kamakura, Japan: info@j-views.biz

FG-JP0007-L2
ISBN-13: 978-4-902075-08-3

KURODAHAN PRESS
KURODAHAN.COM

Kaiki:
Uncanny Tales from Japan

Volume 1 – Tales of Old Edo

Foreword by Robert Weinberg
Introduction by Higashi Masao

Contents

CONTENTS

An Ordinary World, Interrupted

Robert Weinberg

PERHAPS THE GREATEST failing of anthologies and collections of supernatural fiction published in the past one hundred years has been the lack of representation of stories from Asia and the Pacific Rim. Volumes and volumes of ghost and spook stories are filled with tales from North America, the United Kingdom and Western Europe. Less common but still included in the more comprehensive collections are narratives from South America, Eastern Europe, and Africa. However, few if any books contain stories from China or Japan. Though supernatural fiction is a mainstay of Oriental storytelling and culture, just about none of it has ever been published in the West. Until now.

This volume, *Kaiki, Uncanny Tales from Japan*, is the first of three collections of uncanny stories edited by Higashi Masao, scheduled to be published by Kurodahan Press. It offers a fascinating and informative glimpse at the best supernatural fiction printed in Japan during the past hundred years. Unlike books of western ghost stories, which are usually arranged in strict chronological order, each Kurodahan collection gathers together stories sorted by time and location. Thus, this first volume is devoted to tales of "Old Edo," the capital of the Tokugawa Shogunate, which ruled Japan from 1603 to 1868, when the city was renamed Tokyo. The two following books will contain stories about "the provinces," and "Tokyo."

This collection begins with an exhaustive and informative introduction by the editor, Higashi Masao, on the origin and history of the Japanese supernatural story. Masao makes the interesting point that while there is a long tradition of strange and unusual fiction in Japan, the classic horror elements so common in the English and European ghost story are not always present in the Japanese story. Thus, this volume contains tales that are not the least bit horrific – such as "The Pointer" by Kōda Rohan. The long narrative tells of two fishermen who find what they suspect is a haunted fishing pole, and what they do with it. Told in a relaxed narrative style and filled with a wealth of information about how to fish Japanese rivers using all manners of equipment and what sort of fish one might expect to catch doing so, the story's supernatural element is so mild that it hardly registers on the reader's awareness. Indeed, except for the minor supernatural riff at the conclusion of the story, the tale might have been categorized as a "fishing story" instead of a "ghost story." Which perhaps is the point.

Not all Japanese ghost stories are horrific, or even violent, in nature. Most of them treat the ghostly manifestations as a part of the natural order of things. Though, sometimes that order is helter-skelter and not what we expect it to be. Take, for example, the tale titled "The Face in the Hearth" by Tanaka Kōtarō, written in 1938. The story begins with a high-born samurai warrior on vacation at a hot springs, playing a game of go with the manager of the spring. From there, it takes a slightly unexpected turn as a wandering monk comes along and challenges the samurai to a game. The story drifts along at a slow but steady pace until the samurai makes an unexpected and horrific discovery in the woods. Suddenly, the tale speeds up and another, greater and more unexpected horrible event takes place, leaving the reader to wonder if the events of the story were an example of destiny taking hold of a situation or was the gruesome end a result of the samurai not listening to the advice given to him early on in the story by the monk? No hint to an answer is given, leaving the reader to puzzle out the true nature of the horror encountered.

One of the most fascinating aspects of this collection is that the stories contained within are very similar and yet oddly different than the English ghost story as best demonstrated by M.R. James that were all the rage in England at approximately the same time as these were written. Though there is no evidence of crossed-storytelling, it is astonishing to read the best of James and then pick up this book and read several stories which, except for the unusual settings, could have been written by the master himself.

In all such cases, the basic genesis of the plot comes from the notion of "an ordinary occurrence, interrupted." By ordinary, we mean, the usual, normal aspect of life as practiced in both England and Japan. Thus, the event could be a man going on a long needed vacation trip in Europe, or a samurai balancing the books at his master's estate in Edo. The normalcy of the setting is extremely important, as without it, the uncanny events that follow would not be as powerful.

An ordinary occurrence could be the events of a day, the passage of time, the normalcy of life in a well-defined surrounding. What is most important is the feeling of absolute calm, that life is what it is and reality is unchanging. The violation of that principle is what makes the horror of the situation so much more frightening. Take, for example, the most unusual story in this entire collection, Kyōgoku Natsuhiko's very, very strange tale, "Where Had She Been?"

In this deceptively simple story, a beautiful young servant working in the mansion of a wealthy samurai disappears one day. No one can find her. She has not returned home, nor does she seem to have run off with some bandit. She had no quarrels with anyone and there is no reason to think she has died. It is a mystery as to where she has gone. Until, weeks later, the girl is discovered alive and living in a place no one would have ever suspected. (We will leave that discovery to the reader!) Here is where the Japanese and British ghost story veer in different directions. If composed by M.R. James, once the girl's location is found, supernatural violence would follow. There would be deaths and some explanation of what had taken place.

But, this being a Japanese weird story, there is no violence. More important, while the story hints at supernatural events, no supernatural events actually take place in the entire adventure. Questions are raised but there are no answers given. An explanation is mentioned but never verified. Still, the story makes a strong impression long after the book is closed. Is it a horror story? Or is it merely a strange story, an uncanny story? Or more precisely, a Japanese ghost story?

We'll leave that decision to the reader. Prepare then, to be captivated, puzzled, enchanted, and, from time to time, horrified. This is a collection of stories that you won't soon forget. These are tales of an ordinary world, interrupted by intruders from somewhere else. Enjoy.

Robert Weinberg
July 28, 2009

The Origins of Japanese Weird Fiction

Higashi Masao　　　　　　　　　　東 雅夫
Translated and with footnotes by Miri Nakamura

Uncanny Tales from Japan (Nihon kaiki shōsetsushū, 日本怪奇小説集) is an anthology of seminal fantastic fiction works, carefully handpicked from numerous modern and contemporary texts, ranging from the Meiji (1868–1911) and Taishō (1912–1925) eras through Shōwa (1926–1988) and Heisei (1989–). The three volumes are divided into the spatial categories of "Edo," "The Provinces," and "Tokyo."

As the editor, I endeavored to find works with great literary value, ignoring such so-called divisions as "pure literature" and "popular literature."[1] By reading this anthology, I believe that the reader will be able to experience first-hand the quality and the level of Japanese weird fiction.

At the end of each volume, I have also included a manga that has captured the essence of the Japanese fantastic in creative ways. My hope is that this will allow foreign readers who may not be familiar with Japanese culture, history, or customs to grasp the iconography of Japanese fantastic fiction in a more concrete manner.

---

1. This divide is one that was created in the Taishō era. "Pure literature" (*junsui bungaku*) refers to "canonical" literature, considered by the literary circle and critics to possess more aesthetic value than its opposite, "popular literature" or "mass literature" (*taishū bungaku*).

IN THIS OPENING volume, I would like to begin by explaining the term *kaiki shōsetsu* (怪奇小説, uncanny/strange/fantastic fiction).

First of all, in Japan, there were no specific genre names that corresponded to the Western "horror and supernatural fiction." Until World War II, the word *kaidan* (怪談, strange tales or ghost stories) was widely used, but this terminology was a fairly vague one that encompassed not only fiction but also folklore and oral performances. Thus, in the postwar era, on top of *kaidan*, genre names like *kai'i shōsetsu* (怪異小説, tales of the strange), *kyōfu shōsetsu* (恐怖小説, horror stories), *kaiki shōsetsu* (uncanny fiction) and *gensō to kaiki* (幻想と怪奇, the fantastic and the strange) also appeared as its equivalent, and in the mid-eighties, *horā* (horror) came to represent the field as its entirety.

Having said that, even today, ghost stories (including real tales) are often called *kaidan*, and classical horror (in the West, this would be fiction through Shirley Jackson and Robert Aickman) is also still referred to as *kaiki shōsetsu*. It is for this reason that in this anthology, I have chosen to use the term *kaiki shōsetsu* in order to capture the tradition of Japanese horror fiction that dates back to *kaidan* art forms.

THE BIRTH OF Japanese weird fiction (*kaiki shōsetsu*) as a modern literary genre can be traced back to the mid-seventeenth century. Of course, even before that period, one can point out classical texts that may qualify as such: the "Aoi" chapter in the famed *Tale of Genji* (Genji monogatari, ca. 11th century) where a spirit possession occurs, the numerous folkloric monster tales (*yōkai hengadan*) in short story format (*setsuwa*) that first appeared in the *Record of Ancient Matters* (Kojiki, 712) and continued through *Tales of Times Now Past* (Konjaku monogatari, ca. 12th century), *The Tale of the Heike* (Heike monogatari, ca. 13th century), and Muromachi era short fiction (Otogi zōshi, ca. 14th–16th century). There were also noh plays about ghost stories. Classical works that may be seen as being the origin of fantastic fiction are thus numerous, but the rise of the kind of weird fiction that specifically aimed at providing its audience with horrific pleasure had to wait, as in the West, until the modern era.

The year 1600 saw the division of Japan by the two great warrior forces who vied at the Battle of Sekigahara.[2] The victor Tokugawa Ieyasu then established the shogunate in Edo (present Tokyo) and thus the peaceful Edo period, which would continue for the next two hundred sixty-five years, was begun. During this period, Japanese culture developed rapidly, as did that of the West.

This development was especially evident in the field of publishing. Woodblock printing techniques in the Kan'ei era (1624–1644) helped to disseminate written works at a rate that was not possible with the older method of hand-copying texts (*shahon*). The readership also grew, as the new merchant class emerged. Popular texts written in kana[3] called "kana story-books" (*kana zōshi*) then arose to answer to the needs of this new readership, and in the 1660s, ghost story (*kaidan*) story-books based in the *setsuwa* tradition of ancient and medieval times became popularized.

IN 1661, THE famed Zen monk Suzuki Shōsan published *Tales of Cause and Effect* (Inga mongatari, 因果物語; his disciple later published a revised, enlarged hiragana edition). This was followed two years later by *The Tale of Sorori* (Sorori monogatari, 曾呂利物語, anonymous), celebrating the legendary storyteller Sorori Shinzaemon, who served under Toyotomi Hideyoshi as an *otogishū* (entertainers who served as storytellers for their lords). In 1666, Asai Ryōi, also a renowned monk and the representative author of mid-era kana storybooks, produced his masterpiece *Hand Puppets* (Otogi ōbōko, 伽婢子).

Literary scholar Takada Mamoru, editor of the seminal anthology in the field of early modern ghost stories, *Anthology of Edo Ghost Stories* (Edo kaidanshū, 江戸怪談集, 1989), has situated the three books as the forefathers of "Buddhist Lecture Style Ghost Stories," (*shōdō bukkyōkei kaidan*), "Folkloric Ghost Stories" (*minzokukei kaidan*), and "Chinese Style Ghost Stories" (*chūgoku shōsetsukei kaidan)*, respectively. He astutely

---

2. Famous battle that is often seen as the beginning of the Tokugawa shogunate. "The two great warrior forces" that Higashi mentions are the western forces of Ishida Mitsunori, one of the top advisors under Toyotomi Hideyoshi, and the eastern forces of Ieyasu.

3. Simplified handwriting derived from Chinese characters.

defines early modern ghost story anthologies as a mixture of these three types of tales.

Following the period above, in 1677, an anonymous collection of ghost stories called *One Hundred Tales of the Country* (Shokoku hyaku monogatari, 諸国百物語) was printed by a Kyoto publisher. Its preface states that it is a record of a one hundred ghost storytelling event, which took place one rainy night amongst a rōnin from Suwa (Shinshū province) named Takeda Nobuyuki and his fellow samurai warriors. The number of stories amount exactly to one hundred, with twenty stories in each of the five volumes. In other words, it is like a ghost story version of Chaucer's *Canterbury Tales*.

The very last story in *Hand Puppets*, "When One Narrates the Strange, the Strange Shall Arrive" (Kai o katareba kai itaru), explains this Japanese tradition of one hundred ghost storytelling:

> There is a set format to the one hundred storytelling. One must light candles wrapped in blue paper on a moonless night. After each story has been narrated, one must blow out a candle. Eventually, the space will become dark. The paper will reflect the blue color all around, and it will bring about an eerie atmosphere. They say that if one continues to tell the ghost stories even under those conditions, a strange occurrence or a frightening one will take place without fail.

Along with this "One Hundred Tales" format, there was another popular style of early modern ghost story anthology called "Country Tales" (*shokoku banashi*). These anthologies would have traveling literati or famous monks as their main characters, who would go around to various regions of Japan, collecting ghost stories and strange tales. The anthologies were then presented as "real" stories compiled into books by these travelers. Some representative works of this style are *Country Tales of Ikkyū* (Ikkyū shokoku monogatari, 一休諸国物語, ca. 1670) and *Country Tales of Sōgi* (Sōgi shokoku monogatari, 宗祇諸国物語, 1685).

The one writer who adapted this style and wrote a serialized short story collection (rather than a ghost story anthology) and brought about a great literary development was the early modern literati Ihara Saikaku with his *Country Tales of Saikaku*

(Saikaku shokoku banashi, 西鶴諸国ばなし, 1685) and *Portable Inkstone* (Futokoro suzuri, 懐硯, 1687). His works, renowned for his unique character portrayals and plots that are premeditated on the reader's reaction, are comparable to the fantastic stories by nineteenth-century Western writers like Mérimée, Gogol, and Maupassant.

After the kana storybooks (*kana zōshi*) and the genre of floating world storybooks (*ukiyo zōshi*) created by Saikaku, a new fictional genre called "reading books" (*yomihon*) emerged in the Kyoto region in the mid-eighteenth century. These "reading books" came about as Chinese vernacular tales called "baihua" (popular tales written in the vernacular language) were imported into Japan. In *Garland of Heroes* (Hanabusa zōshi, 英草紙, 1749), a collection of strange tales, Tsuga Teishō (a.k.a. Kinro Gyōja), the father of the genre, altered the original Chinese vernacular tales to set them in medieval Japan.

The representative author of early "reading books" Ueda Akinari's *Tales of Moonlight and Rain* (Ugetsu monogatari, 雨月物語, 1776) is a celebrated work of Edo period ghostly literature. Not only that, it is not an overstatement to say that the book is one of the top three all time best works of Japanese weird fiction. Many of you too may recall that it was the original text for director Mizoguchi Kenji's Ugetsu.[4]

In "White Peak" (Shiramine) a traveling monk visits the grave of an emperor and converses with his ghost. In the emotional tale of "The Reed-Choked House" (Asaji ga yado) a wife waits for the return of her husband from the capital even after her death. In "The Cauldron of Kibitsu" (Kibitsu no kama), a wife betrayed by her husband turns into a demon to haunt and brutally murder him and his lover. In "A Serpent's Lust" (Jasei no in) a snake spirit disguised as a beautiful woman stalks a handsome young man. "The Chrysanthemum Pledge" (Kikka no chigiri, 菊花の約) ends with a ghostly encounter that is brought about by the logic of bushido and its emphasis on righteousness. It may be described as one of the best works of early modern Japanese ghost tales. The beauty of the climactic scene where the ghost appears is simply one of a kind.

---

4. Mizoguchi's film, produced in 1953, is mainly based on two of the stories from *Moonlight and Rain* and weaves them together: "The Reed-Choked House" and "A Serpent's Lust."

IN THE EARLY nineteenth century, the so-called "Cultural Progress Eastern Advance" (*bun'un tōzen*) movement took place, where the cultural center moved from Western Japan to Eastern Japan, along with the rise of Edo as the shogunate's city. Along with this shift, the production of "reading books" also moved to Edo from the Kamigata region (today's Kyoto and Osaka area), and long serials referred to as "later reading books" (*kōki yomihon*) emerged.

These later works are represented by their creator Santō Kyōden (山東京伝), who wrote *Loyal Servants' Water Margin* (Chūshin suikoden, 忠臣水滸伝, 1799) and by the writer Takizawa Bakin (曲亭馬琴) with his epic work *The Eight Dogs of the House of Satomi* (Nansō satomi hakkenden, 南総里見 八犬伝, 1814-42). These texts were also influenced by Chinese vernacular tales as with their earlier counterparts, but they were also based on concepts such as karmic retribution and "reward the good punish the evil" theme.[5] The later "reading books" were enormous and complex: worlds full of heroes, villains, beautiful princesses, vengeful ghosts, spirits, magicians, and various demons. In a way, they were similar to their contemporary, Western gothic fiction.

The following seminal works of the genre have greatly influenced contemporary writers: Kyōden's *Revenge Tale of Asaka no Numa* (Fukushū kidan Asaka no Numa, 復讐奇談安積沼, 1803), *The Complete Legend of Princess Sakura* (Sakurahime zenden akebono zōshi, 桜姫全伝曙草紙, 1805), *Tales of the Past: Booklets of Lightning* (Mukashi banashi inazuma byōshi, 昔話 稲妻表紙, 1806), *Legend of the Loyal Servant Utō Yasutaka* (Utō Yasukata chūgiden, 善知安方忠義伝, 1806), Bakin's *Strange Tales of Moon and Ice* (Geppyō kien, 月氷奇縁, 1804), *The Complete Legend of Sankatsu and Hanshichi: The Dream of Nanka* (Sanshichi zenden nanka no yume, 三七全伝南柯夢, 1808), *Legend of Spiritual Master Raigō and His Rat Magic* (Raigō ajari kaisoden, 頼豪阿闍梨怪鼠伝, 1808), Ryūtei Tanehiko's (柳 亭種彦) *Early Modern Ghost Tales: Star of Dewey Night* (Kinsei kaidan shimoyo no hoshi, 近世怪談霜夜星, 1808), and *The Image of Asama Ravine* (Asamagatake omokage zōshi, 浅間 嶽面影草紙, 1809). These works have recently been "remade"

---

5. *Kanzen chōaku* was a common theme in later Edo literature, where good always triumphed and evil was always punished.

by contemporary writers, such as Terayama Shūji's (寺山修司) *New Version: Booklets of Lightning* (Shinshaku inazuma sōshi, 新釈稲妻草紙, 1974), Minagawa Hiroko's (皆川博子) *The Record of Mysterious Cherry Blossoms* (Yōōki, 妖櫻記, 1993), and Kyōgoku Natsuhiko's *Peeping Koheiji* (Nozoki Koheiji, 覘き小平次, 2002). In this manner, these works have created an uncanny lineage within Japanese literature, one that may be dubbed as "Japanese gothic tradition."

These "reading books" also came with numerous illustration and paper crafts, and one can see the fantastic imagination of ukiyo-e print artists like Katsushika Hokusai. The innovation and the details of their expressions of the strange often go beyond the content of the written works (see the illustration at the end of this introduction).

British literature scholar Andrew Lang once claimed in a chapter called "Some Japanese Bogie-Books" in *Books and Bookmen* (1886), "But our ogres are nothing to the bogies which make not only night but day terrible to the studious infants of Japan and China."[6] I hope that the reader will be able to observe the unleashing of demonic transformations in the artwork, ones proclaimed to be the most fearful in the world.

DURING THE BUNKA and Bunsei eras (1804–29), when Kyōden, Bakin, and Tanehiko were competing to produce later "reading books," the world of kabuki theater had also moved to the city of Edo. Playwright Tsuruya Nanboku IV (四世鶴屋南北), a scenario writer of kabuki kyōgen[7] acclaimed as a genius, also brought about a movement that may be thought of as a revolution in ghost story theater.

Nanboku's first play, *Foreign Tales of Tenjiku Tokubei* (Tenjiku Tokubei ikoku banashi, 天竺徳兵衛韓噺), was performed in the summer of 1804. It starred Onoe Matsusuke, known for his kabuki roles as ghosts and demons. The kyōgen belonged to the "samurai warrior house conflict" (*oie sōdō*) subgenre, and it had a magician who could transform himself into a gravestone by chanting magical words. It became famous because of the powerful acting that shocked the audience, and

---

6. See http://www.gutenberg.org/ebooks/1961
7. Literally "mad words"—a comic noh play often performed in the middle of day(s)-long noh performances.

after its production, ghostly kyōgen played during the summer, written by Nanboku and performed by the father-son combination of Matsusuke and his son Eizaburō (later Onoe Kikugorō III), became a set venue.

Nanboku began to incorporate real ghost tales, disseminating around Edo, in his plays. *Kasane* (累) is a Japanese exorcist-type story, where a farmer's wife is brutally murdered by her husband at a river. Her spirit then possesses her stepdaughter to haunt him, but the spirit is eventually exorcised by the prayers of a high-ranking monk. *Plate Mansion* (Sara yashiki, 皿屋敷) revolves around another female curse. This time, a young girl is beaten to death at a samurai house because she accidentally broke the house treasure, a set of decorated plates. Her curse brings about the fall of the entire house. *Kohada Koheiji* (木幡小平次) tells of an actor, who is assassinated by his fellow theater members. He manifests in front of his wife, who was having an affair with the murderer. Nanboku thus created a unique style of realistic theater called "live social issues" (*kizewa*) that mixed together fictional elements with actual events.

During the Bunka and Bunsei eras, popular art forms like *kōdan* and *rakugo*[8] also flourished, along with kabuki plays. It is thought that around one hundred twenty-five *yose* (theaters where these storytelling performances took place) stood in the city of Edo. Among these performances, ghost stories like the aforementioned *Kasane*, *Plate Mansion*, and *Kohada Koheiji* attracted especially large audiences.

It was during this height of this "ghost story boom," where ghost stories became a form of entertainment across literary, visual, and performative arts, that Tsuruya Nanboku IV's masterpiece *Ghost Tale of Yotsuya* (Tōkaidō Yotsuya kaidan, 東海道四谷怪談) came out in July of 1825.

The story tells of a warrior class wife Oiwa, whose father is murdered by her selfish and cruel husband Tamiya Iemon. Iemon also poisons and kills Oiwa, and her begrudging ghost haunts Iemon and all around him. The story was based on an actual happening, one listed in *A Collection of Various Yotsuya Tales* (Yotsuya zōtanshū, 四谷雑談集), and it is thought that

---

8. *Kōdan* refers to public readings, whereas *rakugo* refers to one-man storytelling performances.

Nanboku wrote it as a mixture of various strange tales that his audience would have been familiar with at the time.

The tale of Oiwa is one of the most famous ghost stories in Japan, and it has been remade into numerous films and television dramas in the modern and contemporary eras, going beyond the early modern genres of storytelling and "reading books." Oiwa's grudge is so famous that every time one performs the tale, one must go to Oiwa Inari Tamiya Shrine in the Yotsuya Samonchō district of Tokyo, where her spirit is enshrined, and pray to her spirit before the performance. It is believed that if one does not go through this process, one will incur her wrath.

James S. de Benneville, who introduced the story early on in *The Yotsuya Kwaidan: or O'Iwa Inari* (1917), states in his preface:

> Curiously enough, it can be said that most Nipponese ghost stories are true. When a sword is found enshrined, itself the malevolent influence—as is the Muramasa blade of the Hamamatsu Suwa Jinja, the subject of the Komatsu Onryū of Matsubayashi Hakuchi—and with such tradition attached to it, it is difficult to deny a basis of fact attaching to the tradition.[9]

This nature where the border between fiction and nonfiction is blurred, where one could always intrude on the other, came to be an important characteristic of Japanese fantastic fiction that has lasted to this day. This blurring may be based in Eastern animism and worldview where we locate deities among mountains, rivers, and trees and recognize the existence of ancestral spirits in the shadows of meadows or faraway mountains. It may also have its foundation in the artistic theory of the puppet theater master Chikamatsu Monzaemon (近松門左衛門), who upheld the theory of "Skin Thin Falsehood and Truth" (*kyojitsu himaku*), which contended that art abides in a realm that is neither truth nor fiction.[10]

The ghost story boom of Bunka and Bunsei eras came to be viewed as outmoded after 1853, when Commodore Perry arrived in Japan, ending Japan's isolation policy and bringing much confusion to the late Edo era. The end of the shogunate was finalized by the "The Restoration of Imperial Rule" treaty

9. See http://www.gutenberg.org/etext/19944

10. 虚実皮膜論. See http://ja.wikipedia.org/wiki/近松門左衛門

(*taisei hōkan*), and the new Meiji government was established via the rapid importation of Western policies.

The late Meiji era, mainly in the 1900s, then witnessed a new kind of literary movement brought about by modern writers that revived the genre of ghost stories, taking in various aspects of Western culture and rationalist thought. I will comment more on this development in the introductions of Volumes 2 and 3.

I WILL NOW comment on the authors and the works compiled into this volume.

Let me begin with Lafcadio Hearn, whom I have selected as the prologue for the entire series as the author of "In a Cup of Tea." Hearn was born in Greece and grew up in Ireland, but he later moved to the United States to begin his career as a journalist and a literary critic. In 1890, he immigrated to Japan and married a Japanese woman. Hearn was a born wanderer, and his ashes are thus buried in a foreign land.

Hearn came to Japan during the Meiji era when older folkloric traditions were being pushed aside and forgotten by the rapid modernization process. Hearn, a fan of the mystical and the ghostly, decried this lamentable shift and praised the beautiful nature of ancient Japan. He obsessively collected early modern fantastic tales, and using them as the source of his inspiration, with the help of his wife, he produced wonderful retellings like *Kotto: Being Japanese Curious, with Sundry Cobwebs* (1902) and *Kwaidan: Stories and Studies of Strange Things* (1904).

"In a Cup of Tea" was compiled in *Kotto*, and its original source is thought to be the story "A Young Man's Face Appears in a Cup at a Tea Shop" (Chamise no suiwan jakunen no omote) found in *New Collection of Things Written and Heard* (Shin chomonjū, 新著聞集). The strange occurrence in the retelling is identical to that of the original, but Hearn adds a gothic style preface at the beginning. He also brings out the tale's fantastic and nonsensical nature by intentionally editing out the last parts.

Hearn also lectured on the appeal of Western fantastic fiction in the English Department of Tokyo Imperial University,[11]

---

11. Current Tokyo University

inspiring many youths of his time. His achievements in this field were progressive and amazing.

I HAVE ALREADY discussed Ueda Akinari's *Tales of Moonlight and Rain*. The English version of the entire work exists,[12] so I urge those interested to read the whole work. You will be impressed by the wonderful literary world of *Moonlight and Rain*, where each chapter is carefully arranged to reflect one another and create a mysteriously beautiful work as a whole.

AS I MENTIONED before, Japanese strange tales often adapted older "true" ghost stories and folklore and re-arranged actual Chinese tales in unique ways. There was a whole literary tradition of "Skin Thin Falsehood and Truth," and it has carried over. The writers compiled in this series are all those who represent this tradition.

Kyōgoku Natsuhiko is a famous contemporary writer, whose debut work *The Summer of Ubume* (Ubume no natsu, 姑獲鳥の夏) sold over million copies. His *Old Ghost Tales* (Furui kaidan, 旧怪談, 2007) is a work that consciously situates itself in the tradition as its successor. The original text is the seminal Edo period collection of strange tales, *Tales Heard* (Mimi bukuro, 耳袋, 1814). This was an enormous ten-volume set of stories recorded by Negishi Yasumori, a high-ranking Edo official who went around and collected the strange stories over many years. *Tales Heard* has been regarded as one of the origins of today's "real ghost tale" type books, and it goes without saying that the name of Kihara Hirokatsu and Nakayama Ichirō's series *New Tales Heard* (Shin mimi bukuro, 新耳袋, 1998) is derived from the original Edo version.

Kyōgoku's story was originally serialized in *Yoo* (幽, Ghostly), a magazine that specializes in ghostly literature for which I am the chief editor. Kyōgoku actually tried to reproduce the original tales of *Tales Heard* in a written style reminiscent of *New Tales Heard*, and he achieved this difficult task in his serialization. I hope that you will enjoy his careful narration, which has

---

12. There are two translations of the English version: Leon Zolbrod's *Tales of Moonlight and Rain: Japanese Gothic Tales* (1972) and the more recent version by Anthony Chambers, *Tales of Moonlight and Rain: A Study and Translation* (2006).

turned the original "In a Cup of Tea" into a modern day ghost story marked by absurdity. I will just add that Kyōgoku has also produced long serialized works such as *Laughing Iemon* (Warau Iemon, 嗤う伊右衛門, 1997), which draws from *Ghost Tale of Yotsuya* and *Peeping Koheiji* (覘き小平次, 2002), based on *Kohada Koheiji*.

MIYABE MIYUKI IS another writer as popular as Kyōgoku, and has repeatedly revealed her love for Edo period ghost stories in her works. *Trembling Rock* (Furueru iwa, 震える岩, 1993) describes a cunning city girl who must solve mysteries with her psychic powers, and Miyabe apparently based the story on the strange tales in *Tales Heard*. Her works often take place in Fukagawa, a downtown area where she grew up that still has remnants of Edo, and her tales reveal a kind of sympathy towards those who struggle as the bottom ranks of society. *Sticking out the Tongue* (Akanbei, あかんべえ, 2002), for example, is what I call a "gentle ghost story"[13] that belongs to this category. "The Futon Room" (Futon beya, 布団部屋) in her collection of Edo strange tales *The Strange* (Ayashi, あやし, 2000) can also be categorized as such. This is why it is always shocking when the supernatural in her work reveal its merciless side, ruthlessly attacking her characters' weaknesses and faults. One cannot forget this double-sidedness of her supernatural.

Miyabe, furthermore, is an aficionado of Western supernatural tales, and she has even edited an excellent anthology called *Tales to be Gifted: Terror* (Okuru monogatari Terror, 贈る物語Terror, 2002). In one of the passages in the work in this series, two sisters converse in a dream, saying "It… is extremely hungry," which is an allusion to L. P. Hartley's short story "Podolo."

MIYABE MIYUKI HAS contantly expressed her admiration towards Okamoto Kidō, who started the tradition of referencing Edo ghost stories before her. Kidō was one of the earliest writers to revive the genre in the Meiji and Taishō eras, along with Izumi Kyōka and Yanagita Kunio. He wrote a story for the special issue of the journal *Bungei Kurabu*, which was called "Real Ghost Stories in Japan/Real Ghost Stories in the West" (Nihon

---

13. A story with a kind ghost instead of a malevolent one.

yōkai jitsudan/Seiyō yōkai jitsudan 日本妖怪実譚／西洋妖怪実譚) in 1902. This collection became one of the earliest modern "real ghost story" examples, and after its publication, Kidō began to devote himself to the dissemination of both foreign and domestic supernatural stories, writing novels and plays and introducing translated works.

Among his novels, the best known are *Strange Tales at Blue Frog Temple* (Seiadō kidan, 青蛙堂鬼談, 1926), which is a collection of supernatural tales, and his earlier lengthy work *The Ghost Story of Hida* (Hida no kaidan, 飛騨の怪談, 1913). His plays tend to mix together Western supernatural tales and traditional Japanese lore. *Blue Frog Deity* (Seiajin, 青蛙神, 1931) is an adaptation of W. W. Jacobs' "The Monkey's Paw," and *Werewolf* (Jinrō, 人狼, 1931) is based on Frederick Marryat's "The White Wolf of the Harz Mountains." He also published anthologies of translated foreign works, which are now seen as classics. These include *Masterpiece Collection of Supernatural Tales from Around the World* (Sekai kaidan meisakushū, 世界怪談名作集, 1929) and *A Collection of Chinese Strange Tales* (Shina kaiki shōsetsushū, 支那怪奇小説集, 1935). All of these works reveal Kidō's encyclopedic knowledge and mastery of Japanese, Chinese, and Western fiction.

"Here Lies a Flute" (Fuezuka, 笛塚) in this volume is one of the best tales among the wonderful stories of *Blue Frog Temple*. The collection is written in an Edo-style actual hearsay format about a "one hundred ghost storytelling" performance that took place at the Blue Frog Temple in the Koishikawa district of Tokyo. For this reason, the Japanese begins with the phrase "The eleventh man narrates," meaning that this was the story of the eleventh speaker among the one hundred. The speaker refers to a story from *Tales Heard* in the beginning, but he then adds, "The story I'm about to tell is somewhat similar but a more complicated and mysterious tale." This passage, to me, hints at the author's endeavor to produce a kind of supernatural tale that would be applicable to the new modern world.

TANAKA KŌTARŌ, AUTHOR of "The Face in the Hearth" (Kamado no naka no kao, 竈の中の顔) was also a master of supernatural tales in the Taishō era, a leading figure who rivaled

Kidō. He began to publish strange tales after publishing his short story "Mysteries of Fish/Strangeness of Insects" (Sakana no yō, mushi no kai, 魚の妖・虫の怪) in the opinion-leader magazine *Chūō Kōron*. Versed in Japanese and Chinese classics and folklore, he wrote an impressive amount of historical fiction, contemporary fiction, Chinese tales, and "real" ghost stories. He also edited large series like *The Collection of Japanese Ghost Stories* (Nihon kaidan zenshū, 日本怪談全集, 4 vols., 1934), *New Collection of Ghost Stories (Fictions and Real Accounts)* (Shin kaidanshū (monogatarihen/jitsuwahen), 新怪談集 (物語篇・実話篇), 2 vols., 1938), and *A Complete Anthology of Chinese Ghost Stories* (Shina kaidan zenshū, 支那怪談全集, 1931).

Tanaka is known for his *kanbun*-esque[14] orthography that captures the mindset of those haunted by the strange. As with "The Face in the Hearth," many of his works portray absurd, strange occurrences that strike terror in one's heart.

Similar to Kyōgoku Natsuhiko's short story "What Does He Want?" (Nani ga shitai, 何がしたい) "The Face in the Hearth" was inspired by a story in the fifth volume of *Tales Heard* called "About the Strange Stove" (Kaisō no koto, 怪竈の事). However, Tanaka exhibits a completely different viewpoint from that of Kyōgoku, and the comparison of the two works should prove to be interesting for the reader.

THE ONE WRITER who cannot go without being mentioned, when speaking of encyclopedic knowledge of Japanese and Chinese classics and *kanbun* writing style, is the renowned Meiji writer Kōda Rohan. He is often cited alongside Izumi Kyōka (included in Volume II) as one of the major figures in Japanese fantastic fiction. Spanning from the Meiji era through the Shōwa era, Rohan produced both fictional and critical works, exhibiting a profound understanding of Eastern occultism. While Kyōka immersed himself into a ghostly, mysterious, and beautiful fantasy world, using a feminine writing style, Rohan wandered around in a mystifying dream-like world, writing in a more daring and masculine style taken

---

14. *Kanbun* (漢文), orthography based on classical Chinese; in the classical era, this was the orthography of men, as opposed to kana, which female writers used.

from Japanese and Chinese classics. The two thus complement one another in perfect unison.

In "The Skull" (Tsui dokuro, 対髑髏, 1890), a young traveler seeks shelter for the night at a hut in the mountains, where a beautiful woman resides all by her lonesome. She tells him stories about her past, but the next morning, when the young man wakes up, both the house and the woman have disappeared, and all that remains is a skull by his feet. After he climbs down the mountain, the man hears a story from an innkeeper about a beggar woman who went mad. This strange tale became one of the most celebrated of all modern fantastic fiction.

Rohan wrote the story included in this volume, "The Pointer" (Gendan, 幻談, 1938), during his last years. It is a masterpiece, written in a dictation-type style, where the narrator tells of a strange occurrence surrounding a haunted fishing rod in a well-composed rhythmic manner. The text thus masterfully creates an uncanny atmosphere. The numerous information about the fishing rod and the depiction of the rivers that is truly reminiscent of the Edo past both add a realistic touch to the work, bringing the supernatural occurrence to life. No matter how many times I read this work, I am always impressed by it. It is truly a work of art.

INAGAKI TARUHO DEBUTED in the 1920s as a writer of *modanizumu* literature. Beginning with his first work, *Tale of One Thousand and One Seconds* (Issen ichibyō monogatari, 一千一秒物語, 1923), he produced numerous futurist fantastic fiction. At the same time, he is also known for strange stories focusing on his own time, and this volume's "The Inō Residence, Or, The Competition with a Ghost" (Inōke=bakemono concours, 稲生家＝化物コンクール, 1972) is representative of the latter category. In this story, a young samurai disturbs an old mound he finds in the mountains and becomes the target of numerous supernatural activities. He, however, faces them without any fear, bravely conquering every strange, supernatural obstacle. It sounds like a purely original work, but it is actually based on a story that is said to have taken place during the mid-Edo era in a town called Miyoshi in Hiroshima prefecture. The story was recorded in *An Account of Inō and the Spirit* (Inō mononoke roku, 稲生物怪録), and Taruho wrote a newer version, closely adapting from the original.

An Account of Inō and the Spirit was an object of study for early modern nativist scholars like Hirata Atsutane, modern folklorist Orikuchi Shinobu, and writers like Iwaya Sazanami and Izumi Kyōka. In fact, these writers have produced their own versions of the story in various manners, the most notable of which are Taruho's story and Kyōka's novel *Grass Labyrinth* (Kusa meikyū, 草迷宮, 1908). *Account* was also reproduced as picture scrolls.

I should also note that for "Inō Residence," there exist a couple of variant versions, one called "Nostalgic July" (Natsukashi no shichigatsu, 懐しの七月, 1956) and the other called "San-moto Gorōzaemon Retreats" (Sanmoto Gorōzaemon tadaima taisan tsukamatsuru, 山ン本五郎左衛門只今退散仕る, 1968). There are interesting editorial changes in both, but for this compilation, I have opted to use the final version.

A PHENOMENON CALLED "deity kidnap" (*kamikakushi*) is common in Japanese folklore[15]. It is used to describe strange occurrences where an infant or young girl suddenly goes missing without a trace. Sometimes, the children never come back, and sometimes, they appear after many years. These incidents are also referred to as "*tengu* kidnap" because those who make it back oftentimes insist that they were kidnapped by the *tengu*[16] and resided in their mystical world.

Yamamoto Shūgorō's "Through the Wooden Door" (Sono kido o tōtte, その木戸を通って, 1959) is a work that captures the mysticism and the fear towards this phenomenon of "deity kidnap." He succeeds in depicting subtleties of human emotions and explores the truths of life. Yamamoto is actually known, not as a supernatural fiction writer, but as a historical fiction writer. He has written fiction revolving about the laments of the ordinary, marginal beings and also highly popular epic works like *The Fir Tree Remained* (Mominoki wa

---

15. The Japanese title of Miyazaki Hayao's film "Spirited Away" is *Kamikakushi*.

16. A *tengu* is a human-like goblin with wings and a long nose. There are many stories in Japanese folklore about *tengu* who kidnap people and eat them.

nokotta, 樅ノ木は残った), which was eventually turned into a TV movie.

"Wooden Door" will move you and arouse awe. This feat could not have been achieved by anyone but a masterful historical fiction writer like Yamamoto. His story eloquently demonstrates how a good supernatural tale is not just about fear or strange, entertaining things.

For a volume entitled Tales of Old Edo, there is no one more befitting for its conclusion than the manga artist and critic Sugiura Hinako. Throughout her short life, she spoke openly of her love for Edo culture and customs, calling herself an "Edo person" (*edojin*) and devoting herself to Edo period philosophy. She produced an epic manga collection of ninety-nine tales called *One Hundred Ghost Stories* (Hyaku monogatari, 百物語, 1988–93), and the manga "Three Eerie Tales of Dark Nights" (Yamiyo no kai sanwa, 闇夜の怪三話) was taken from that collection.

One Hundred Ghost Stories begins with the words:

> From ancient times, people performed something called
>   "One Hundred Ghost Stories"
> When one hundred mysterious tales are collected,
>   They say monsters appear without fail.

Sugiura had mastered the art of "One Hundred Ghost Stories," an Edo-period tradition. With various brilliant techniques, she succeeded in capturing the essence of the Japanese supernatural in a visual medium.

BY READING THIS volume, I hope the reader will be able to experience first-hand the profundity and uncertainty that belonged to the darkness of Edo nights.

Tokyo
June, 2009

have seen in any books, but which is of great philosophical importance; there is something ghostly in all great art, whether of literature, music, sculpture, or architecture.

But now let me speak to you about this word 'ghostly'; it is a much bigger word, perhaps, than some of you imagine. The old English had no other word for 'spiritual' or 'supernatural' – which terms you know, are not English but Latin. Everything that religion to-day calls divine, holy, miraculous, was sufficiently explained for the old Anglo-Saxons by the term ghostly. They spoke of a man's ghost, instead of speaking of his spirit or soul; and everything relating to religious knowledge they called ghostly. In the modern formula of the Catholic confession, which has remained almost unchanged for nearly two thousand years, you will find that the priest is always called a 'ghostly' father—which means that his business is to take care of the ghosts or souls of men as a father does. In addressing the priest, the penitent really calls him 'Father of my ghost.' You will see, therefore, that a very large meaning really attaches to the adjective. It means everything relating to the supernatural. It means to the Christian even God himself, for the Giver of Life is always called in English the Holy Ghost.

Accepting the evolutional philosophy which teaches that the modern idea of God as held by western nations is really but a development from the primitive belief in a shadow-soul, the term ghost in its reference to the supreme being certainly could not be found fault with. On the contrary, there is a weirdness about the use of this word which adds greatly to its solemnity. But whatever belief we have, or have not, as regards religious creeds, one thing that modern science has done for us, is to prove beyond question that everything which we used to consider material and solid is essentially ghostly, as is any ghost. If we do not believe in old-fashioned stories and theories about ghosts, we are nevertheless obliged to recognise to-day that we are ghosts of ourselves—and utterly incomprehensible. The mystery of the universe is now weighing upon us, becoming heavier and heavier, more and more awful, as our knowledge expands, and it is especially a ghostly mystery. All great art reminds us in some way of this universal riddle; that is why I say that all great art has something ghostly in it. It touches something in us which relates to infinity. When you read a very great thought, when you see a wonderful picture or statue or building, and when you hear certain kinds of music, you feel a thrill in the heart and mind much like the thrill which in all times men felt when they thought they saw a ghost or a god. Only the modern thrill is incomparably larger and longer and deeper. And this is why, in spite of all knowledge, the world still finds pleasure in the literature of the supernatural, and will continue to find pleasure in it for hundreds of years to come. The ghostly represents always some shadow of truth, and no amount of disbelief in what used to be called ghosts can ever diminish human interest in what relates to that truth.

So you will see that the subject is not altogether trifling. Certainly it is of very great moment in relation to great literature. The poet or the story-teller who can not give the reader a little ghostly pleasure at times never can be either a really great writer or a great thinker. I have already said that I know of no exception to this rule in the whole of English literature. Take, for instance, Macaulay, the most practical, hard-headed, logical writer of the century, the last man in whom you would expect to find the least trace of superstition. Had you read only certain of his essays, you would scarcely think him capable of touching the chords of the supernatural. But he has done this in a masterly way in several of the 'Lays of Ancient Rome'—for example, in speaking of the apparition of the Twin Brethren at the battle of Lake Regillus, and of Tarquin haunted by the phantom of his victim Lucretia. Both of these passages give the ghostly thrill in a strong way; and there is a fainter thrill of the same sort to be experienced from the reading of parts of the 'Prophecy of Capys.' It is because Macaulay had this power, though using it sparingly, that his work is so great. If he had not been able to write these lines of poetry which I referred to, he could not even have made his history of England the living history that it is. A man who has no ghostly feeling can not make anything alive, not even a page of history or a page of oratory. To touch men's souls, you must know all that those souls can be made to feel by words; and to know that, you must yourself have a 'ghost' in you that can be touched in the same way.

Now leaving the theoretical for the practical part of the theme, let us turn to the subject of the relation between ghosts and dreams.

No good writer—no great writer—ever makes a study of the supernatural according to anything which has been done before by other writers. This is one of those subjects upon which you can not get real help from books. It is not from books, nor from traditions, nor from legends, nor from anything of that kind that you can learn how to give your reader a ghostly thrill. I do not mean that it is of no use for you to read what has been written upon the subject, so far as mere methods of expression, mere effects of literary workmanship, are concerned. On the contrary, it is very important that you should read all you can of what is good in literature upon these subjects; you will learn from them a great deal about curious values of words, about compactness and power of sentences, about peculiarities of beliefs and of terrors relating to those beliefs. But you must never try to use another man's ideas or feelings, taken from a book, in order to make a supernatural effect. If you do, the work will never be sincere, and will never make a thrill. You must use your own ideas and feelings only, under all possible circumstances. And where are you to get these ideas and feelings from, if you do not believe in ghosts? From your dreams. Whether you believe in ghosts or not, all the artistic elements of ghostly literature exist in your dreams, and form a veritable treasury of literary material for the man who knows how to use them.

All the great effects obtained by the poets and story writers, and even by religious teachers, in the treatment of supernatural fear or mystery, have been obtained, directly or indirectly, through dreams. Study any great ghost story in any literature, and you will find that no matter how surprising or unfamiliar the incidents seem, a little patient examination will prove to you that every one of them has occurred, at different times, in different combinations, in dreams of your own. They give you a thrill. But why? Because they remind you of experiences, imaginative or emotional, which you had forgotten. There can be no exception to this rule—absolutely none. I was speaking to you the other day about a short story by Bulwer Lytton, as being the best ghost story in the English language.[2] The reason

2 'One of his short stories is generally acknowledged to be the greatest ghost story that was ever written... I mean the little story called first 'The House and the Brains,' but afterwards called 'The Haunted and the Haunters.'

why it is the best story of this kind is simply because it represents with astonishing faithfulness the experiences of nightmare. The terror of all great stories of the supernatural is really the terror of nightmare, projected into waking consciousness. And the beauty or tenderness of other ghost stories or fairy-stories, or even of certain famous and delightful religious legends, is the tenderness and beauty of dreams of a happier kind, dreams inspired by love or hope or regret. But in all cases where the supernatural is well treated in literature, dream experience is the source of the treatment.

I know that I am now speaking to an audience acquainted with literature of which I know practically nothing. But I believe that there can be no exception to these rules even in the Far East. I do not mean to say that there may not be in Chinese and in Japanese literature many ghost stories which are not derived from dream-experience. But I will say that if there are any of this kind, they are not worth reading, and can not belong to any good class of literature. I have read translations of a number of Chinese ghost stories in French, also a wonderful English translation of ghostly Chinese stories in two volumes, entitled 'Strange Stories from a Chinese Studio,' by Herbert Giles.[3] These stories, translated by a great scholar, are very wonderful; but I noticed that in every successful treatment of a supernatural subject, the incidents of the story invariably corresponded with the phenomena of dreams. Therefore I think that I can not be mistaken in my judgement of the matter. Such Japanese stories as I could get translations of, obeyed the same rule. The other day, in a story which I read for the first time, I was very much interested to find an exact parallel between the treatment of a supernatural idea by the Japanese author, and by the best English author of dream studies. The story was about a picture, painted upon a screen, representing a river and a landscape. In the Japanese story (perhaps it has a Chi-

---

From Hearn's lecture 'English Fiction in the First Half of the Nineteenth Century' (Erskine edition, vol. 1). Bulwer Lytton (1803–1873) first published this story in Blackwell's Magazine in August, 1859; it was edited for republication by his son in 1875.

3 'Strange Stories from a Chinese Studio,' by Herbert Giles (1845–1935) appeared in four editions between 1880 and 1926. A reprint edition—apparently based on the third (1916) edition – was much later issued by Cheng Wen Publishing in Taiwan.

nese origin) the painter makes a sign to the screen; and a little boat begins to sail down the river, and sails out of the picture into the room, and the room becomes full or water, and the painter, or magician, or whoever he is, gets into the boat and sails away into the picture again, and disappears forever. This is exactly, in every detail, a dream story, and the excellence of it is in its truth to dream experience. The same phenomena you will find, under another form, in 'Alice in Wonderland,' and 'Through the Looking Glass.'

But to return to the point where we left off. I was saying that all successful treatment of the ghostly or the impossible must be made to correspond as much as possible with the truth of dream experience, and that Bulwer Lytton's story of the haunted house illustrates that rule. Let us now consider especially the literary value of nightmare. Nightmare, the most awful form of dream, is also one of the most peculiar. It has probably furnished all the important elements of religious and supernatural terror which are to be found in all really great literature. It is a mysterious thing in itself; and scientific psychology has not yet been able to explain many facts in regard to it. We can take the phenomena of nightmare separately, one by one, and show their curious relation to various kinds of superstitious fear and supernatural belief.

The first remarkable fact in nightmare is the beginning of it. It begins with a kind of suspicion, usually. You feel afraid without knowing why. Then you have the impression that something is acting upon you from a distance—something like fascination, yet not exactly fascination, for there may be no visible fascinator. But feeling uneasy, you wish to escape, to get away from the influence that is making you afraid. Then you find it is not easy to escape. You move with great difficulty. Presently the difficulty increases—you cannot move at all. You want to cry out, and you can not; you have lost your voice. You are actually in a state of trance—seeing, hearing, feeling, but unable to move or speak. This is the beginning. It forms one of the most terrible emotions from which a man can suffer. If it continued more than a certain length of time, this fear might kill. Nightmare does sometimes kill, in cases where the health has been very much affected by other causes.

Of course we have nothing in waking life of such experience—the feeling of being deprived of will and held fast from a great distance by some viewless power. This is the real experience of magnetism, mesmerism; and it is the origin of certain horrible beliefs of the Middle Ages in regard to magical power. Suppose we call it supernatural mesmerism, for want of a better word. It is not true mesmerism, because in real hypnotic conditions, the patient does not feel or think or act mentally according to his own personality; he acts by the will of another. In nightmare the will is only suspended, and the personal consciousness remains; this is what makes the horror of it. So we shall call the first stage supernatural mesmerism, only with the above qualification. Now let us see how Bulwer Lytton uses this experience in his story.

A man is sitting in a chair, with a lamp on the table beside him, and is reading Macaulay's essays, when he suddenly becomes uneasy. A shadow falls upon the page. He rises, and tries to call; but he cannot raise his voice above a whisper. He tries to move; and he can not stir hand or foot. The spell is already upon him. This is the first part of the nightmare.

The second stage of the phenomenon, which sometimes mingles with the first stage, is the experience of terrible and unnatural appearances. There is always a darkening of the visible, sometimes a disappearance or a dimming of the light. In Bulwer Lytton's story there is a fire burning in the room and a very bright lamp. Gradually both fire and lamp become dimmer and dimmer; at last all light completely vanishes, and the room becomes absolutely dark, except for spectral and unnatural luminosities that begin to make their appearance. This also is a very good study of dream experience. The third stage of nightmare, the final struggle, is chiefly characterised by impossible occurrences, which bring to the dreamer the extreme form of horror, while convincing him of his own impotence. For example, you try to fire a pistol or to use a steel weapon. If a pistol, the bullet will not project itself more than a few inches from the muzzle; then it drops down limply, and there is no report. If a sword or dagger, the blade becomes soft, like cotton or paper. Terrible appearances, monstrous or unnatural figures, reach out hands to touch; if human figures, they will grow to the ceiling, and bend themselves fantastically as they approach. There is one more stage, which is not often reached—the climax of the horror. That is when you are caught or touched. The touch in nightmare is a very peculiar sensation, almost like an electric shock, but unnaturally prolonged. It is not pain, but something worse than pain, an experience never felt in waking hours.

The third and fourth stages have been artistically mixed together by Bulwer Lytton. The phantom towers from floor to ceiling, vague and threatening; the man attempts to use a weapon, and at the same time receives a touch or shock that renders him absolutely powerless. He describes the feeling as resembling the sensation of some ghostly electricity. The study is exactly true to dream-experience. I need not here mention this story further, since from this point a great many other elements enter into it which, though not altogether foreign to our subject, do not illustrate that subject so well as some of the stories of Poe. Poe has given us other peculiar details of nightmare-experience, such as horrible sounds. Often we hear in such dreams terrible muffled noises, as of steps coming. This you will find very well studied in the story called 'The Fall of the House of Usher.' Again in these dreams inanimate objects either become alive, or suggest to us, by their motion, the hiding of some horrible life behind them – curtains, for example, doors left half open, alcoves imperfectly closed. Poe has studied these in 'Eleonora' and in some other sketches.

Dreams of the terrible have beyond question had a good deal to do with the inspiration both of religious and of superstitious literature. The returning of the dead, visions of heavenly or infernal beings,—these, when well described, are almost always exact reproductions of dream-experience. But occasionally we find an element of waking fear mixed with them—for example, in one of the oldest ghost stories of the world, the story in 'The Book of Job.' The poet speaks of feeling intense cold, and feeling the hairs of his head stand up with fear. These experiences are absolutely true, and they belong to waking life. The sensation of cold and the sensation of horror are not sensations of dreams. They come from extraordinary terror felt in felt in active existence, while we are awake. You will observe the very same signs of fear in a horse, a dog, or a cat—and there is reason to suppose that in these animal cases, also, supernatural fear is sometimes a cause. I have seen a dog—a brave dog, too—terribly frightened by seeing a mass of paper moved by a slight current of air. This slight wind did not reach the place where the dog was lying; he could not therefore associate the motion of the paper with a motion of the wind; he did not understand what was moving the paper; the mystery alarmed him, and the hair on his back stood up with fear. But the mingling of such sensations of waking fear with dream sensations of fear, in a story or poem, may be very effectually managed, so as to give the story an air of reality, of actuality, which could not be obtained in any other way.

A great many of our old fairy ballads and goblin stories mixed the two experiences together with the most excellent results. I should say that the fine German story of 'Undine' is a good example of this kind.[4] The sight of the faces in the water of the river, the changing of waterfalls and cataracts into ghostly people, the rising from the closed well of the form of Undine herself, the rising of the flood behind her, and the way in which she 'weeps her lover to death'—all this is pure dream; and it seems real because most of us have had some such experiences of fancy in our own dreams. But the other part of the story, dealing with human emotions, fears, passions—these are of waking life, and the mixture is accomplished in a most artistic way. Speaking of Undine obliges me also to speak of Undine's predecessors in mediaeval literature—the mediaeval spirits, the succubae and incubi, the sylphs and salamanders or salamandrines, the whole wonderful goblin population of water, air, forest, and fire. All the good stories about them are really dream studies.

And coming down to the most romantic literature of our own day, the same thing must be said of those strange and delightful stories by Gautier, 'La Morte Amoureuse,' 'Arria Marcella,' 'Le Pied de Momie.'[5] The most remarkable is perhaps 'La Morte Amoureuse'; but there is in this a study of double personality, which complicates it too much for the purposes of present illustration. I shall therefore speak of 'Arria Mar-

---

4. 'Undine', by Friedrich de la Motte Fouque (1777–1843). Numerous English translations and versions have appeared over the years.

5. Hearn's translations of the stories mentioned here by Théophile Gautier (1811–1872) were first published in 1882, and appeared in a number of reprint editions since.

cella' instead. Some young students visit the city of Pompeii, to study the ruins and the curiosities preserved in the museum of Naples, nearby. All of them are familiar with classic literature and classic history; moreover, they are artists, able to appreciate the beauty of what they see. At the time of the eruption, which occurred nearly two thousand years ago, many people perished by being smothered under the rain of ashes; but their bodies were encased in the deposit so that the form was perfectly preserved as in a mould. Some of these moulds are to be seen in the museum mentioned; and one is the mould of the body of a beautiful young woman. The younger of the three students sees this mould, and romantically wishes that he could see and love the real person, so many centuries dead. That night, while his companions are asleep, he leaves his room and wanders into the ruined city, for the pleasure of thinking all by himself. But presently, as he turns the corner of a street, he finds that the city looks quite different from what it had appeared by day; the houses seem to have grown taller; they look new, bright, clean. While he is thus wandering, suddenly the sun rises, and the streets fill with people—not the people of to-day, but the people of two thousand years ago, all dressed in the old Greek and Roman costumes. After a time a young Greek comes up to the student and speaks to him in Latin. He has learned enough Latin at the university to be able to answer, and a conversation begins, of which the result is that he is invited to the theatre of Pompeii to see the gladiators and other amusements of the time. While in this theatre, he suddenly sees the woman that he wanted to see, the woman whose figure was preserved in the Naples museum. After the theatre, he is invited to her house; and everything is very delightful until suddenly the girl's father appears on the scene. The old man is a Christian, and he is very angry that the ghost of his daughter should deceive a young man in this manner. He makes a sign of the cross, and immediately poor Arria crumbles into dust, and the young man finds himself alone in the ruins of Pompeii.

Very beautiful this story is; but every detail in it is dream study. I have given so much mention to it only because it seems to me the very finest French example of this artistic use of dream experience. But how many other romances belong in the same category? I need only mention among others Irving's 'The Adalantado of the Seven Cities,' which is pure dream, so realistically told that it gives the reader the sensation of being asleep. Although such romances as 'The Seven Sleepers,' 'Rip Van Winkle,' and 'Urashima,'[6] are not, on the other hand, pure dreams, yet the charm of them is just in that part where dream experience is used. The true romance in all is in the old man's dream of being young, and waking up to cold and grave realities. By the way, in the old French lays of Marie de France, there is an almost precisely similar story to the Japanese one— similar, at least, at all points except the story of the tortoise. It is utterly impossible that the oriental and the occidental story-tellers could have, either of them, borrowed from the other; more probably each story is a spontaneous growth. But it is curious to find the legend substantially the same in other literatures—Indian and Arabian and Javanese. In all of the versions the one romantic truth is ever the same—a dream truth.

Now besides the artistic elements of terror and of romance, dreams certainly furnish us with the most penetrating and beautiful qualities of ghostly tenderness that literature contains. For the dead people that we loved all come back to us occasionally in dreams, and look and talk as if they were actually alive, and become to us everything that we could have wished them to be. In a dream-meeting with the dead, you must have observed how everything is gentle and beautiful, and yet how real, how true it seems. From the most ancient times such visions of the dead have furnished literature with the most touching and the most exquisite passages of unselfish affection. We find this experience in nearly all the ancient ballad-literature of Europe; we find it in every kind of superior poetry; and modern literature draws from it more and

---

6. The story of the Seven Sleepers and Washington Irving's 'Rip Van Winkle' will be familiar to English readers; 'Urashima' refers to the story of Urashima Tarō, a Japanese fisherman, who was taken to the palace of the Dragon King on the back of a giant tortoise. After a long and happy stay under the ocean, Urashima desired to return home. He was sent on his way with a great box, under instructions not to open it, lest something terrible happen to him. The tortoise took Urashima home, but everything was different, and no-one knew him. Finally he opened the box, and all the years he had spent in the magic kingdom flew out – and poor Urashima Tarō crumbled to dust.

more as the years go by. Even in such strange compositions as the 'Kalevala' of the Finns, an epic totally unlike any other ever written in this world, the one really beautiful passage in an emotional sense is the coming back of the dead mother to comfort the wicked son, which is a dream study, though not so represented in the poem.

Yet one thing more. Our dreams of heaven, what are they in literature but reflections in us of the more beautiful class of dreams? In the world of sleep all the dead people we loved meet us again; the father recovers his long-buried child, the husband his lost wife, separated lovers find the union that was impossible in this world, those whom we lost sight of in early years—dead sisters, brothers, friends—all come back to us just as they were then, just as loving, and as young, and perhaps even more beautiful than they could really have been. In the world of sleep there is no growing old; there is immortality, there is everlasting youth. And again how soft, how happy everything is; even the persons unkind to us in waking life become affectionate to us in dreams. Well, what is heaven but this? Religion in painting perfect happiness for the good, only describes the best of our dream life, which is also the best of our waking life; and I think you will find that the closer religion has kept to dream experience in these descriptions, the happier has been the result. Perhaps you will say that I have forgotten how religion teaches the apparition of supernatural powers of a very particular kind. But I think that you will find the suggestion for these powers also in dream life. Do we not pass through the air in dreams, pass through solid substances, perform all kinds of miracles, achieve all sorts of impossible things? I think we do. At all events, I am certain that when, as men-of-letters, you have to deal with any form of supernatural subject—whether terrible, or tender, or pathetic, or splendid – you will do well, if you have a good imagination, not to trust books for your inspiration. Trust to your own dream-life; study it carefully, and draw your inspiration from that. For dreams are the primary source of almost everything that is beautiful in the literature which treats of what lies beyond mere daily experience.

In a Cup of Tea

Lafcadio Hearn (1902)

HAVE YOU EVER attempted to mount some old tower stairway, spiring up through darkness, and in the heart of that darkness found yourself at the cobwebbed edge of nothing? Or have you followed some coast path, cut along the face of a cliff, only to discover yourself, at a turn, on the jagged verge of a break? The emotional worth of such experience—from a literary point of view—is proved by the force of the sensations aroused, and by the vividness with which they are remembered.

Now there have been curiously preserved, in old Japanese story—books, certain fragments of fiction that produce an almost similar emotional experience... Perhaps the writer was lazy; perhaps he had a quarrel with the publisher; perhaps he was suddenly called away from his little table, and never came back; perhaps death stopped the writing-brush in the very middle of a sentence. But no mortal man can ever tell us exactly why these things were left unfinished... I select a typical example.

ON THE FOURTH day of the first month of the third Tenwa—that is to say, about two hundred and twenty years ago—the Lord Nakagawa Sado, while on his way to make a New Year's visit, halted with his train at a tea-house in Hakusan, in the Hongō district of Yedo.[1] While the party were resting there, one of the lord's attendants—a *wakatō*[2] named Sekinai—feeling very thirsty, filled for <u>himself a large wa</u>ter-cup with tea. He was raising the cup to his

1. Yedo is the old spelling of Edo (江戸), the capital city called Tokyo today.
2. Wakatō (若党) is a retainer to a samurai, and often was an heir to the samurai's position.

lips when he suddenly perceived, in the transparent yellow infusion, the image or reflection of a face that was not his own. Startled, he looked around, but could see no one near him. The face in the tea appeared, from the coiffure, to be the face of a young samurai: it was strangely distinct, and very handsome—delicate as the face of a girl. And it seemed the reflection of a living face; for the eyes and the lips were moving. Bewildered by this mysterious apparition, Sekinai threw away the tea, and carefully examined the cup. It proved to be a very cheap water-cup, with no artistic devices of any sort. He found and filled another cup; and again the face appeared in the tea. He then ordered fresh tea, and refilled the cup; and once more the strange face appeared—this time with a mocking smile. But Sekinai did not allow himself to be frightened. "Whoever you are," he muttered, "you shall delude me no further!"—then he swallowed the tea, face and all, and went his way, wondering whether he had swallowed a ghost.

Late in the evening of the same day, while on watch in the palace of the Lord Nakagawa, Sekinai was surprised by the soundless coming of a stranger into the apartment. This stranger, a richly dressed young samurai, seated himself directly in front of Sekinai, and, saluting the *wakatō* with a slight bow, observed:

"I am Shikibu Heinai—met you to-day for the first time... You do not seem to recognize me."

He spoke in a very low, but penetrating voice. And Sekinai was astonished to find before him the same sinister, handsome face of which he had seen, and swallowed, the apparition in a cup of tea. It was smiling now, as the phantom had smiled; but the steady gaze of the eyes, above the smiling lips, was at once a challenge and an insult.

"No, I do not recognize you," returned Sekinai, angry but cool;—"and perhaps you will now be good enough to inform me how you obtained admission to this house?"

[In feudal times the residence of a lord was strictly guarded at all hours; and no one could enter unannounced, except through some unpardonable negligence on the part of the armed watch.]

"Ah, you do not recognize me!" exclaimed the visitor, in a tone of irony, drawing a little nearer as he spoke. "No, you do not recognize me! Yet you took upon yourself this morning to do me a deadly injury! ..."

34

Sekinai instantly seized the *tantō*[3] at his girdle, and made a fierce thrust at the throat of the man. But the blade seemed to touch no substance. Simultaneously and soundlessly the intruder leaped sideward to the chamber-wall, and through it!... The wall showed no trace of his exit. He had traversed it only as the light of a candle passes through lantern-paper.

WHEN SEKINAI MADE report of the incident, his recital astonished and puzzled the retainers. No stranger had been seen either to enter or to leave the palace at the hour of the occurrence; and no one in the service of the Lord Nakagawa had ever heard of the name "Shikibu Heinai."

ON THE FOLLOWING night Sekinai was off duty, and remained at home with his parents. At a rather late hour he was informed that some strangers had called at the house, and desired to speak with him for a moment. Taking his sword, he went to the entrance, and there found three armed men—apparently retainers—waiting in front of the doorstep. The three bowed respectfully to Sekinai and one of them said:

"Our names are Matsuoka Bungo, Tsuchibashi Bungo, and Okamura Heiroku. We are retainers of the noble Shikibu Heinai. When our master last night deigned to pay you a visit, you struck him with a sword. He was much hurt, and has been obliged to go to the hot springs, where his wound is now being treated. But on the sixteenth day of the coming month he will return; and he will then fitly repay you for the injury done him..."

Without waiting to hear more, Sekinai leaped out, sword in hand, and slashed right and left, at the strangers. But the three men sprang to the wall of the adjoining building, and flitted up the wall like shadows, and...

HERE THE OLD narrative breaks off; the rest of the story existed only in some brain that has been dust for a century.

I am able to imagine several possible endings; but none of them would satisfy an Occidental imagination. I prefer to let the reader attempt to decide for himself the probable consequence of swallowing a Soul.

---

3. Short sword (短刀)

The Chrysanthemum Pledge

菊花の約 (Kikka no chigiri)

Ueda Akinari (1776)　　　　　　　　　　上田秋成
English translation by Pamela Ikegami

DO NOT PLANT the willow, so lushly green in spring, in your garden. Do not associate yourself with superficial people. The willow thrives and turns a rich green early in spring, but when the first winds telling of autumn begin to blow, it cannot endure and the leaves scatter. Superficial people are easy to associate with, but these ties are also soon broken. As each spring comes, the willow's leaves turn green again, but once the connection with a superficial man has been broken he will not come to visit again.

In the town of Kako in Harima province lived a scholar named Hasebe Samon. He was poor but satisfied with the purity of his life. Aside from the books that were his companions day and night, he did not like to have too many things in his surroundings. He had an elderly mother who was wise and whose strong principles were in no way inferior to those of the mother of the Chinese philosopher Mencius. She worked tirelessly spinning thread and weaving cloth and she supported Samon's lofty ambitions. Samon's younger sister had married into the Sayō family in their village. The Sayō family was extremely wealthy, but they were so impressed by this wise mother and her children that they took the daughter into their house as a wife and became relatives. Sometimes the Sayō sent goods to Samon, but he would never accept them, saying, "I will not rely on others for my livelihood."

One day Samon went to visit a man living in the same village. They chatted about events past and current. As they were chatting the sound of someone moaning in pain could be heard through the wall. It sounded as though the person was truly suffering. When Samon asked the owner of the house about it, the man replied, "He seems to be a man from a province west of here. He fell behind his companions and asked me if he could spend a night here. He looked like he had the bearing of a samurai and didn't seem to be a vulgar sort, so I let him stay. But that night he ran a vicious high fever and it came to be that he couldn't even get up or move as he wished. He has spent three or four days in that sorry state. I don't even really know where he is from. I didn't realize what I was getting myself into when I let him stay here and don't know what to do about it now."

Hearing that, Samon said, "That is a sad story. It's true that you are troubled by this, but that man suffering from illness, strucken sick on the road where he knows no one—how pitiful he must feel. I would like to see him."

The man stopped him and said, "They say an epidemic will harm people, so I am not allowing anyone from my house to go in there. You must not let yourself fall to harm."

Samon laughed. "The span of a human life is decided by fate, just as the saying goes. I wonder if there really are things like diseases that spread to people. That's the kind of thing said by stupid, common folk. People like me, we don't believe that," he said, and pushed the door open. When he looked at the man he saw indeed, just as the home owner had said, this was no average person, but he appeared gravely ill with a yellowed facial complexion and gaunt with darkened skin, laying prone and writhing atop an old futon. He looked at Samon as though looking at an old friend and said, " I'd like a cup of hot water."

Samon drew near and said, "Don't worry. I will certainly help you." Samon consulted with the home owner, selected medicines, created and decocted his own preparations and administered them himself. Not only that, but he fed the man rice gruel and nursed him as if he were his own brother. It was quite a remarkable situation.

The warrior shed tears at the generous kindness shown by Samon. "You have so wholeheartedly offered your aid to this traveller passing through. Even if it kills me, I want to repay you for your kindness," he said.

Samon spoke to encourage him. "Please don't say such weak-hearted things. A plague has a fixed period. Once that period has passed, there is no loss of life. I will come here every day and take care of you," Samon promised wholeheartedly. And he did just that. The illness gradually waned and the man's spirits recovered as well. The warrior voiced his gracious thanks to the home owner. He respected Samon's quiet acts of goodwill and helped him in his work. He also spoke of his own self as follows:

"I am Akana Sōemon from Matsue in the province of Izumo. I have studied the ways of war and so taught these ways to Enya Kamonnosuke, the lord of Tomita Castle. However, I was chosen to be a secret emissary to Sasaki Ujitsuna of Ōmi, and while I was staying in that residence, Amako Tsunehisa, the previous lord of the castle, fell in with the Yamanaka clan and devised a plot. On the night of New Year's Eve they launched a surprise attack and took over the castle, and Lord Kamonnosuke was slain. The province of Izumo was originally controlled by the Sasaki clan, and Kamonnosuke was the official representing the Governor. I counseled Ujitsuna to help both Misawa and Mitoya and destroy Tsunehisa. However, despite his brave appearance, inside Ujitsuna is a cowardly and stupid military commander, so he did not heed those words. What's worse, I was stranded there. I thought there was no reason to stick around someplace I had no reason to be. As I was surreptitiously making my way back home alone, I was stricken by this illness and then unexpectedly troubled you with it. I am eternally indebted for your kindness. I will spend the rest of my life repaying this kindness to you."

Samon replied, "It's only natural human emotion that did not allow me to turn away from another's misfortune. There is no reason for me to receive such gracious words. Please stay here and regain your health." Akana put his trust in those sincere words and within several days his physical strength and vigor returned almost to normal.

Over the course of these days Samon came to see he had gained a good friend. As they spent both day and night together talking, Akana spoke from time to time about the

Hundred Schools of Thought, and his questions about it and comprehension were excellent. The theories of military tactics about which Akana spoke came from his vast experience and were excellent. There was nothing about which the men disagreed. They admired and felt joy and at last they pledged a bond of brotherhood.

Akana was five years older than Samon and so was called Elder Brother by Samon. Akana said to Samon, "It has been a long time since I parted from my parents. Since your aged mother is now my mother too, I would like to visit her as her adopted son. I hope Mother will take pity on my childish heart and accept me as hers." Very pleased to hear this, Samon said, "Mother worries that I am always alone. When she hears your words filled with sincerity such reassurance will surely add years to her life," and brought Akana back to his home. His mother was pleased to greet them and said, " My son has no talents and his scholarly pursuits do not fit these times. He has lost the opportunity to go out into the world. Please do not abandon him and please offer him guidance as his pledged older brother." Akana reverently bowed his head and said, "A man values righteousness above all else. To become famous or rich is so trivial it goes without saying. Mother, I now have your affection and the respect of Samon. There is nothing more I could desire." Happily and joyously they spent several days there.

The cherry blossoms of Onoe, which were in blossom only yesterday, or was it today? They have all scattered. It was also evident in the waves pulled in by the cool breezes that early summer had arrived. One day Akana said to Samon and his mother, "The reason I broke free from Ōmi was because I wanted to see what was happening in Izumo. I would like to return to my hometown just this once and then I will come right back here, and even though I am poor, I will do my best to serve you and repay your kindness to me. Please allow me to go for a short while."

Samon asked, "Well, when will you come back, Elder Brother?"

Akana replied, "The months go by quickly, but at the latest, I will return by autumn of this year."

Samon said, "Could you decide on a date in autumn that I shall wait for? Please decide that before you leave."

Akana replied, "Let's make it the ninth day of the Ninth Month, the day of the Chrysanthemum Festival."

Samon said, "Brother, please do not forget this date. I will be waiting for you with a single chrysanthemum and a small gift of saké." Making their intentions apparent to each other, they made this promise and Akana left for his home in the west.

The months passed by quickly, and then the fruit on the lower branches of the silverberry became tinged red and the wild chrysanthemums blossomed beautifully in the hedges. The Ninth Month came. On the ninth day Samon woke up earlier than usual. He cleaned and straightened the sitting room of his simple home, put a few white and yellow chrysanthemums in a small vase, and emptied his wallet to buy food and drink. His elderly mother said, "That town of Yakumotatsu in Izumo is at the other end of the San-in Road. I hear it's over one hundred *ri*[1] from here, so don't set your heart on his arriving today. It wouldn't be too late to prepare things after you see he has come."

Saying, "Akana is a warrior true to his word. There is no way he will fail to keep his promise. I would be ashamed of what he would think if I rushed around to prepare after seeing he has arrived," Samon bought good wine and prepared some fresh fish so it was all ready in the kitchen.

That day the sky was clear, with not a cloud in sight. Groups of travellers conversed while walking. Listening to their conversations you could hear things like, "What a fine day! Perfect for so-and-so's trip to the Capital. This must be a sign that this next venture will be profitable." A warrior of about fifty said to his companion, "With the ocean this calm today, if we had gone by ship and set out from Akashi this morning we would have been on our way to Ushimado Bay now. What kind of young man wastes money so frivolously and is such a coward?" As they passed by, the companion, a young man in his twenties dressed in a similar fashion, tried to mollify him, saying, "I heard from someone who accompanied the lord on a trip to the Capital. They made the crossing from Shodoshima to Murotsu, but the currents were running and it was a terrible time. When you think about that, anyone would be afraid of crossing around here. Please don't begrudge me. I'll buy you

1. A *ri* is about 3,930 meters, or about 2.4 miles.

soba noodles at the station at Sakanagahashi." A packhorse man angrily said, "You damn dead horse. Can't you even open your eyes?" as he re-positioned the pack saddles and followed after the horse. It was well past noon, but the person Samon was waiting for did not come. As he watched while the sun started to set in the west and the travellers hurried by on their way to their lodgings, only other people caught his eye and it was as if his heart was drunk.

Samon's mother called to him, "As long as his heart has not changed like the capricious autumn skies, today is not the only day when the chrysanthemum blooms deeply of your pact. As long as he has the sincere intention to come back, how can you begrudge him even if he returns under rainy skies? Come inside and lie down and wait for tomorrow." Without a word of protest, he humored his mother and saw her off to bed. Then, when he went outside to see, just in case, the sparkling lights of the Milky Way shone faintly. The moon shone forlornly upon his solitary figure and he heard the barks of a watchdog coming from somewhere in the distance. The sound of the waves on the shore sounded as though they came all the way to him.¥

The light of the moon sank behind the edge of the mountain and it grew dark. Samon decided that was enough for that day, and as he closed the gate and went to go back into the house, he glanced and saw a person approaching from the misty dark shadows as though he was being blown by the wind. Wondering who it could be, he looked closely and saw it was Akana Sōemon. Samon felt like dancing for joy, and said, "I have been waiting for you since early this morning. I am so glad you came and kept our pact. Please come in." Akana simply nodded without saying a word. Samon entered first and guided Akana to his seat in front of the southern window of the sitting room. When Samon said, "Elder Brother, you arrived late and Mother was tired out from waiting. She went to bed saying, 'He will certainly come tomorrow.' Shall I go wake her?" Akana shook his head to stop Samon, but he still did not say anything.

Saying, "You travelled both day and night to get here so you must be tired in body and soul. Please have something to eat and drink and rest," Samon warmed the saké and set out the fish, but Akana covered his face with his sleeve as though avoiding a disagreeable smell.

Samon said, "It is a poor meal that I made myself and is inadequate for a guest, but I made it with all my heart. Please don't be scornful of it. Please eat."

Akana still did not answer and let out a long sigh. Then after a short while he finally started to speak. "I do not intend to refuse this feast you have prepared for me with all your heart. And I have no words with which to lie to you, so I shall speak the truth. Please don't think this is strange. I am not a person of this world. I have appeared in the form of a person temporarily in the body of an unclean ghost."

Samon was quite surprised. "Elder brother, why do you say such a bizarre thing? I really don't think I could be dreaming this."

Akana said, "I left you and went to my homeland but most of the people there were afraid of Amako Tsunehisa's vigor and followed him. Nobody remembered their debt to Kamonnosuke. When I inquired for my cousin Akana Tanji at Tomita Castle, Tanji tried to explain to me who it was advantageous or disadvantageous to side with, and then he brought me to Tsunehisa. First I listened to his persuasion and then I closely watched what Tsunehisa did. He possessed outstanding bravery and led his troops impressively. But although he employed wise men he did so with a deeply suspicious nature, and none of his retainers were moved to serve their master from deep within their hearts. I thought it wouldn't do any good to stay there for a long time, so I explained my pledge to meet you on the day of the Chrysanthemum Festival, but when I made my way to leave Tsunehisa became suspicious and bore a grudge against me. He ordered Tanji to imprison me in the castle and that is how it has been to this day. My heart sank when I thought of what you would think if I broke our pledge, but there was no way for me to escape. The ancients said, 'A man cannot go one thousand *ri* in one day, but the spirit can go one thousand *ri* in a day.' I remembered this logic, took my own life and rode all this way tonight on a dark wind to get here and keep our pledge for the Chrysanthemum Festival. Please take these feelings of mine into account." After saying this, Akana's tears flowed ceaselessly. "This is our final parting. Please take good care of Mother," he said and when he went to stand up instead he disappeared without a trace.

Samon hurried to stop him, but his eyes were clouded by a wind redolent of rank, raw flesh and he lost sight of where Akana went. He stumbled, fell prostrate and cried there violently. His mother was roused by his cries. Startled awake she went to Samon. When she saw where he was, she saw many cups and plates of saké and fish and Samon fallen down and laying prostrate in the middle of it. She hurried and picked him up and asked what had happened, but he stifled his voice and continued to cry without answering. His mother asked, "If you're going to hold a grudge because your elder brother Akana didn't keep his pledge, what are you going to say if he shows up tomorrow?" With strong reproach she said, "I didn't know you were this obsessed and foolish." Then Samon finally spoke to her in reply. "Elder Brother did come tonight to keep his pledge to meet on the day of the Chrysanthemum Festival. I greeted him and offered saké and fish. I offered many times but he refused, saying 'See now, there's a reason for this and I would be breaking my promise to you, so I ended my life with a blade and have became a ghostly spirit travelling over a hundred *ri*.' And then he disappeared. That is why I disturbed your sleep. Please forgive me." Then he broke down in tears again.

Mother said, "People who are locked up in jail see dreams about being pardoned and the thirsty drink water in their dreams. You must have just had that kind of dream. Please calm down." But Samon shook his head and said, "It really wasn't anything as uncertain as a dream. Elder Brother was definitely here." He fell down sobbing in tears again. Mother no longer had any doubts and they both spent the evening sobbing in tears.

The next day Samon regained his sense of propriety and said to his mother, "I have followed the scholarly path since I was a child, but I have no reputation for having shown loyalty to our land. I have been unable to be dutiful to my parents at home. I have merely lived a meaningless existence in this world. Compared to this, my adopted brother Akana ended his life persistently adhering to his loyalty. Today I will set out for Izumo. At the very least I want to be true in my fidelity as a brother and bury his remains. Mother, please take good care of yourself and please allow me this time to fulfill my duty."

Mother answered, "My son, go to Izumo if you must, but

please come back soon and put my mind at ease. Please don't remain there for a long time and make today's parting our final one."

Samon said, "A person's life is like foam that floats upon the water. No one knows if it will disappear in the morning or evening. It is a fleeting thing. But I will come back home soon." Wiping his tears, he departed. He went by the Sayō home and asked them to look after the mother he left behind, then he set out for Izumo. Along the way he didn't stop to eat even when starving. He was unconcerned with clothing even when it became cold. Whenever he dozed off he saw Akana in his dreams and wept through the night. Ten days later he reached the Tomita Castle.

Samon first went to Akana Tanji's home. He gave his full name and requested an audience and Tanji let him in. "How could you possibly know about Sōemon's death? A bird or something didn't tell you. There is no way," he said repeatedly. Samon said, "A warrior should not make an issue of the vicissitudes of wealth and rank. He should only prize fidelity. My brother Sōemon honored a pledge that he spoke only one time. He died, became a spirit and travelled one hundred *ri* to my home to keep his promise. To repay this I have travelled day and night to reach this place. It is something I learned in an ordinary manner, but there is something I would like to ask you about. I would like to receive a straight answer. Long ago in China when the Chancellor of Wei was ill the King of Wei himself went to visit at his bedside and took the chancellor's hand and said, 'If anything were to happen to you, to whom could I entrust state affairs? Please tell me.' When asked this, the Chancellor replied with sincerity, 'Shōō may be young but he possesses a rare talent. If you do not recruit him do not let him leave our borders, even if you have to kill him. If he is allowed to go to another land, that will surely become the source of disaster for our nation.'

Then the Chancellor secretly called for Shōō and told him, 'I recommended you to the King, but it doesn't look as though he will take you in. Then I told him if he will not recruit you he had better kill you rather than let you go elsewhere. I said this on the principle of first thinking of the Ruler and then of his retainers. You should escape to another country quickly and avoid harm.'

How would you compare this story to the situation between yourself and Sōemon?"

Tanji dropped his head, speechless.

Samon moved forward and closer. "My elder brother Sōemon's consideration of his longstanding obligation to Kamonnosuke and refusal to serve Amako Tsunehisa was the conduct of a loyal warrior. Your abandonment of your old master Kamonnosuke in order to follow Tsunehisa means you do not possess loyalty as a warrior. My brother gave his life to travel one hundred *ri* to honor a pledge to reunite on the day of the Chrysanthemum Festival. That is the pinnacle of loyalty. You now fawn over Tsunehisa and caused your blood relative Sōemon to suffer and die a pitiful death. You have no loyalty as a friend. Even if Tsunehisa had been able to force Sōemon to stop, if you had thought about your long relationship with him you would have shown your loyalty in secret, like the Chancellor did to Shōō. Instead you just ran to your own profit and advancement. Your lack of character as a warrior shows exactly what the Amako clan's tradition is about. That is why my brother tried to put a stop to them. Honoring my loyalty, I have come here with a purpose. You will leave a legacy of dishonor because of your injustice." Before he finished talking, he drew his sword and slashed, felling Tanji on the spot with a single stroke. While his retainers ran about in a panic, Samon quickly left the premises and concealed his whereabouts. When Amako Tsunehisa heard about this incident he was so moved by the depth of the fraternal loyalty he did not have Samon pursued. Alas, the saying "Do not associate yourself with superficial people" is precisely correct.

Three Old Tales of Terror

旧耳袋 (Furui mimi bukuro)

Kyōgoku Natsuhiko (2005)　　　　　　京極夏彦
English translation by Rossa O'Muireartaigh

Who made them?
誰が作った

MR. U, THE chief attendant to the samurai, had a great number of servants in his house.

One day, Miss A, a servant-girl who had worked in the house for many years, took ill.

Great efforts were made to cure her, but to no avail, and her condition did not improve. She was in great pain, so she made a request to Mr. U that she be excused from her work.

As it was essential to her survival that the utmost efforts be made to nurse her back to health, Mr. U gave her an unlimited period of rest to recuperate. With assurances that she could return to work when she fully recovered, Mr. U told Miss A not to worry, but to rest and get well.

After some time past, Miss A unexpectedly came to the room where Mr. U's mother lived in retirement.

Miss A bowed her head deeply towards Mrs. U and said:

"Thanks to your kindness, I was able to rest during all this time. I am so grateful to you for all the generosity you have shown me for so long." Mrs. U had always been quite fond of Miss A and so she was greatly pleased to hear this report of her recuperation. However, when Mrs. U looked at Miss A, she found that she still presented a sickly mien.

So she said, "You still don't look very well. Please rest some more. One needs to take even more care of oneself after an illness. When you are well again you can then come back to us. As we promised, you will still be able to work for us."

Miss A then smiled and said, "Don't worry, I can now work," and with that she unwrapped a cloth-covered parcel she had brought, to reveal a two-tiered *jūbako*[1].

"I have brought you this as an expression of my gratitude. I hope you like them."

Mrs. U opened the *jūbako* and found it stuffed full with snow-white rice dumplings.

Mrs. U remarked that the rice-dumplings looked delicious indeed, to which Miss A smiled and told her, "I made them myself."

They did in fact look freshly made. "Well, if she can make rice dumplings as lovely as these, no doubt she must have recovered. I dare say she can indeed resume her work," Mrs. U mused to herself.

And given Miss A's own eagerness to return, it would be churlish to refuse.

So after a few moments of reflection, Mrs. U relented saying, "Very well. I suppose we can let you work again. But please promise not to exhaust yourself." Miss A was greatly pleased. She profusely professed her gratitude to Mrs. U once more and then took her leave, saying, "Well. I must be off to say hello to everyone else in the house." With that she headed off in the direction of the main residence.

Looking at her from behind as she moved off, Mrs. U felt that she looked healthy enough. But still she felt some apprehension about her wellbeing, and so shortly afterwards she took the liberty of calling on the kitchen where Miss A worked.

She approached the head servant of the kitchen and said to her, "Miss A came to me a while ago. She may have told you herself but she starts work again from today. She tells me she has recovered from her illness but I am still a little concerned and would like everyone to assist her."

When she said this, all the servants standing around listening cocked their heads in surprise and reported that they had

---

1. *Jūbako*: A traditional box for carrying prepared food, usually consisting of a stack of box-like trays.

not seen Miss A anywhere about at all. Then Mrs. U, wondering if Miss A had perhaps gone around to another part of the house to say hello, looked for her all over. Absolutely no one, it seemed, had laid eyes on her at all—either inside or outside the house.

This was all very peculiar, so Mrs. U sent a messenger to visit Miss A's family home. Mrs. U thought to herself, "She must not have been recovering after all; she probably had a relapse and went back to her family".

It would be most regrettable if she had collapsed on the way.

At that moment Mrs. U was overcome by a sense of foreboding, so she went to check again the box Miss A had given her.

The box was there, all right.

When she opened it, the rice dumplings were still inside.

Beautiful, shimmering-white, fresh rice dumplings enticing her eyes with their deliciousness.

Eventually the messenger returned.

"Miss A is dead."

So Mrs. U's frightful premonition had been right after all. She felt shocked and saddened.

The messenger continued, "She died two or three days ago. It was very sudden, so the family have delayed reporting it."

Mr. U does not know if his mother ate the rice dumplings or not.

What does he want?
何がしたい

I DON'T KNOW how old this tale is, but it concerns a workman named Mr. B who lived in Kaitaichō (present-day Shinjuku in Tokyo). Mr. B was a hardworking man and often cooked his own meals.

One day, Mr. B bought a second-hand *kamado*[2] stove.

It was still in considerably good condition, so without further ado he set it down in the earthen floor just inside the entrance to his house and boiled some water.

The next evening, Mr. B sensed something peculiar about the stove and inadvertently took a glance at the base of it.

Just then, he saw a hand come slithering out.

Naturally, he thought this an illusion. But something had definitely come out at him. This he was sure of.

He stepped down into the kitchen area and bent down to take a look. What he saw, in the bottom of the stove, was nothing other than a rather dirty-looking monk with his hand stretched out.

Mr. B was astounded by this spectacle, although he felt more confused than scared by what he saw. He left things as they were and went to sleep.

The next morning, the stove looked as normal as it should be. His mind filled up with absurd and idle thoughts such as whether the cavity at the bottom of the stove would be big enough for a person to squeeze into, or whether shoving in some sticks of firewood could perturb any further intrusions. He smiled wryly to himself at these wild musings, and set off for work.

When he came back later that day, he made his dinner. Shortly after he finished eating, the hand appeared again.

Seeing it now for the second time, he was sure there was indeed a mangy monk inside. This was very odd, as a fire had just been burning only a short time ago under that very stove. But strange and all as it may be, there was no denying what was there. The monk himself actually did nothing – just put out his hand. Mr. B did not feel so surprised now that he was seeing this strange sight for the second time. There was nothing to be done about it, and he had no inclination to strike up a conver-

---

2. *Kamado* stove: A traditional Japanese stove with a large ceramic base.

sation with his new-found freakish visitor. So this day, too, he left things as they were and went to sleep.

Waking up early the next morning, Mr. B thought to himself, "He is not doing any harm, this monk, but still it does feel rather grotesque."

With that, he went to the second-hand shop where he had bought the stove and said to the shopkeeper, "This stove is no good. I don't like it. I want to exchange it." The shopkeeper looked displeased and replied, "The stove is well crafted and the price very reasonable. It may be second-hand, but it is still clean and intact".

Mr. B did not try to explain himself but just simply said, "Whatever you say, I just don't like it". He decided not to tell the shopkeeper his story as he felt it was too strange to be believed. On top of that, Mr. B also suspected that it may well have been his own delusions. When he thought rationally about it now, it all seemed so impossible and absurd.

Even so, he still felt quite disturbed by the whole affair.

The shopkeeper then said, "Well, fine. I will give you your money back." Mr. B asked the shopkeeper again if he could do a direct exchange for another stove, but the shopkeeper told him that there was no other stove for that price.

In fact, all the other stoves were slightly more expensive. And indeed, the more persistent Mr. B became, the more the shopkeeper grew suspicious of him. So Mr. B agreed that this time the sale would be final, paid the balance of the exchange, and brought away a different stove.

With that, matters were resolved for now.

A short while after this episode, Mr. B heard that his colleague at work, Mr. C, had bought a stove. Not thinking it would be the same stove, he was nevertheless curious and asked Mr. C about it. He then realized from listening to Mr. C that the stove was actually from the same shop where Mr. B had bought and returned his.

According to Mr. C, the stove was a good bargain.

Two or three days later, Mr. B visited Mr. C. Mr. B had a vague inkling that the stove his friend had bought was the same stove he once had. As anticipated, Mr. C had a disturbed expression on his face when Mr. B met him. It seemed something strange had indeed happened.

Asking if anything was up, Mr. C replied, "You may laugh. But every evening something a bit scary happens." Mr. C made a strained and weary face.

Every evening, it seemed that something, whatever it was, appeared out from under the stove. Mr. C felt unnerved by it and never checked to see what it was.

Mr. B slapped his knees, and exclaimed, "Aha! That's what I thought would happen," and began to relate his own experiences with the stove.

"Maybe that's the same stove I bought. The same thing kept happening with mine. It gave me the creeps, so I changed it. Maybe you should exchange yours as well."

"Yes. It is a bit unnerving."

Mr. C followed Mr. B's advice, and the next day brought the stove back to the second-hand shop and paid the extra amount to change it for another stove.

The whole event played on Mr. B's mind, so driven by his own curiosity, he went back again to the second-hand shop and, feigning ignorance, struck up a casual conversation with the shopkeeper to try and find out something about the stove.

After a while, he managed to broach the subject, saying, "By the way, whatever happened to that stove? It was a good stove and very cheap, so I'm sure you were able to sell it off immediately."

"Well, actually, it was sold again but then returned again. The customer felt the same way about it as you did. What is actually so unattractive about that stove, I ask you!"

The shopkeeper was puzzled so Mr. B made up his mind to tell him what had happened, and proceeded to recount all the details.

At this the second-hand shopkeeper was furious.

"Sir! There is no need for such rubbish lies. Is it your intention, sir, to criticize my goods?"

"These are no lies. Instead of getting angry with me, why don't you try it for yourself?"

With that, Mr. B cut short the conversation and went home.

After some time, the shopkeeper from the second-hand store called on Mr. B.

The shopkeeper had a perplexed expression as he showed Mr. B some gold coins.

"What are those?" Mr. B asked him, wondering why he was being suddenly shown this gold.

The shopkeeper started off with an apology to Mr. B, saying "Well, I must beg your forgiveness for my anger the last time I met you. It was most regrettable of me."

"At first, I thought you were just trying to annoy me. But you did actually pay me extra to change the stove. And it was very strange that another customer came back with the exact same stove a second time. So I began to think things over and wondered if there was some reason for all this. So, what I did was, I brought the stove into my own kitchen and brewed some tea on it. Anyway, that evening..."

The hand, naturally, appeared again for the shopkeeper to see.

"Not only that," continued the shopkeeper, "but it then started to crawl around".

"What started to crawl around?"

"This disgusting, filthy monk. He was there crawling around so I just couldn't bear it."

"The next morning, straightaway I took the stove to the shop and smashed it up. But when I did that these gold coins fell out."

The shopkeeper went on, "I don't know. Maybe what this apparition was, was the worldly attachments or something of a religious devotee who died and left the gold hidden in the stove."

Mr. B did not say anything, but felt himself that this wasn't quite correct.

He did not believe that whoever it was had wanted the hidden gold to be found. It is not a happy thing to give over gold to a complete stranger. Nor did he think either it was the regrets of someone who had died without having a chance to use the gold.

"I don't know if it was a dead spirit or what it was. I have no idea what it wanted, putting its hands out like that and crawling around."

"It sure was a dirty and horrible thing, whatever it was," said B.

Where had she been?
どこに居た

IT WAS THE winter of 1795, in the seventh year of the Kansei era.

In the house of Mr. O there resided a servant girl of rare and wondrous beauty. Indeed, her pulchritude was such that it was an object of some public renown.

However, one day, quite suddenly, she just disappeared without a trace, and was nowhere to be found.

Being the pretty and alluring maiden that she was, she was assumed by many to have been whisked away by a secret admirer. However, this did not make sense, as Mr. O's house was no ordinary town house, but a splendid samurai's residence. It was hard to see how anyone could be so bold as to creep in and actually snatch away one of the servant girls. Furthermore, Mr. O was of a high-born family entitled to one hundred thousand *koku*[3] of rice, and so his residence, unlike those of lower-ranking samurai, was enclosed by four formidable walls. As such, any infiltration from the outside would have been impossible. The only way to abduct her would have been when she was outside the house. But there were no indications that she had ever left the premises.

She had simply vanished without a trace.

But surely it is impossible for a person to just disappear like a puff of smoke. She must just have taken off of her own accord. There was no other way. Sneaking in would be impossible, so she must have sneaked out.

But there was no reason on earth for her to have done so.

So speculation then emerged that someone must have fallen for her, and they had eloped in secret.

Enquiries were made at her family home, but no one there had any idea either where she might be.

There was no trace of her, and absolutely no way of knowing where she was.

Just twenty days after her disappearance, another servant girl, who slept in the same wing of the house as the girl who

---

3. *Koku*: A unit of measurement traditionally equal to a year's supply of rice, about five bushels. In pre-modern Japan, a samurai's stipend was measured and allocated by *koku*.

had disappeared, went to the bathroom. This wing was effectively one long terraced row partitioned into smaller houses. It was here that all the domestic servant girls lived.

As this servant girl was washing her hands at the water trough located outside, just beside the row of houses, she was startled to see a white hand suddenly appear beside her.

The hand was thin and pale white, and it held a seashell, which it was apparently attempting to fill with water.

The servant girl screamed and fainted.

Hearing the screaming, the other servant girls from the same rooms, along with others from around the house, came rushing over to see what had happened. As they came crowding around, they beheld a grotesque figure trying to scamper away under the elevated floor of the house. Thinking it to be a thief or vagabond of some sort, the crowd seized upon this intruder.

It was the missing girl.

It was all very bizarre. Right away, she was brought over to the parlor and given warm water. After she became more relaxed, the people around started asking her questions about where she had been.

But no matter what she was asked, she did not answer. She completely shunned their interrogation.

However, after more questions and much prodding, she began to open up, albeit with some reluctance, telling them, "I found the man chosen for me. We are now married – my husband and I."

She stated that she was now wedded into an opulent and splendid house.

However, she would not tell them anything about where this house was. Or indeed who it was she had married.

More questions were leveled at her, but her answers were all the time vague and opaque, and volunteered only half-heartedly at that. The name and address she revealed to them were also obscure. It was all quite senseless. It wasn't so much that her responses were evasive as simply inchoate.

They pleaded with her for clearer answers, comforting her and cajoling her, until she eventually relented, saying, "Fine. As you all want to know, I shall bring you to see where I live."

She stood up and beckoned to them all, "Please, this way."

With that, she crouched down and started to make her way in underneath the floorboards of the house.

Two or three of the others followed her, as it seemed to be the only thing they could do in this situation. She crawled on her belly and went deeper and deeper into the space under the floor of the house.

Finally, she stopped and announced to them, "Well. This is my home."

There were straw and rush mats laid around.

She placed some teacups and bowls on top of one of the rush mats.

"It is such a lovely place, isn't it?" she enthused.

The others who had followed felt exasperated and dumbfounded.

One of them ventured to enquire, "This is the house...so who exactly is your husband?"

"Haven't I already told you? A splendid, wonderful man," she answered, and proceeded to utter a name that no one could make head nor tail of. Again, she was answering their questions, all right, but she was not making any sense whatsoever.

Her behavior was so odd.

She must have gone insane, was what they all thought. They managed to pull her out from under the floor after enticing her with reassurances that they understood perfectly what she had been telling them.

Whatever else, everyone was glad to see that she was alive.

But it was now impossible for her to continue working in the house as before. The authorities were informed of her reappearance and also of the fact that she had effectively gone mad. Mr. O contacted the girl's family and had her taken away. She was relieved of her duties.

The girl's parents were greatly relieved to have her back safely, whatever state she may be in. They were sure she would recover in due course from her present derangement. They gave her medicines and cared for her. But for all their efforts, alas the girl soon died.

Her grieving parents wondered if she had not been tricked by some fox or *tanuki*.[4]

---

4. Foxes (*kitsune*), and racoon dogs (*tanuki*; similar to a badger) were, ac-

When Mr. O heard this, he just frowned and shook his head, saying, "Be that as it may, was our servant girl really under those floorboards for the twenty days she was missing?"

In the space under those floorboards, the mats were still laid out, but absolutely no traces of food were found. Or indeed any signs whatsoever of anyone ever having lived there.

---

cording to Japanese folklore, shape-shifters who would transform themselves and play nasty tricks on human beings.

The Futon Room

布団部屋 (Futon beya)

Miyabe Miyuki (2000) 宮部みゆき
English translation by Stephen A. Carter

KANEKOYA, THE SAKÉ merchant in Eitaiji Monzen Higashi-chō in Fukagawa, was known for the short lifespans of its succession of owners.

The first one founded the business at this location in the year Hōei 6 (1709), but in the interval of fifty and a hundred years since then, the number of heads of the household climbed to seven. In the normal course of things, there would have been four or five at most.

Still, the ways in which the previous six owners died had not been notably untoward. Although there was one exception, five had died peacefully, passing away with such tranquility that all who knew them would have considered them natural deaths had only they lived to the fullness of age. This was because they had all simply gone to bed at night and never awakened—come morning, when their wives went to rouse them, they were each found to have died.

If one had to attach a reason, it may have been that the men of Kanekoya were unfortunate enough to have had a weak heart passed down from generation to generation. In truth, the second- and third-born sons who were not in line to inherit the shop tended to die while still in childhood. Only the eldest sons managed to live on to adulthood. Then, when each son reached the age of sixteen or seventeen, the father would die young, and the son would hurriedly take over the shop, marry quickly, and produce offspring, and when that child somehow clung to life to reach the age of sixteen or seventeen, the father himself would suddenly pass on—this was the cycle that repeated.

The daughters, meanwhile, always grew up healthy and strong. The wives taken in each generation were also robust and hardy, blessed with many children, which they bore with ease.

Gossipmongers would say that the women of Kanekoya were *too* strong, and so the menfolk had their vitality drained away and died young. This certainly seemed plausible. In fact, the young masters who had only recently taken over as head of the household on inheriting the shop were surrounded not just by old women but by very old women, all healthy and spry, each sharp and bright of eye, and so maybe it wasn't entirely possible to laugh this off as exaggeration. However, the rumors that Kanekoya was filled with *hinouma* women who were born in the darkly inauspicious "fire-horse" year of the Chinese zodiac and were said to devour men, and that the house only took in brides born in the fire-horse year, and that only daughters born in the fire-horse year were produced— these were all baseless, and in fact the household had not a single woman born in the fire-horse year.

Another rumor was also heard. Of the six prior owners, one alone was said to have died in a different way. That was Kiemon, the fourth head of the house, who at the age of thirty-three had died of measles after the turn of the year. Measles contracted in adulthood is a fearsome disease, and not uncommonly life-ending.

At the time, however, Kiemon's death was widely rumored to be divine retribution. The smiting god was held to be Lord Tsunayoshi, the fifth shōgun. Lord Tsunayoshi had died of measles in 1709, after the turn of the year. The year 1709 happened to be the year Kanekoya was founded. Simply stated, the deified spirit of Lord Tsunayoshi was angered by Kanekoya heedlessly launching a saké shop in the year of his death, and had meted out punishment.

In any event, this was an extremely far-fetched tale, and so it is little surprise that it failed to gain much credence. Lord Tsunayoshi, the fifth shōgun, was a draconian ruler who made the common people suffer in many ways, and many would have liked to see him punished. What's more, even if the spirit of Lord Tsunayoshi really had become a peevish god and meted out retribution to an insolent Kanekoya, he hardly would have waited until the fourth generation to do so. There were a few who long-windedly held that because the first, second, and third generations had all uneventfully experienced measles in childhood, waiting until the fourth generation had been necessary, but taking quibbling to such levels made it ridiculous, and all who heard it clutched their bellies in laughter.

Be that as it may, the reputation for dying young took hold, and the spread of unfunny rumors each time the master of the house died was bad for business. Talk concerning death smacked of religion, which was all the more unacceptable because the product being traded was saké. That is why, for generation after generation, Kanekoya kept itself more deferential than other dealers, accepting difficult orders that others turned away, earning the trust of their clientèle by demonstrating honesty and a willingness to work all-out as traders.

This inevitably made them strict with their workers. Thus, although it never reached the same prominence as their reputation for owners who died young, Kanekoya also earned a another reputation—one for treating its employees unsparingly. It wasn't that they made up for being demanding by paying well. They were simply demanding.

Nonetheless, for seven generations, Kanekoya had never had a scandal due to workers running off, not even once. What's more, Kanekoya's employees were genuinely hard-working and never grumbled or caused trouble.

Worker discipline is the biggest headache of a shop-owner, and prevailing belief holds that nothing can be done to ensure perfection. If a shop hires ten employees and spends ten years grooming them, the business will be lucky if one or two grow into able workers of use to the shop—that's how difficult the matter is held to be. Many quit, and many simply run off because of the demanding work. Not a few are sidelined by disease or injury.

In the worst cases, some wretches even abscond with pilfered funds, sink into roguery, or rob the shop that took them in and try to make off with the its property. That the law decrees that any worker who harms his master or attempts to set his master's house on fire, no matter what reason or excuse is proffered, is sure to be sentenced to having his head cut off and exposed to public view, is, when seen from the opposite angle, evidence that the number of such instances is too high to brush off as a fluke.

Workers are not all adults; apprentices and nursemaids may be taken on while still in childhood. The shop must take the role of the parent in disciplining them, and this, too, is a difficult task. Scolding, admonishing, and, at times, applying severe physical punishment to children who shirk their tasks to play, or sneak bites of food when no one is looking, or doze off requires considerable time and effort. Yet even so, more times than otherwise it is ineffective.

Kanekoya accomplished this difficult task with consummate ease, generation after generation. On coming to work at Kanekoya, even rough young men who had until then been intractable troublemakers, and weepy, timorous children, were, in a span of no more than ten days, completely transformed into dependable shop workers. They also became uncommonly resistant to illness and injury.

It is no surprise that this aroused wonder and envy among nearby merchants. But when asked what tricks they used, the master, or his wife, or the head clerk would just smile and look away, which only served to deepen the mystery. Would could the secret be?

As it happened, though, a young housemaid suddenly spouted a gushing nosebleed and fell dead. This event took place around the tenth month of the year Bunka 11 (1814), when the seventh head of Kanekoya, Shichibē, was thirty-five years old.

THE HOUSEMAID WHO had suddenly dropped dead was named Osato.

The oldest daughter of a tenant farmer in the village of Ōshima in Ozaimokugura-higashi in Sarue, she had been taken on as a nursemaid at Kanekoya at the age of eleven, and at the time of her death, she was working as a maid in the household and was sixteen years old. She had been in training at Kanekoya for five years in all. A sweet-tempered and indus-

trious worker, she was overly thin but appeared more self-pos-
sessed than her years, conducting herself like a adult, and at a
quick glance she gave the impression of a grown-up woman of
twenty years or more.

Kanekoya was not a large shop. It was, at most, of medi-
um-small size. Eating establishments and samurai houses
numbered among its clientèle, but it naturally also did a brisk
business in in-store sales. Because it made keeping its front
door open longer than any other place in Fukagawa its strong
point, the employees often missed the last call for bathing at
the public bathhouses. The people at the bathhouses they pa-
tronized learned to keep their front doors open until the help
from Kanekoya hurried in at a run.

On the night in question, that was how Osato, too, rushed
to the last bath of the day. She hurriedly used the bath, bid
the man at the watch stand a good night, and left, and her
demeanor during this time was said to be as brisk as always,
showing nothing out of the ordinary. Not more than a few moments after leaving the bathhouse, however, she suddenly developed a copious nosebleed, and toppled over like a stick at
the side of the road, her hands still pressed to her face.

She was all alone at the time, and a gatekeeper who had
been nearby came to her aid; he carried her back to Kanekoya
on his shoulders, but by the time they arrived she was no longer breathing.

According to the gatekeeper, however, over all the roads
they went down as she was carried to Kanekoya, Osato at his
back appeared not to suffer at all, but whispered this in a sing-
song voice the entire way:

This way, Sir Demon, toward the clapping hands.
This way, Sir Demon, toward the clapping hands.

With these words ringing in his ears, the gatekeeper thereafter slept for three full days.

By no means is it as if nothing was tried at Kanekoya—the lay
police assistant jumped into action, as did the town officials—
but despite all this, the cause behind why Osato died remained
undetermined. She had eaten the same things as everyone
else for supper, so food poisoning seemed unlikely, and it was
likewise inconceivable that she had been deliberately poi-
soned. Her body had no wounds, and no strange spots arose

on her cold skin. Her face in death was peaceful, and once the aftermath of the nosebleed had been wiped away, she even looked as if she could be asleep.

Kanekoya's employees were simply dumbfounded by her sudden death and could only shake their heads, saying they had had no inkling of any disease or injury or anything of the like. Leading the employees whose work was in the household was a woman named Omitsu, the chief housemaid, who was forty-three years old, sturdy of body and forceful of temperament, and not of a nature easily shaken, but even this Omitsu, when questioned by the master and his wife, could merely report timidly that nothing about Osato had seemed amiss.

Osato was fine right up until she left for the bathhouse, tidily eating a late supper, just as always, and hadn't seemed to be feeling out of sorts in any way—Omitsu repeated this over and over, and apologized in tears to the master and mistress, saying she had failed to notice whatever had been wrong. Omitsu was an exemplary housemaid, with the master and his wife relying on her to an unusual degree, and because having a head maid as outstanding as Omitsu aroused the envy of other shops, it never even occurred to them to blame her; indeed, they turned instead toward consoling her.

At Kanekoya, they decided to return Osato's remains to her parents quickly, including a modest sum as a token of their condolences. The notifications made to the town officials wrapped everything up tidily as "death from disease." The merchant houses in the Monzen-chō area clamorously passed all sorts of rumors about the unexpected and mysterious death of a Kanekoya worker, but as the town officials had already been placated, these efforts were doomed from the outset. At most, they could only watch the day-to-day doings of Kanekoya with eyes of redoubled avidness; however, few shops were affluent enough to be able to do only that all the day long, and so even the whispers died down of their own accord.

Osato's parents, who had taken an advance on her wages, were naturally in no position to raise strong words against Kanekoya because she had died suddenly while in their employ. On the contrary—to make up for the loss of Osato, they offered to place their youngest girl into service, asking that they make use of her. The mediating employment service also was aware that Osato had been a conscientious worker, and knew that the parents were desperately poor, and enthusiastically pursued the matter with the master and his wife at Kanekoya on their behalf.

In this way, half a month after Osato's death, her youngest sister Oyū came to be employed at Kanekoya. She too was eleven years old. Her parents took an advance equal to her wages until she reached the age at which her sister had died, and sent her off from home carrying a single small cloth-wrapped bundle.

It was decided that Oyū, on becoming a member of Kanekoya, was to be provided with everything her sister had used, just as it was. Her futon and bedding, her meal-tray box, rice bowl, and chopsticks, and even her work apron were hand-me-downs from Osato. She also slept and arose in the same corner of the maid's room that had been given to Osato.

This room was for three persons, and the other two had no doubt known Osato well when she was alive. They were also closer in age to Osato. But the two girls never once spoke in reminiscence of Osato. Though they surely knew that Oyū was Osato's younger sister, they never even spoke a word of condolence.

It seemed just as if they had completely forgotten about Osato.

Although she was never mistreated, neither was she ever shown special kindness. Up close, in fact, the two housemaids did not appear to be all that close to one another. They seemed remote and detached.

Kanekoya at present had no children of an age needing minding, and so right from the start the tasks assigned to Oyū were the same as those of the older housemaids. Fetching water, cleaning, airing the futons, washing up, running errands— Oyū worked as hard as she could, but tasks beyond the abilities of an eleven-year-old girl popped up one after another, in unending succession.

Even in her child's mind, Oyū understood quite well that she was a useless girl who fell far short of her dead sister. That's why she also did what she could to devise ways that would enable her to master her tasks as quickly. That much insight she had. And the person who had given her that insight was none other than Osato.

Oyū's family was dirt-poor and had six children, but Osato and Oyū were the only girls. The parents being preoccupied with eking out a living, Oyū had been brought up almost single-handedly by Osato. When Osato had gone off to work, Oyū had run after and wept fiercely, and when Osato came back on servants' holidays, Oyū had been so filled with joy that she even begrudged the time lost to sleep at night.

At such times, they huddled together in the same futon and talked together through the night. Selecting only the aspects that were entertaining or enjoyable, Osato told her sister about her place of employment.

Yes. For the most part, Osato spoke only of the fun things. But sometimes she would get a bit of a serious look and say something like this:

When you get to be my age, of course you'll also be sent off to work somewhere. When that happens, you work just as hard as you can. Because it's the hard workers who come out ahead.

Oyū took these words of her sister completely to her young heart.

Sometimes she grew lonely and tears came. Sometimes she missed her home. At such times, she would pull the bedding over her head and lie huddled there, unmoving. When she did this, Oyū felt enveloped by the body warmth of living Osato that still remained in the bedding. This brought to mind the times back home when the two had both slept on a single futon, and she even felt as if she could hear her sister's voice. She believed her sister was always at her side and watching over her. When eventually the tears subsided, Oyū would mutter a good-night to her sister and go to sleep.

By the time a month had passed, Oyū had more or less mastered her tasks.

One morning, as she was doing the washing by the well, Omitsu, the head housemaid, strode heavily up to her. Thinking she was in for a scolding, Oyū hunched her shoulders. This large-framed head housemaid normally almost never deigned to speak to Oyū. At Kanekoya, the housemaids maintained a firm hierarchy, and Omitsu directly spoke and gave instructions to only the senior housemaids directly under her. These senior housemaids assigned jobs to Oyū and the two young maids who shared the same room. The young housemaids then ordered about Oyū, at the very bottom, by gesturing with their chins.

This was not the case, though, when she was being reproved. Omitsu would skip over two levels and suddenly appear before her.

However, this morning was different. To Oyū, who had stopped work, stood up, and quietly waited with bowed head to accept a rebuke, Omitsu said something unexpected. *The mistress is pleased with your work*, she said.

Oyū had addressed the master and his wife only once, when she joined the employ of the household; most days, girls at Oyū's level never even saw them. But it seemed the mistress had noted to Omitsu that Osato's newly arrived sister was quite a hard worker.

Oyū, filled with joy, felt a warm glow rise in her bosom. She thought that the praise had come not just to her, but also to the spirit of her sister who was always with her and watching out for her. She bowed her head deeply and said *Thank you very much* in a quiet voice.

Because Omitsu remained unmoving beside her, blocking her way, Oyū raised her face and timidly looked up at the woman. Omitsu had narrowed both eyes to lines and was staring fixedly at Oyū.

Omitsu was not only large in body, but also had oversize facial features. She had a striking face that, although not beautiful, drew the eye. When reprimanding the housemaids, she would goggle her giant eyes, open her mouth a huge distance, and shout angrily.

Now, however, she seemed a completely different person. It even almost seemed as if she was wearing a mask.

Oyū suddenly became afraid, and not knowing whether she should say something or whether she should look down again, she dithered. At this, Omitsu, perceiving these flustered thoughts, spoke flatly, as if interrupting:

You're scared of me.

Oyū was unable to speak, as if her tongue had pulled back into her throat.

Without waiting for a reply, Omitsu spoke again.

Tonight, when I call you, you follow me with your bedding. Because you're going to sleep in the inner futon room.

On saying only this, she turned on her heel and went off. Only when Omitsu's broad back had disappeared from view did Oyū break out in a sweat.

Because you're going to sleep in the inner futon room.
It was a strange command, but Oyū was not all that surprised. That was because she had an idea what those words signified.

It had been maybe ten days after Oyū had joined the household. The two housemaids with whom she shared a room were whispering back and forth to one another, ignoring Oyū.

Omitsu hasn't taken her into the inner futon room yet.
How strange. It usually doesn't take this long.
I got taken in there on my third day her.
For me, it was on my very first day.
I wonder why Oyū doesn't get taken in there.

As the days passed, the whispers between the two housemaids became more frequent, and the brightness of their eyes as well as the amount of twist of their lips as they whispred back and forth also increased.

Apparently, being "taken into the inner futon room" was, for the housemaids, a feared punishment or something. That must be why the other two thought it peculiar that Oyū had not yet experienced it even though they themselves had experienced it early on.

But if so, that in itself would be odd. Oyū had already been soundly rebuked by Omitsu. If she moved just a little slowly or failed to grasp what she was told the first time, Omitsu would shout at her unsparingly, and sometimes hit her. If being "taken into the futon room" was punishment intended to demonstrate the authority of the head housemaid to new maids, then, just as the two housemaids said, it was strange that Oyū herself hadn't been taken there long ago.

After much thought, Oyū tried asking the housemaids sharing the room while the three of them were lying on their futons at night, with Oyū in the middle. Without lifting their heads from their pillows, the other two exchanged startled glances. The expressions of the two became uncharacteristically avid.

After a bit, while remaining constantly guarded, they asked her why she wanted to know such a thing. Oyū shrewdly answered that she had gathered from overhearing the two that the reason why Oyū had not been taken into the futon room was because she wasn't yet fully accepted as a housemaid at Kanekoya, and so she wondered whether sooner or later she would be let go and sent back to her parents, which worried her no end.

The two housemaids seemed somewhat mollified. They then explained that taking new workers into the futon room was a tradition at this shop.

It's not as if it's just housemaids. The male workers get taken in there, too.

Oyū already knew what the inner futon room was. It was a dim room, four and a half tatami mats in size, at the northeast corner of the house. Having neither windows nor closets, it was an empty room now used for nothing at all, but because it was said to have once been used as a room for storing futons, that is what it was called.

It's the room in the kimon, the unlucky northeastern corner, so sleeping in it all alone was a little creepy, but it's not like it's haunted. I even slept more soundly than I do in my own room.

One housemaid said this with a self-satisfied air.

Maybe it's just a game to test the nerves of the new workers.

The other agreed, nodding vigorously.

So that's why on those nights Omitsu sits at the paper sliding doors to the hall to the futon room, keeping watch to make sure the worker sleeping doesn't get out.

The two said it was an odd custom, but that that was all there was to it, and laughed together. But that laughter soon came to a sudden stop, as if it had been chopped off. When Oyū threw a glance toward the two in surprise, the two were both identically staring unmoving up at the ceiling, eyes wide. They looked just like marionettes who had lost their puppeteers.

Asking no further questions, Oyū simply thanked them for telling her and donned her nightclothes.

Then that night, Oyū had a terribly vivid dream. In the dream, she was walking hand in hand with Osato in some dark place—she couldn't tell exactly where. As she gently swung their clasped hands back and forth, Osato murmured the same words over and over and over.

I'm here with you, so it'll be all right.

Oyū tried to ask *what* would be all right, but in the dream she had no voice. Both in front and behind was blackness in which nothing could be seen, and yet a presence was felt. In the dark at her back, some unknown thing was tracking Osato and Oyū, following close behind. The dragging sound of the thing's footsteps and its harsh breathing seemed audible in the darkness.

Despite awareness that this was a dream, Oyū trembled with fear, and her hand grasping her sister's felt slick with sweat. The thing at their backs seemed to be walking with terrible slowness, and also seemed occasionally to hasten its pace and close the distance between them. When it had come so close it was right at their heels, some smell came from the darkness. It may have been the fetor of the thing's breath. The breath was horribly hot, and could now and again be heard to wheeze in its throat.

Something smells bad.

Walking straight ahead, Osato spoke in cold tones out of character for her.

That thing is awfully hungry.

For a moment, Oyū wanted to turn around and see for herself what it was that her sister had called a *thing* with evident loathing. But just before she turned, the sound of the *thing* emitting a groaning cry reached her, and she lost her nerve.

The *thing* behind them seemed to slow its pace, and the sound of its dragging footsteps began to recede. Nonetheless, Osato, without slowing, kept advancing steadily. At that moment Oyū suddenly realized that the *thing* was not fearsomely hungry, but fearsomely lonely.

The next morning, on waking, she unaccountably felt intense sadness. Even after the sun had climbed high and the details of the dream were forgotten, a twinge of sadness, an aftertaste, like biting down on a leaf of ginger, stayed with her for a long while.

Between recalling her previous dream and wondering what "sleeping in the futon room" was like, that day Oyū worked with hands that were not very productive. Three times within half a day she made blunders that brought sharp words from Omitsu.

That is why when Omitsu, true to her words at the well,

came for her that night, so late that it was already nearing midnight, she actually felt something akin to slight relief. Getting it over with quickly was better than fretting over things. As commanded by Omitsu, Oyū obediently folded her bedding, placed a pillow atop it, and cradling it in her arms, followed along behind Omitsu until they reached the inner futon room.

During the walk down the corridor, Omitsu spoke not a word. When they reached the futon room, as she extended her hand toward the sliding paper doors, and without looking in Oyū's direction, she suddenly said something unexpected.

The forty-nine days for Osato are definitely over, right?

That was right—yesterday had been the forty-ninth day. It was said that when someone dies, the person's soul lingers in this world for forty-nine days, and afterward moves on to the next world. Oyū had therefore carefully kept count until the forty-ninth day for her sister. She had been filled with worry that after that day she would no longer feel her sister's presence.

Yes, it was yesterday.

At Oyū's response, Omitsu nodded and slid open the paper doors.

Go on in, Oyū was urged, and she set foot inside the room. Musty, moist air enveloped Oyū. It felt stifling.

"Set down your pillow, lie down, and get under the covers. There's no futon, so you'll have to sleep on the bare tatami mat."

Holding a candle just before the threshold of the sliding doors at the entrance without setting foot in the room herself, Omitsu gave orders in a brisk voice. When Oyū lay down as instructed, Omitsu continued to speak while remaining unmoving from where she stood.

Don't try to slip out. I'll be keeping watch in the corridor all night, so I'll know right away if you try to leave.

After reminding her that slipping out would mean the end of her service at the shop, Omitsu shut the sliding doors. The darkness, damp and thick, sank down onto Oyū as if it had been expectantly waiting for her.

At first, she thought she would never be able to sleep. The darkness was unchanged whether her eyes were open or closed, and the silence was unbroken. She had grown completely used to the snores and teeth-grinding of the maids who shared her room, so the current situation had the opposite effect of making her feel even more awake, and Oyū kept tossing and turning as she lay curled up under the covers. As she moved around in this way, Oyū began to feel that the fragrance of Osato's hair on the bedclothes seemed especially strong that night.

I'm here with you, so it'll be all right.

This is what her sister's words in the dream had signified. Her sister had come to work here at the same age as she, and had no doubt been subjected to the same test of nerves. She must have been terribly afraid. She must have felt all alone. But in Oyū's dream, Osato had come to comfort her, and told her not to be afraid, because her spirit was here with her.

Thinking of this brought relief and let her close her eyes. In a short while her breathing became deep and regular, and Oyū fell into sound sleep.

Then she dreamt again.

It was the same dream as before. She was holding hands with Osato and walking through impenetrable darkness ahead and behind. Her sister's hand gripped Oyū's tightly, but their pace seemed slightly faster than in the earlier dream.

Something was tracking them from behind. The sense of its presence, too, seemed just as in the dream before—or even stronger. When she listened closely, she could hear the *scrape scrape scrape* of the thing's footfalls.

You mustn't turn around.

Osato spoke beside her. Her sister was smiling, but her eyes glittered forcefully, as if in defiance, and the corners of her eyes turned down with what looked like a touch of anger.

Scrape, scrape, scrape. The footsteps approached. A sickening stench, perhaps the thing's exhalations or the breath in its nostrils, clutched at the back of Oyū's neck. The smell reminded her of when her grandfather had died three years before. Her grandfather had died of an ailment that made his belly fill with fluid. Even after becoming bedridden, he had remained as kind and gentle as ever, a patient who troubled his caretakers little, but in his final hours his breath turned so foul it made one dizzy. When she asked her father about it later, he had told her that no matter how pure of heart a person may be, when they approached death their innards went bad, and so their breath turned foul.

Did that mean this thing that followed them was someone who was dying? Was that why its footsteps were so ponderous?

Just then Osato suddenly began to sing.

This way, Sir Demon, toward the clapping hands.

Her voice was loud. Her voice was vital and strong. It seemed that her sister knew what the thing pursuing them actually was, and to get away from it, she was singing to give herself courage, as if to show that she wasn't afraid of the thing that pursued them, so Oyū began to sing along with her.

This way, Sir Demon, toward the clapping hands.
This way, Sir Demon, toward the clapping hands.

Osato walked on, tugging Oyū's hand. Every now and then she glanced down at Oyū with a gentle look, as if to encourage her. Oyū also looked up at her sister, smiling with her eyes, thinking only of placing one foot ahead of the other.

There was no telling how far they had walked. At length, in the inky-black darkness ahead of them, a faint white glow began to be seen.

Oh, the day is breaking!

Osato spoke with elation.

Run, Oyū!

Pulled by the hand by Osato, Oyū started to run. As the two picked up speed, the white light rushed closer. As it spread and became a strong light that reached to just over their heads, Osato let out a shout of joy.

We did it! We got away!

With a shout, Osato jumped into the white radiance, bringing Oyū into it with her. Blinding light surrounded Oyū.

That is when she awoke. Oyū sat up with a start. The room was still fully dark. Behind her, however, Oyū sensed something unstill.

Oyū whipped around. In the darkness, at Oyū's pillow, crouched something even blacker than the shadows. That it was something that seemed to exude malevolence, Oyū was able to discern not merely by sight, but as vividly as if her hand were touching it.

The thing let out a cry like a groan.

"But the forty-nine days are over!" it spat out with evident frustration, then suddenly disappeared. Left behind was only darkness.

Oyū wrapped the bedcovers around her and continued to sit, still and alert. After a while, Omitsu spoke outside the paper doors. Asked if she was awake, Oyū answered yes.

The sliding doors were opened. The light of daybreak filled the corridor. Omitsu kneeled there at the floor in the formal way, fixing Oyū with an unwavering scowl.

Her eyes were bloodshot and completely red, as if she hadn't had a moment's sleep all night.

THAT DAY, IN the afternoon, Oyū was again summoned by Omitsu. She was commanded to help clean up the storehouse.

The maids were puzzled. By convention, cleaning of the storehouse was done only by the senior housemaids, under Omitsu's direction. The storehouse contained many items that were important or valuable, so that was only natural.

However, no one could contradict Omitsu. Oyū nervously entered the storehouse with Omitsu. As soon as the two were inside, Omitsu soundly shut the storehouse door. Through windows cut high in the walls to let in light, golden sunbeams slanted in, and in them danced fine motes of dust. They were the only things moving inside the storehouse.

Sit there.

Omitsu pointed at the floor, then sat herself down first. This action seemed slower and more laborious than usual. Recalling Omitsu's blood-red eyes early that morning, Oyū thought it true after all that Omitsu hadn't slept a wink the night before.

I didn't call you here to clean. I did it because there's something I want to tell you.

Omitsu began to speak in slow tones. Seen up close, the skin under Omitsu's cheeks and eyes was chapped and rough, and her color was poor. Yet her eyes were still and settled, and fixed on Oyū.

There's nothing to be afraid of, said Omitsu, smiling slightly. This was the first time since coming to Kanekoya that Oyū had seen the head housemaid smile.

Last night you did a fine job of besting me, said Omitsu. Then she raised her right hand and wearily rubbed the back of her neck.

The thing that was chasing you was me. I wanted to pluck your soul from your body, but Osato's spirit thwarted me, and in the end I wasn't able to do it. I thought that because the forty-nine days were over, Osato's spirit would no longer be with you, but it was still close by, and protected you.

But the forty-nine days are over!

Recalling the words the malevolent entity spat out in the darkness of the futon room, Oyū felt the hairs at the back of her neck stand up.

So that had been Omitsu.

That's right—that was me, Omitsu said with a nod. *Though it might be better to say it was me, and yet it wasn't. Listen to me carefully. I'm telling you this because I want you to help me.*

Kanekoya was cursed, Omitsu began to explain.

The current master is the seventh head of this house. This is a fine house. But a very long time ago, to establish the shop, the first master murdered a man and hid his corpse. It's likely he did it for money. Not even I know the details.

The ghost of the murdered man, repressing its resentment and remaining in this world, attached itself to Kanekoya, which had been built on his blood. It is said that this was why Kanekoya's owners, one after the other, had all died young.

But in time, the thing that haunts and brings misfortune to this house became no longer content just to shorten the lives of the masters. To take form and stay in this world, it must consume the souls of the living. Just as we must eat to live. So to do this, it has come to first move into the body of one of the workers and get inside the house, then pluck out the soul of another worker.

In each generation, she said, one worker had been possessed. Sometimes that was the head clerk, and sometimes the head housemaid. The "tradition" had arisen that the possessed person would arrange to take the workers into the futon room to be robbed of their souls.

And now it's me. My body is possessed by a lingering evil spirit intent on doing harm to this shop and this household.

Omitsu said she had been hired when she was twelve years old. She had been twenty when the evil entity possessed her, and at that time she had just become the youngest head housemaid in Kanekoya's history. Proud of her rise, the open haughtiness she showed toward her other workers created an unbridgeable distance between them, she said, her mouth twisted as if she had bitten into something bitter.

When the soul has been stolen, a person no longer complains, said Omitsu. *Laziness goes away, too, and so does ambition. The childlike desire to play also disappears, and longing for home goes away as well. At a glance they look like ordinary people, and act like ordinary people, but inside they're empty. They're just like wooden puppets. And that's how the employees at Kanekoya can be made into such diligent workers that the other shops watch out for them. They never fall ill and they never get hurt. Because, after all, they're no longer more than half-living.*

That was why the house prospered. The outside world admired the formidable discipline inculcated in Kanekoya's workers.

But the succession of owners were unable to enjoy this prosperity and acclaim wholeheartedly. The reason for this was that they each knew he would have to leave this world with his life taken from at about half the age of ordinary men. After having been predeceased at an early age by his predecessor, and the one before, and the one before that, at around age thirty the current head of the household would naturally begin to wonder when he himself would be taken.

At a certain point in their lives, the master's wife and children, too, would have to live their days in fear of the sudden death of their husband or father. No matter how well-off one may be, living with Death's scythe pressed against the back of the neck is not pleasurable. The mind is truly never at ease.

You're going to be dismissed tomorrow.

Turning again toward Oyū, Omitsu spoke. Her eyes were slightly moist.

That's what I'm going to tell the master and mistress. I'm going to tell them that something bad will happen to the shop if you're here. They'll let you go for sure. But that's fine. You can no longer stay here.

But before she left, there was something she wanted her to do for her, said Omitsu, leaning forward on her knees.

I'm going to hide a wand of sacred sakaki twigs and a small packet of salt behind the water jug in the kitchen, so in the dead of night tonight, you go the futon room without letting yourself be seen, and throw those into the room and come right back. Now listen—you be sure to do it. As long as you do, you'll have nothing more to fear.

Saying she was counting on her, Omitsu tightly gripped Oyū's shoulder. Even more than the force of that grip, the chill of that hand, felt clearly even through the layers of kimono, made Oyū shiver.

I promise, she answered in a quavering her voice. At this, Omitsu smiled widely, released Oyū's shoulder, and stood.

Osato's spirit is with you, so you don't have to be afraid. That girl was too much for me. She was a strong one with a lot of pluck, she said in a tones that had grown slightly gentle.

Last night in the futon room, I dreamed of my sister, said Oyū.

Is that so?

Omitsu nodded, whereupon she tilted her head to the side as if falling into thought for a moment, then murmured that she was sorry.

To be honest, your sister's soul was the only one the bad thing attached to me was never able to take. More than five years had passed since she started working here, but no matter how many times I made her sleep in the futon room, it always ended in failure. It must have been because Osato never stopped caring about you, her sister, and your family back home.

Oyū thought of her sister, and her chest grew tight.

She was like a mother to me, she said impulsively.

Is that so? Even when you were apart, Osato must never have stopped thinking about you, not even for a moment. That's why there never was an opportunity.

Omitsu closed her eyes as if convinced. For a few moments she held that pose, unmoving.

But listen—that's why Osato died the way she did. She was haunted and killed. I think I've had enough of such things.

Muttering this, Omitsu suddenly opened her eyes as if coming to a decision, then placed her hand on the door to the storehouse and forcefully pushed it open. When she went into the sunlight outside, her shadow fell onto the ground. Oyū happened to glance down at it, and barely managed to contain a scream.

Omitsu's shadow, reflecting the large-framed woman, was black and big, and from its head grew two horns.

THAT EVENING, IN the dead of the night, Oyū did as Omitsu had requested. The strong scent of greenery of the *sakaki* wand she threw into the futon room was comforting.

The next morning, as soon as she awoke from light sleep, she was summoned by Omitsu and taken to the master and his wife. Told her work was inadequate, she was dismissed. The master and mistress, looking bewildered, kept looking at Omitsu as if for confirmation.

Oyū, making no complaint, bowed fully, gathered up her things in a small cloth-wrapped bundle, and left Kanekoya. No one saw her off.

When she had almost reached the village of Ōshima, Oyū grew afraid for the first time; her knees knocking, she became unable to walk one step more. A man from the village passing by found Oyū and carried her, piggyback, back to her house.

Some ten days after that, the rumor came that a fire had occurred at Kanekoya. The fire had no clear origin, but the master had burned to death, and both the house and the shop had burned to the ground, it was said. A few days before that, the head housemaid Omitsu had run off and vanished, and so the town officials and hired thief-takers, suspecting her to be connected with the suspicious fire, were said to be seeking her whereabouts.

Omitsu's flight had also been mysterious. Her belongings were all left in her room, and no one had witnessed her departure from Kanekoya. The same day she had disappeared, however, one of the housemaids had spotted a red-kimonoed woman of around twenty, a stranger, appear from Omitsu's room and slip outside. On hearing what the maid had to say, the head clerk noted that the figure and kimono pattern of the mysterious woman closely resembled Omitsu in her youth, but because people do not suddenly become young again, such talk ended there.

Some time after the fire, digging at the site where Kanekoya had stood unearthed human bones at the northeast corner. The bones were said to be very old and quite misshapen, retaining almost none of their original form. Because of this, it was held, the head was shaped as if it had grown horns.

No one had the least idea where the bones had come from, or whose they were. Or maybe they weren't even human.

Oyū found employment at another shop. The head house-maid there, too, was a formidable woman whose rebukes were fearsome. But her shadow was always human in form, and so Oyū was never afraid of her.

Before long, she forgot about the events at Kanekoya. The dreams also stopped. Yet she remembered the bedding filled with the sent of Osato. If she had known there would be a fire, that's the one thing she would have liked to have save, Oyū pensively thought, with feelings of gentle regret.

Here Lies a Flute

笛塚 (Fuezuka)

Okamoto Kidō (1925)　　　　　　　　岡本綺堂
English translation by Nancy H. Ross
  (winner of the 2008 Kurodahan Press Translation Prize)

One

I'M FROM THE North, and this ghost story is told among the members of my clan. But before I tell you the story, I'd like to recount a tale told in *Mimibukuro*, the essays of Negishi Yasumori, the famous magistrate in Edo. In Mino, when the house of Kanemori was stripped of its rank and had its property confiscated by the shogunate, a certain chief retainer was ordered to commit suicide. The retainer turned to the investigator and said he had a clear conscience as he prepared to commit hara-kiri to atone for the sins of his lord. Indeed, he said, as a samurai it was his pleasure to do so.

"But," he continued, "to tell the truth, I committed a crime I have never told anyone about. When I was young I once stopped at an inn where an itinerant priest was also staying. In the course of telling some story, he unsheathed his sword and showed it to me. It was a fine specimen and the work of a famous swordsmith, and I wanted it badly. I offered him a good price for it, but he said it had been in his family for generations and refused to sell it to me. Still, I couldn't get it out of my mind. So the next morning I set out with the priest, and when we came to a lonely pine grove, I attacked and killed him, took his sword and fled. This happened long ago, and, fortunately,

81

no one ever found out about it. But thinking of it now, it was a sinful deed, and it is fitting that I should meet this fate, if only for that reason." Then he committed hara-kiri. The story I'm about to tell is somewhat similar but a more complicated and mysterious tale.

In my homeland, noh songs and comic dramas have been popular for many years, so there are many masters of those arts. And I suppose that is why there are some samurai who can perform noh dances as well as noh songs. There are also those who play the flute or the hand drum. Yagara Kihei, a young samurai of nineteen who worked as a mounted guard for his lord, was one of them. His father, who was also called Kihei, died the summer his only son was sixteen, so the youth, who had only just been initiated into manhood, took his father's name and succeeded to his post. For the next four years the younger Kihei fulfilled his duties without difficulty, and as he was held in fairly high regard, his mother and other relatives resolved among themselves to find a proper bride for him the following year, when he would turn twenty.

Our homeland being the sort of place I've described, Kihei had been playing the flute since he was a boy. Had it been another clan, perhaps he would have been accused of being unmanly, but in our clan men of refinement are considered more samurai-like than those with no artistic accomplishments at all, so no one criticized him for his enthusiasm for the flute.

Since olden times it has been said that those born early in the year have even teeth and thus are well-suited to playing the flute. Perhaps because he was born in February, Kihei was quite a good player. Since childhood he had been praised for his playing, and his parents boasted of his talent, so it was the one indulgence he couldn't give up.

One fall evening in the early 1830s, captivated by the lovely moon, Kihei went out, taking his prized flute with him. He walked over the dew-covered path to the riverbank outside the castle grounds. The tassels on the tall grass and the reeds appeared white beneath the bright moon. Somewhere insects chirped. Kihei walked a long way downstream, playing his flute as he went, until he heard the sound of another flute coming from the direction in which he was going.

It could not have been the echo of his own flute on the water. He had no doubt that someone else was playing somewhere. He listened carefully for a few moments. The clear sound of the flute that reached the riverbank seemed to come from far away. The player was not unskillful, but Kihei realized that the flute itself was a splendid instrument, and he wanted to know who its owner was.

It is not only deer that are attracted by the sound of a flute in the fall: Kihei too was entranced. And as he followed the sound he discovered that it was coming from amid the grass that grew along the lower reaches of the river. He was fascinated by the idea that, like him, someone else had been captivated by the moon and ventured out to enjoy playing the flute in the evening mist. He tiptoed into the tall grass at the river's edge where there was a small, low hut made of bamboo covered with straw mats. He knew a wandering beggar was living there.

It seemed quite strange that such a sound should be coming from the hut, so he hesitated to proceed.

"Can it be that I'm being deceived by a fox or a *tanuki*?" he wondered.

Perhaps a fox or an otter had seized this opportunity to play a trick on him. Kihei plucked up his courage, reminding himself that he was a samurai and that he had his precious family sword tucked into his sash. If it were some kind of apparition, he was prepared to do it in with a single stroke. He parted the grass and entered the thicket to find the thatch covering the entrance to the hut had been lifted and a man was seated there playing the flute.

"Hey, you!"

The man stopped playing, then stiffened and looked up when Kihei called out to him.

Seen in the moonlight his appearance was unmistakably that of a beggar, but he appeared to be only about twenty-seven or twenty-eight. Kihei could tell at once that he was different from the ordinary vagabonds or beggars who hung about there, so he addressed the man again more politely.

"Were you playing the flute just now?"

"Yes," replied the flute player in a low voice.

"The sound was so beautiful I followed it here," Kihei said with a smile.

The man's gaze went to Kihei's flute, and he seemed to relax a bit. His tone softened.

"I'm embarrassed to have you hear my poor playing."

"On the contrary, I've been listening for a while, and I can tell you've practiced quite a lot. Would you mind showing me your flute?"

"It's just something I play to amuse myself and hardly something to be shown to a gentleman such as you."

Nevertheless, with no apparent unwillingness, he carefully wiped off his flute with leaves from some of the tall grass growing there and proffered it to Kihei.

His manner was not one of a mere beggar. Kihei thought perhaps he was a *ronin* who had fallen on hard times for some reason, so he spoke even more politely.

"Kindly allow me to have a look."

He took the flute and held it up to the moonlight. Then, after getting permission to do so, he tried playing it. Its tone was extraordinary; it was a singularly exceptional flute, so Kihei was even more inclined to believe the other man was not just anyone. Of course, Kihei's own flute was a fine instrument, but it could hardly compare to this one. He wanted to know how the man had come to have such a flute. Motivated in part by his curiosity, as he handed the flute back to its owner he broke off some grass, laid it on the ground and sat down on it next to the other man.

"How long have you been here?"

"About two weeks."

"Where were you before this?" Kihei asked.

"Because of my circumstances, I don't stay long in any one particular place. I wandered from the Chūgoku Region to Osaka and Kyoto and then through Ise and Ōmi.

"You are a samurai, aren't you?" Kihei said suddenly.

The man was silent. Kihei took the lack of a denial as an affirmation of the fact, so he edged nearer and said, "There must be a reason why you are wandering about with such a splendid flute. If you don't mind, won't you tell me what it is?"

The man remained silent, but after Kihei repeatedly pressed him to reply, he began reluctantly to speak.

"I am cursed by this flute."

Two

HE WAS A samurai from Shikoku by the name of Iwami Ya-jiemon. Like Kihei, he had enjoyed playing the flute since he was a boy.

One spring evening when he was nineteen, Yajiemon was on his way home from worshipping at his family temple when he came upon a pilgrim who had collapsed in a field through which people seldom passed. Upon approaching him, Ya-jiemon found that the pilgrim was a man of around forty who was in pain from some sort of sickness. Yajiemon fetched some water from a nearby spring and gave it to him. He removed some medicine from his *inro*, administered it to the pilgrim and performed various other ministrations, but the man's suffering only increased.

He was grateful to Yajiemon, a total stranger, for his kindness and for going to such lengths to care for him. Saying there was no way he could properly express his gratitude, the pilgrim took from his sash a flute in a bag and offered it to Ya-jiemon as a token of his appreciation.

"There is no other flute like this in the world," he said. "But take care that you do not end up like me."

With this cryptic utterance, he died. Yajiemon had asked the man's name and his hometown, but he had merely shaken his head. Thinking it must be fate, Yajiemon took the body to his family temple, where he had it buried.

The flute the pilgrim had left behind was of the finest quality and unlike any other. Yajiemon thought it strange that the man should have been in possession of such an instrument, but in any case he was happy that this treasure had fallen into his hands as a result of this chance event. One day about six months later, Yajiemon was once again returning from a visit to his family temple. As he entered the field where he had found the pilgrim, he saw a young samurai dressed as a traveler standing there waiting for him. The samurai approached and said, "Are you Iwami Yajiemon?"

When Yajiemon replied that he was, the samurai drew nearer. "I heard you cared for a sick pilgrim here and were given his flute," he said. "That pilgrim was my enemy, and I have come a long way in search of him to take his head and his flute. If he is dead, there is nothing I can do about that, but I would at least like to have the flute, and that is why I have been waiting here for you."

Spoken to in this way without the slightest warning, Ya-jiemon could not simply hand over the flute.

He said to the young samurai, "I don't know who you are, where you are from or why you had a grudge against the pilgrim, and without hearing that I cannot offer a proper reply." But the samurai gave no further explanation and merely insisted that Yajiemon give him the flute.

This only served to raise more doubts in Yajiemon's mind, and he began to think that perhaps the samurai was making all this up in an effort to trick him out of the precious flute. He flatly refused, saying, "As long as I don't know who you are or why you are seeking vengeance, I shall not give you the flute." The samurai's expression changed.

"In that case...," he said, and grasped the hilt of his sword. There seemed to be no point in discussing it any further, so Yajiemon also made ready to fight. After a short heated exchange, their swords were drawn, and the young samurai fell before Yajiemon, covered in blood.

"That flute will bring a curse upon you," he said, and died.

Having killed the man without really knowing why, Ya-jiemon felt for a moment as if he were in a dream. But when he reported what had occurred, in light of the circumstances, Yajiemon was found blameless for the other man's senseless death, and that was the end of the matter. Needless to say, Ya-jiemon didn't know the identities of the pilgrim who had given him the flute or the young samurai.

The matter of the slaying of the samurai was thus settled, but then a difficulty arose. This incident became well known throughout the domain, and when word of it reached the lord, he ordered Yajiemon to show him the flute. If the lord merely wanted to see the flute, there would be no problem, but one of the lord's concubines enjoyed playing the flute, and Yajiemon knew that money was no object to her when it came to acquiring a good one. If he were so foolish as to hand the flute over, it might be taken from him on the pretext that it was the lord's wish, and then given to the concubine. As a retainer, Yajiemon was in no position to refuse an order from the lord. He was at a loss as to what to do, but in any case he hated the thought of parting with the flute.

So, he had no choice but to take it and flee. Thus the young samurai forsook his ancestral fief for a flute.

Because the lords in those days were not as well-off as in times past, they rarely took on new retainers. So Yajiemon was obliged to set off with his flute and wander the land as a *ronin*. He crossed over to Kyushu, traveled through the Chūgoku Region and roamed Kyoto and Osaka trying to find a way to support himself. He met with one misfortune after another, falling ill and being robbed, until at last he was reduced to begging.

He even sold his swords, but he never thought to part with the flute. Then he wandered to the North and had been enjoying playing the flute that moonlit evening when Yagara Kihei happened to hear it.

When he reached that point in his story, Yajiemon sighed.

"Just as the pilgrim said before he died, this flute seems to have some sort of curse upon it. I know nothing of its previous owners, but I do know that the pilgrim who owned it died by the side of the road, and the traveling samurai who came to get it died by my hand. And I find myself in these circumstances on account of this flute. I shudder to think what lies ahead. Many times I have vowed to sell this flute or break it and throw it away, but it seems a shame to sell it, and throwing it away seems an even greater shame. So, though I know it will bring only misfortune, I've kept it."

Kihei could not listen to this story without sighing himself. Over the years he had heard strange tales like this about swords, but he never imagined there could be such mystery surrounding a flute.

But he soon dismissed that notion. Perhaps this beggar of a *ronin* feared that Kihei might covet his flute and so had made up this strange story when, in fact, nothing of the sort had happened.

"Knowing it will bring you misfortune, I can't understand why you wouldn't part with the flute, no matter how hard it might be to do so," he said to Yajiemon accusingly.

"I don't understand it myself," Yajiemon said. "I can't get rid of it even if I try. I suppose it is both a misfortune and a curse. On account of this I've endured ten years of unrelieved misery."

"Unrelieved misery, you say..."

"It must seem absurd. Even if I tried to explain it, no one would believe me."

At that Yajiemon fell silent. Kihei was silent also. All that could be heard was the chirping of insects. The moonlight that bathed the riverbank was as white as frost.

"It's late," Yajiemon said, gazing at the sky.

"Yes, it's late," Kihei repeated and stood up to go.

Three

NOT LONG AFTER parting from the *ronin* and returning home, Kihei appeared on the riverbank again. Lightly clad and wearing a mask, he crept up to the hut like the vengeful samurai in a scene from a famous play.

Kihei wanted the flute badly, but from what the *ronin* had said it seemed he was unlikely to hand it over. So he concluded he had no choice but to attack Yajiemon in the dark and take the flute. Of course, he had wavered before reaching that decision, but Kihei was determined to have the flute. Though a *ronin*, Yajiemon had been reduced to a mere wandering beggar. If Kihei killed him without being seen, there would be no unpleasant investigation. Thinking of it that way, he had become even more fiendish. He went home, prepared and then waited until the dead of night before returning to attack.

Kihei wasn't sure whether it was true or not, but based on what he had heard earlier, Yajiemon was apparently a highly skilled swordsman. He didn't seem to have a weapon of any sort, but nevertheless Kihei thought it best not to take any chances. He had had the usual training in swordsmanship, but he was young, after all, and of course he had never been in a real fight. He supposed a certain amount of preparation was necessary, even for a sneak attack, so he broke off a stalk of bamboo in a thicket along the way, made a spear from it, put it under his arm and approached stealthily. Taking care not to rustle the leaves, he made his way through the tall grass to the hut. A straw mat had been pulled down over the entrance, and the sound of the flute could no longer be heard. All was quiet.

Or so Kihei thought until he heard a low moan. It grew gradually louder, as if Yajiemon were in great pain – not from a sickness but rather as if he were in the throes of some sort of nightmare. Kihei hesitated slightly. Reminded of the story he had heard earlier of how Yajiemon had endured unrelieved misery for ten long years on account of the flute, he felt vaguely apprehensive.

Kihei held his breath and waited. The cries from within the hut grew piercing, as if Yajiemon were writhing in even more pain, and then he tore aside the straw mat at the entrance and tumbled out of the hut. Awakened from his frightening dream, he uttered a sigh of relief and looked about.

Kihei had no time to hide. As luck would have it, the moonlight cast a glow over the entire area, so standing there with his bamboo spear he was plainly visible to the *ronin*.

Kihei was thrown into confusion. He had been discovered, and he had to act quickly. He took up his spear and lunged at Yajiemon, who nimbly sidestepped, grabbed the spearhead and pulled hard, toppling Kihei onto his knees on the grass.

His opponent was much more formidable than he had imagined, so Kihei was thrown into even greater confusion. He tossed aside the spear and went for his sword. As he did so Yajiemon called out, "No, wait. Is it my flute you want?"

Kihei had been caught out, so he made no reply. He took his hand from his sword, and hesitated for a moment.

"If you want it that badly, I'll give it to you," Yajiemon said softly. He went into the hut, returned with the flute and handed it to Kihei, who was kneeling in silence.

"Do not forget the story I told you earlier. Take care that no misfortune befalls you."

"Thank you," Kihei stammered.

"You must go home before anyone sees you," Yajiemon warned.

At that point Kihei could do nothing but obey. He humbly accepted the flute, rose to his feet mechanically, bowed politely in silence and left.

On the way home he was seized by shame and remorse. While quite pleased that he had obtained the singularly splendid flute, at the same time he regretted his shameful behavior of that evening. The other man had handed over the flute so readily that Kihei was tormented by a terrible sense of guilt, no different than if he had killed the man for the instrument. His only consolation was that he hadn't made the mistake of doing that.

Kihei resolved to visit the *ronin* again the following morning, apologize for his behavior that evening and offer some token of gratitude for the flute. He quickened his pace and soon reached home, but he was wide awake and passed a sleepless night.

He couldn't wait for dawn, so very early in the morning he returned to the scene of the previous night's events carrying three gold coins in his breast pocket. The morning mist of autumn still hung over the riverbank, and the cries of geese could be heard in the distance.

As he parted the tall grass and approached the hut, Kihei was brought up short: Iwami Yajiemon lay dead before the hut. He had stabbed himself through the throat with the bamboo spear that Kihei had left behind and was still clutching it in both hands.

The following spring Kihei married. He and his wife were happy together and were blessed with two sons. They lived peacefully until one autumn day seven years after the incident I've just described, when Kihei was ordered to commit hara-kiri on account of a blunder he had made in the course of performing his duties. While preparing to kill himself, he asked the official who had come to his home to witness his death if he might be allowed to play one last tune on his flute. The official gave his consent.

The flute was the one Kihei had been given by Iwami Yajiemon. He calmly played a tune, and just as he was finishing, the flute suddenly emitted a strange sound and split in two. Surprised, Kihei examined the flute and found these words inscribed inside:

The end will come in nine hundred and ninety years.
Hamanushi

As might be expected of a student of that field, Kihei was familiar with Owari no Hamanushi, who was the first to popularize the flute in Japan and who was revered for his contributions to the field of music. It was now 1838. Thus nine hundred and ninety years before was 848, three years after Hamanushi played the flute at the Imperial Court. Early in his career Hamanushi had made his own flutes. As his name was inscribed in this one, perhaps he had made it. An inscription on the outside would have been one thing, but Kihei could not imagine how Hamanushi could have inscribed this message on the inside of the slender flute.

Even more mysterious was that this seemed to be the year in which it was said the end would come. Had Hamanushi himself made the flute and prescribed its lifespan? Thinking of it now, Kihei realized that the fateful tale Iwami Yajiemon had told must have been true. With its strange destiny this flute had brought misfortune to one owner after another. And as its final owner met his doom, the flute reached the end of its own nine-hundred-ninety-year life.

Kihei was astonished, and at that moment he realized that his fate and that of the flute were inescapably intertwined. He turned to the official, and after telling him all the secrets of the flute's past, committed hara-kiri.

The official told the story to others, and everyone who heard it was struck by a sense of the bizarre. After discussing it with Kihei's family, some of his friends in the clan put the flute back together and buried it at the spot where Iwami Yajiemon was believed to have killed himself. They erected a stone marker and inscribed the words "Here Lies a Flute" on it. I've heard that until some years ago the marker was still there on the riverbank, but after two floods there is no longer any trace of it.

The Face in the Hearth

竈の中の顔 (Kamado no naka no kao)

Tanaka Kōtarō (1928)　　　　　　　　田中貢太郎
English translation by Edward Lipsett

- 1 -

"WANT ME TO beat you again today?" asked Aiba Sanzaemon, grinning at the spa's innkeeper over the go board spread
out between them.

"I was rather soundly thrashed yesterday, wasn't I? I was up
all night thinking up new strategies... I don't think I'll be the
one to lose today."

The innkeeper chuckled quietly, and reached out to place a
stone.

"Have to watch you closely, then, I guess... Never underesti-
mate your opponent, they say," smiled Sanzaemon, watching
the other player's fingers trembling as he placed stones here
and there. A nervous habit.

"I won't be the loser today!"

The innkeeper dearly loved go, but perhaps he loved it so
much because he was really not very good at it. He usually
needed a handicap of four or five stones. Sanzaemon played
him to pass the time between hot soaks in the spa.

"Well then, let's have at it, shall we?"

Sanzaemon had come from Edo to this spa, deep in the Hakone mountains, over twenty days ago.

"I know I'll win today."

The clicks of their stones hitting the board echoed intermittently, almost as if they would suddenly remember to play the next stone. Just outside the open *shōji*[1] doors a country road ran through the mountains in the early summer sun, and the people walking up or down drew faint shadows as if seen through a fine mist.

"Isn't that a customer?" asked Sanzaemon, noticing a shadow that might have been a person, or perhaps a bird.

The innkeeper was still deep in the game.

"You may have to turn him away if he's not a decent fellow," laughed Sanzaemon, glancing through the open *shōji* toward the veranda again. A monk, pale and thin, stood there.

"A traveling monk, I see. And good day to you!" he nodded to the visitor.

"I hope you don't mind me watching a bit... I love a good game of go myself," replied the monk, returning the nod with a small bow. At his voice the innkeeper finally took notice.

"Ah, come in, come in. Please, join us!"

"Thank you. I'll just watch for a bit, then."

The monk was wearing a torn robe. He untied the strings holding on his broad sedge hat, and took a seat on the edge of the veranda, peering diagonally over the go board.

"Then I'll move now, shall I?" asked Sanzaemon, placing the stone he'd been holding.

"My turn now... where shall I go? Where shall I go?"

The innkeeper placed his own stone, the monk forgotten already: "Here! Here's the perfect place!"

Sanzaemon's quiet voice was punctuated by the uncertain tones of the innkeeper.

"Ah! Missed it! These stones have connected now, haven't they! I've lost again!" he said, despondently.

Sanzaemon chuckled, "I thought you couldn't lose today. What happened?"

The innkeeper, bobbing his head and scratching the edge of his ear lightly in embarrassment, glanced at the sitting monk.

"I guess I'm just not very good at go, am I?" he asked.

"I love the game, but I'm hardly any good myself..."

"A new opponent is always interesting... what do you say? Would you like to challenge him?"

---

1. *Shōji* are wooden lattice doors covered with paper in order to allow light in from the outside.

The monk's expression made it clear he was interested as Sanzemon broke in: "Maybe I could make a suggestion?"

"I'm sure I'll not make a worthy opponent...," the monk demurred, swinging his legs up onto the veranda and taking a cross-legged position on the floorboards.

"No, you're sitting on the hard floorboards. Please, step inside," he invited, urging the monk to come into the room and sit on the soft tatami mats instead. The monk shook his head.

"I am used to sitting on stone and boards," he refused.

Sanzaemon brought the go board closer to the veranda, placing one of its legs on top of the runner for the *shōji* doors.

"We seem to be more evenly matched," said the monk, taking the box of go stones that the innkeeper held out.

"I'll go first, if that's all right?" asked Sanzaemon.

"I'll go first," broke in the monk, placing his first stone even as Sanzaemon was speaking.

"I thought I would go first!"

"Next time, then."

The two began to place stones. Sanzaemon was relaxed, playing a slow game, and the monk followed suit. The dry click-clack of the stones hitting the board was the only sound for a while.

At last, the board was packed with black and white stones, and Sanzaemon said: "I've lost the game. By two or three stones, I would say..."

Even so, he had enjoyed the game, and found his opponent intriguing.

"No, surely by no more than two stones," countered the monk. They counted, and just as the monk has said, Sanzaemon had lost by two stones.

"My turn to go first," said Sanzaemon, placing his first stone. The monk let him, placing his own stone in response. The game ended with the monk losing by two stones. Sanzaemon was beginning to truly enjoy himself.

"My turn this time," said the monk.

"What a match!" praised the innkeeper, as happy as if he himself were playing.

- 2 -

SANZAEMON AND THE monk played game after game until the evening, winning alternately...the one who played first always won, and the one who placed the second stone always lost. They were very evenly matched, and that made the competition that much more interesting.

After the last game, as the monk was getting ready to leave, Sanzaemon asked "Are you at one of the temples around here?"

He almost felt sad that the monk was leaving.

"A small hermitage up on the mountain," replied the monk, placing his hat back on his head and standing.

"So we can play again? I do hope you'll give me another chance to beat you tomorrow."

"Of course, I'd be delighted. I cannot resist a good game of go. I'll be happy to play you tomorrow, and the next day, and indeed every day, if you so wish."

"Thank goodness! I've been at a loss for what to do with myself these past days."

"Then let us meet again tomorrow," promised the monk, stepping back to the road and trudging up the hill like a bird flying home in the evening sunlight.

"I don't recall ever seeing that monk around here before," said the innkeeper.

"You don't remember seeing him?" queried Sanzaemon, absently, his mind already turning to thoughts of a warm soak in the spa.

"No, I don't think I've seen him in the area. I wonder where he lives... there are many monks around here, though," warned the innkeeper, "and of all kinds. One must be careful whom one associates with. But he does seem to be a good fellow, doesn't he?"

"Why? Have you heard something about one of these monks?"

"Yes, in fact, there is a rather bizarre tale. They said that a strange monk lives in these mountains, and people suddenly die. The rumor somehow stays alive even though nobody ever seems to have died because of something he did, or even claimed to have seen him."

"Really? Well, even if he is a strange monk, I certainly have no objections as long as he can play go well!"

THE MONK CAME again the following day. Sanzaemon had been eagerly awaiting his arrival, and immediately set up the go board, placing the first stone himself. And, just as had happened the previous day, the person who played first won, and he who placed the second stone lost. The two of them played each other game after game until evening, and finally the monk left for home again.

The monk came to play every day, after that. Sanzaemon began to feel bad about how it was always the monk who made the trip to play, and to feel curiosity about what sort of life the monk led. Finally one day he spoke his thoughts.

"You always take the time to come here to the spa to play me," he pointed out. "I am the one with plenty of spare time, and I would like to come play you at your hermitage one day instead."

"My hermitage is deep in the woods, frequented by wolves and foxes and whatnot," the monk explained. "It offers no beautiful scenery and is, in fact, a quite unpleasant place. Please, you would be better off here."

"I certainly don't want to put you to any trouble, but I feel bad that I've never visited your hermitage even once to play."

"Please, put yourself at ease. I assure you, my hermitage is hardly a place for guests. I appreciate your offer, but I must refuse."

"I see...," replied Sanzaemon, then, turning the conversation back to the game, "In that case, have you time for another match?"

THE MONK CAME for about ten days, then suddenly failed to show up, perhaps because of sudden business. Sanzaemon did not feel like playing go with the innkeeper, so instead went out to find something to do, accompanied by his retainer, a younger man who come with him from Edo.

The mountain in early summer was decorated with young leaves, and he could see the river winding between black rocks at the bottom of the valley to the right of the road, like a silver thread. The cuckoo called from somewhere in the valley.

Sanzaemon, looking for a better place to enjoy the view from, climbed a narrow trail off the main road, leading up to a small peak.

Above them rose the bare and wind-swept heights of what must have been Komagadake Peak. Its heights were en-wrapped in bluish-white wisps of cloud.

The path ran into a small forest of cedar and cypress, which hid the looming mountain and the colors of the sky. The cy-press branches were draped with beard lichen, and the mois-ture of the mist seeped up around them, chilled.

The cedar and cypress trees gave way to a mixed forest with scattered rock outcroppings, and they saw a small stream trac-ing through a valley before them.

"There's a hut over there, sir," called his retainer from be-hind, and Sanzaemon turned to look. The other was pointing at a spot high up on the far side of the valley.

"Where?"

"Right there, sir," replied the other. Sure enough, he could make out what looked like a small hut, right under a rock draped with black branches like a horse's flowing mane.

"Oh, there it is!" Sanzaemon exclaimed, and suddenly re-called the monk. "And maybe this is where he lives."

"Who, sir?"

"The monk, of course, the monk who comes to play go every day."

"Isn't he attached to a temple?"

"He said he was at a hermitage, not a temple, and that might well be it. Let's go and see, shall we? And if it's just the hut of a forest watchman, that's all right, too. I'm getting hungry anyway."

Sanzaemon looked for a way across the stream. Broken rocks were strewn across almost like stepping stones, and it was no great difficulty for the two of them to cross to the other side.

There was a faint path, looking as if it had been created by human beings, winding through the rocks and random trees. They followed it, only to discover it almost blocked by devil's tongue and brambles that forced them to proceed slowly and carefully.

The path ended right in front of the hut, which stood in the shadow of a huge boulder. Sanzaemon paused to catch his breath, then stepped up to the doorway.

"Hello? Anyone here?"

"Who is it?" came a reply from inside, and a face appeared. It was the monk.

"And I told you not to bother coming!" he said, making a face. "Well, since you've come anyway, you might as well come inside."

Sanzaemon recalled the monk's words when he said he would come to visit the spa each day, and suddenly regretted having come.

"I had no intention of coming here, I assure you. When you didn't come today I was bored and merely went for a walk with my man here. Down in the valley I happened to see this hut, and I remembered you. And I just dropped by, that's all."

"It doesn't really matter... In any case, please, come inside and have some tea," invited the monk, and Sanzaemon slipped off his straw sandals and stepped in. The hermitage had a reed floor, and he could see an adjoining room for a Buddhist shrine, but that door was closed. There were two hearths to the left, along with a teapot and kettle.

"I'm terribly sorry to have bothered you in your prayers. I'll be on my way in a flash," said Sanzaemon, following the monk inside and sitting down across from him, in front of the hearths.

"No, it's no imposition at all, it's just... well, let me boil up some tea, then," replied the monk, eyes hard and glittering.

"Please, don't go any trouble on my behalf. Really, I'm not thirsty," refused Sanzaemon, glancing at the teapot. Just for an instant, he saw a human face peering out from the hearth, below the teapot: a pale and frightening visage. Sanzaemon was astonished, but he hid his shock completely as he looked at the monk's expression, silently. Perhaps because the monk had also seen the face, he was glaring in that direction, and the pale face quickly pulled back out of sight.

"Hmph. I live in the midst of the woods, but somehow seem to have managed to run out of firewood. Wait a moment, let me get a few branches," said the monk, standing up and stepping outside.

Sanzaemon pulled his katana, lying on the floor, a bit closer, peering intently around the hut, and especially in the hearth. It would be unlucky to stay here longer, he thought, and decided to leave quickly. As a samurai, of course, it would be embarrassing to leave as if fleeing in fright, so he felt he had to leave an offering in return the monk's kindness... if he tried to just leave through the front door, though, it was likely the monk would find some reason to refuse to accept it, and ask him to stay a bit longer. He had to put something down here, immediately, and use the deed done as an excuse to leave as soon as the monk returned.

I wonder if it would be best to leave it in the Buddhist altar, he thought to himself, still watching the hearth. He decided that would indeed be the best idea to leave a small packet of money on the altar shelf, as was tradition when honoring the dead. He pulled out his wallet, and wrapped a few coins in a piece of paper.

"Genkichi!" he called out to his young attendant, sitting on a rock near the front door.

"Yes?"

Genkichi stood, and quickly approached.

"Put this in the altar, would you?"

"Yes, sir."

Genkichi stepped inside, and took the paper packet from Sanzaemon. Crossing to the Buddhist altar, he reached his hand out to open the altar doors, and suddenly jumped back in astonishment.

"My...! A head! A head!" he cried.

Already on edge by what he had seen in the hearth, Sanzaemon wondered what could have happened now.

"What is it?"

"A head! A severed head!"

Sanzeomon leaped to his feet and ran over. In front of the weathered Buddhist altar, blackened and strange with time, sat a man's head, complete with topknot, facing away.

"Give me that money!" said Sanzaemon, snatching the packet from the man's hand and slapping it down on the altar between the statue of Buddha and the severed head. The statue was bizarre, too, with glinting eyes shining from a multitude of faces and protruding limbs.

"Good! Step back outside and look innocent," he instructed,

quickly closing the altar doors again and returning to his seat. Genkichi returned to his post outside, sitting nonchalantly on the rock as before.

"HOW SILLY OF me... running out of firewood in the middle of the forest...," muttered the monk to himself, returning with a bundle of branches.

"I'm so terribly sorry to have put you to such trouble," said Sanzaemon politely, not letting down his guard for an instant.

"Imagine that! Forgetting to keep firewood stocked even though I'm surrounded by it," exclaimed the monk, beginning to load the dry branches into the hearth. Sanzaemon watched closely, and sure enough, the face slid back into view.

The monk suddenly made a fist, and tried to strike the face, but it quickly pulled back out of sight again. The monk picked up the flint and steel lying nearby, and lit the flame in the hearth.

"It'll boil quickly; it's been on the fire for hours already."

"Really, I must be on my way... please don't go to any more trouble!" said Sanzaemon, watching the monk's every action closely, ready to strike if he tried anything suspicious.

"If you have a go set with you," suggested the monk in the same gentle voice he used at the inn, "I'd love to play a game."

Sanzaemon didn't relax his guard for a moment.

"Ah! The water is boiling!" The monk brought out two tea-cups from somewhere, and a dipper.

"One cup, then, and then I really must be on my way."

"No need to hurry. Please, stay a while."

"No, the road back is difficult, and I really must insist."

"I see," murmured the monk doubtfully, dipping a cupful of tea and placing it in front of Sanzaemon, then carrying another toward the front door. As soon as the monk's face was turned away, Sanzaemon dashed the tea into the reeds.

"Here you are, please, have some tea," came the monk's voice, and the sound of Genkichi accepting.

Sanzaemon grasped his sword and stood as the monk returned.

"I am terribly sorry to have been such a nuisance. We'll be leaving now. If you have time tomorrow perhaps you'll stop by for a game or two?"

"Leaving already? Well, then, let us meet again on the morrow."

Taking care not to turn his back on the monk, Sanzaemon slipped on his straw sandals. Genkichi stood, rubbing his hands together.

- 3 -

STILL CAUTIOUS, SANZAEMON left the hut behind, descending the hillside.

"Did you drink that tea?" asked his man, breathing close on his heels.

"What did you do?"

"I threw it in the bushes."

"The right thing to do, I think. I would never drink that! I pretended to, and dashed it out."

Sanzaemon hurried Genkichi, and they practically flew down the hillside, returning to the inn.

With a sense of foreboding, Sanzaemon called the master of the inn: "We had a terrible day today... Tell me, what do you think of the monk who comes to play me every day at go?"

"Did you see something strange?"

"I'll say! We happened to pass close to his hut, and I saw something I'll not soon forget!"

As if suddenly remembering something, the master raised a hand and motioned Sanzaemon to pause.

"Please, don't speak of it! Your life will surely be forfeit if you speak of that terrible monk to another person! You mustn't say it! Please, leave here at once. I've heard say that you should stay at another inn quietly, and return to Edo as soon as possible tomorrow."

His voice was trembling, and his face had gone pasty white.

"But what in the world is all this! I don't understand what's happening!" cried Sanzaemon, confused at the bizarre happenings.

"I mustn't say! I am sure you've had a strange and terrifying experience, but it would be best if you not talk of it at all, and leave at once. Do not tell a soul, at peril of your life!"

"So you say... but it was strange indeed, today."

"No, please, I beg of you... do not say another word! I am telling you the truth, I swear it! Please, hurry!"

Sanzaemon still didn't quite understand just what the master of the inn was so upset about, but his memories of the bizarre sight he had just seen made him realize there must be a core of truth to the matter, and decided to return to Edo at once. He settled his bill and left.

It was already getting dark. Sanzaemon and his manservant spent the night at a small inn at the foot of the mountain, and after a day of hard traveling, the next night at an inn near Fujisawa.

They rushed on to Kanazawa the following day, and when they arrived at their inn for the night found a few retainers from his estate in Edo waiting.

"Why are you here?" demanded Sanzaemon.

"We were told you'd be returning to Edo today, and came to meet you."

Sanzaemon was curious: "How in the world did you know I'd be here?"

"A monk came yesterday, about forty years of age, and told the men at the gate that you were returning hurriedly from Hakone. He said you'd be arriving today, and that you'd asked him to come tell us. So we came at once to meet you."

"A forty-year-old monk, you say?"

"Yes, wearing a tattered black robe."

Sanzaemon fell silent, and continued on to his residence in Edo, arriving that night. Countless relatives and friends had gathered there to celebrate his return.

Sanzaemon stepped into the house, and everyone came crowding closer. His cherished four-year son, his youngest child, who was standing on the veranda, suddenly gave a shriek, shocking Sanzaemon... The child's headless body collapsed onto the floorboards.

The Pointer

幻談 (Gendan)

Kōda Rohan (1938)　　　　　　　　　幸田露伴
English translation by Ginny Tapley Takemori

WHEN THE DAYS become as hot as this, everyone heads either for the high mountains or the cool of the coast to thereby make the most of this oppressive time, as they rightly should. But once you grow old and decrepit, you can no longer go to either mountains or seaside and instead have to make do with the morning dew in the yard and the evening breeze on the veranda, passing the days in peace and safety—well, it's only natural that elderly folks should take it easy. Mountaineering is truly wonderful. There is often a certain kind of fascination in going deep into mountainous terrain and climbing all manner of perilous peaks. Yet danger always threatens and hair-raising tales also abound. It is the same with the sea. The story I wish to tell you now concerns the sea, but first I will relate an account of mountains.

ON JULY 13, 1865, at five-thirty in the morning, a team of climbers departed from the village of Zermatt with the goal of becoming the first to conquer that most majestic mountain of the Alps, the Matterhorn.[1] Just before dawn the next day, July 14, they redoubled their efforts and reached the peak at one-forty that afternoon. This account is from Edward

---

1. Kōda Rohan mistakenly noted that Whymper's team comprised eight men. However, it was only on the first day that there were eight—one of old Peter Taugwalder's sons returned to Zermatt, leaving seven men in the team to make the ascent.

Whymper's celebrated alpine diary, *Scrambles Amongst the Alps*. Whymper's party was the first to reach the summit of the Matterhorn, and it is thanks to their efforts that the Alps subsequently opened to others.

It is well known from the climbing log, and I hardly need to point it out to you now, but an Italian party led by Carrel[2] had already set out to conquer the mountain, and so the two teams naturally ended up competing against each other to be first. However, Carrel had the misfortune to make a false move, and thus lost out to Whymper. Whymper's party was made up of, in order, Croz[3], old Peter and his son, then the aristocrat Lord Francis Douglas. After him came Hadow, Hudson, and Whymper bringing up the rear.

On the fourteenth, at one-forty, they at length reached the summit of the Matterhorn, the fearsome peak that appeared to touch the heavens, and after much rejoicing they then set about the descent. They made their way slowly down with Croz in the lead, followed by Hadow, Hudson, Lord Francis Douglas, the rather elderly Peter, and Whymper. These same men who had just achieved the most outstanding unparalleled success now gingerly followed the dangerous route down over the ice and snow, twice as daunting as on the ascent. However, the second in line, Hadow, who was relatively inexperienced and also no doubt weary—or perhaps it was just fate—for he slipped and fell against Croz in the lead. This happened in a steep, icy section with few footholds, so Croz was instantly swept off his feet, and the two of them fell together. The men had all attached themselves to each other with a rope so that if one of them fell the others would be able to hold their ground and save him from danger. Be that as it may, the fall occurred on a sheer rock face and, unable to withstand the other two, the third man also fell. And then Lord Francis Douglas in fourth place was swept down by the momentum of the first three. As the remaining men braced themselves, the rope between them and Lord Douglas was pulled taut. But

---

2. Jean-Antoine Carrel
3. The full names are: Michel Croz, old Peter Taugwalder and his son, Lord Francis Douglas, Charles Hadow, Rev. Charles Hudson, and Edward Whymper. In Whymper's account, the order of the climbers changed on the final ascent.

the rope was not robust enough, and snapped midway. At precisely three o'clock the first four were precipitated some four thousand feet down the ice. For the others left there, how must they have felt watching half their team falling headlong before their very eyes down into the depths far below? Left behind, they became half-crazed and paralyzed by despair, unable to move either hands or feet. Mindful of the uncertain fate confronting them, aware that they, too, could slip and fall to their deaths, they eventually inched their way down, finally reaching a place of relative safety at about six in the evening.

They did make it down, but since the comrades with whom they had been until just a short while ago had fallen prey to mountain spirits, their psychological state must have been in turmoil. Those of us with no direct experience of what they had been through, having merely heard the story, cannot even begin to imagine what was going on in their minds. Nevertheless, according to Whymper's diary, at around six in the evening the Taugwalders, who were well accustomed to mountaineering, suddenly saw rising over the Lyskamm a kind of pale arch. Seeing them staring in surprise, Whymper too looked in that direction. As they watched, they distinctly saw two vast crosses forming within the arch in the sky. For Westerners the shape of the cross evokes a different emotion than it does for us in the East. The account states that they all had the sensation that they were seeing a vision from another world. Not just one, but all of those who survived, saw it. The cross is something akin to our five-story pagoda. It does sometimes happen that shapes are seen in phenomena caused by mountain weather, but at any rate these men, whose dead comrades had been alive until just a short while beforehand, had all subsequently seen these crosses—and they all saw them, not just one or two of them. Often in the mountains, depending on the direction of the light, the shadow of your body appears on the opposite side. These men, too, thought it might be such an illusion, and they waved their hands and jumped around, but concluded that it was absolutely unrelated.

And so I come to the end of this account. In the words of the old sutra[4], the mind is like a skillful painter—words that somehow ring true, don't you think?

4. Kegonkyō, or Avatamsaka.

WELL NOW, THE story I shall now relate is one that I heard from a certain old-timer once when we were out fishing. It is from a time when the Tokugawa era had not yet met its demise. This man lived in the Honjo district of Edo. Honjo was home to many low-ranking samurai—minor retainers of the shogun who were, as the Edo saying went, humble folk with incomes of not even a thousand *koku* of rice, but rather just a few hundred. He, too, was of a similar status, and being a capable fellow, he was, for a time, in service. Being in service opened the way to promotion—a good thing, to be sure. Nevertheless, society being the tricky thing it is, competence was no guarantee of promotion—on the contrary, he also attracted the jealousy and enmity of others, and for the most part he was assigned to minor house repairs. As the saying goes, the stake that sticks out will get hammered down, and so this capable man ended up being demoted to handyman. Finding himself with too much time on his hands, his errands few and far between, he passed the time fishing. Living expenses were no problem and he was not given to extravagance, neither was he unduly proud; he was understanding, good-natured, and a fine man by anybody's standards. Being just such a person, he was truly delighted to be able to enjoy fishing unencumbered by any bothersome relationships.

And so, whenever he had some spare time, he would indulge his hobby. There was a boathouse on the Kanda River, and on certain stipulated days the boatmen would steer their craft for Honjo, where he would board one and for a fishing trip. On the return, too, the boat would drop him off directly at Honjo, from whence he could go home, a most convenient arrangement. And on days when the tide was right he would go out daily fishing for black porgy. Nowadays these fish are generally called *kaizu* in Japanese, but in the Edo period they were called *keizu*, and that is the correct term. It is a type of sea bream, called *tai* in Japanese, and this is an abbreviation of *keizudai*. This black sea bream is the one carried by Ebisu, one of the seven gods of good fortune. But I'm sure you'll exclaim that Ebisu carries a red sea bream, not a black one, and scold me for saying such odd things! But this is what I heard from one Mr. Yabitsudai, an expert on such matters. Apart from anything, a red sea bream cannot be fished using the type of pole that Ebisu is carrying, which is precisely the type used for fishing black porgy. Since this story concerns a fishing pole, please excuse me for digressing a little.

One day our friend went out on the boat as usual. The boatman was called Kichi, and was already over fifty. Most customers were none too pleased about having an elderly skipper, but this man was in no hurry to catch fish willy-nilly and while Kichi was getting on in years he was hardly senile, and he was very knowledgeable, so this man always put him to good use. Some may think of boatmen as instructors or guides, but actually they are simply companions for people who enjoy going out fishing—that is, they entertain their customers, so a long-time boatman is good at understanding people and knows their likes and dislikes. A proficient skipper is one who gives his customers a good time. This is especially the case with those specializing in net fishing. Some customers may cast the net themselves, but in any case it involves casting the net to catch fish. But we are not talking about fishermen who make a living from catching fish. The point is not to help customers catch lots of fish, but to help them experience the fun of net fishing. The type of people who don't understand entertainment think that on a visit to the pleasure quarters all they need to do is just look at a geisha's face to make her play the samisen and sing, pour drinks, take her fan and dance, and provide all manner of amusements indiscriminately. These same people, when they go fishing, are too concerned with just the fish—in other words they are second-rate customers. That's not to say that it's okay to go out fishing and not catch anything, but this man was after more than just greedily using the boatman to pile on as many fish as possible, and so he was content even if the boatman was Kichi.

Fishing for black porgy is unlike fishing for other types of fish. As to why this is, take whiting, for example, where you use a method of fishing called *tachikomi*, in which you actually stand in the water, or *kyatatsu-tsuri*, where you stand a long ladder in the sea and sit on top of it waiting for the fish to pass. Some people speak ill of this method, calling it such names as "beggar's fishing," since if the fish fail to appear there is nothing you can do about it and you end up cutting a pitiful figure up there on the ladder. And then there's fishing for gray mullet. Gray mullet is not exactly a superior fish, and it comes in shoals so the catch is heavy. Not only do you catch more than you can carry, but the method for catching them involves slinging a long plank or oar across the gunwales on which you sit, exposed to the elements, looking more uncouth even than a patron in a spit-and-sawdust eatery, so it's not much fun. It really is pathetic ending up looking like someone who makes his living as fisherman. But then again, there are unaffected types who go in for precisely that sort of thing and praise gray mullet fishing as being just grand. However, the man I am talking of is not one of those. Fishing for black porgy is another matter altogether. In those days, fish from Edo Bay would venture far up the Great River,[5] and could be fished even further upstream than the Eitaibashi and Shin Ōhashi bridges. There were even anecdotes that we find hard to imagine today, like the one about the women faithful on Ryōgokubashi Bridge who would drop so many strips of paper bearing the printed image of Jizō, the god of children, into the water in the hope that he would answer their prayers that the porgies' eyes would be quite covered over with them.

Well, when fishing for porgy in the river, if you are in a deep part you use a handline without the need for a pole. You send out a long line from a caster ring, and then fish using two fingers to feel what's going on. When you get tired, you mount a gimlet on the gunwale and fix a piece of whalebone on top of it, and feed the line through the comblike baleen plates while you rest. This was known as *itokake*. Later on a bell was added to the top of the whalebone, which came to be known as a *myaku-suzu*, or pulse bell. These are still used today. Now, however, the rivers are utterly changed: fishing has completely ceased in the Great River, and it seems that nobody knows anything about this type of fishing for porgy. The truth is that even then, you didn't catch much with handline fishing. For our friend, going out fishing every day like this from Honjo to the upper reaches of the Great River right on his doorstep was not much fun, so he preferred fishing with a pole and line at sea over handline fishing in the river. There are also various types of pole fishing, and around the end of Meiji[6] there were

5. The Sumidagawa
6. Meiji period 1868–1912

methods like the one known as *hataki*. This involved standing on the boat off Odaiba and tossing out a hook in a place where the waves were particularly rough. In the midst of the strong southerly wind you had to wave your pole and cast the bait in the white surf of waves crashing onto rocks, so even if you did catch anything it was a pretty laborious way of fishing. But this type of fishing didn't exist at that time—indeed, Odaiba didn't exist at that time. And then there's the trolling method of trailing a baited line along a breakwater or such, but this too is quite exhausting. If you are too intent on catching fish, then fishing becomes less genteel and more of a chore.

That sort of fishing wasn't around in the olden days, either. At that time, people would go fishing in or around the sea channels, in a method called *miyo-zuri*. They would stop the boat against the tide where seawater flows naturally in channels. The customer sat by the wheelhouse—that's the cabin nearest the bow—facing forwards, and with back straight and pole extending beyond the bow, he would wave the fishing pole from side to side in a figure eight. The sweep to the right was known as the righthand pole, and the sweep to the left the lefthand pole. Everybody had his own style, but it was necessary to pause slightly on the tail of the sweep. All the while, the customer kept his eyes fixed on the tip of the pole. The skipper stood behind the customer, much like an attendant, waiting slightly to starboard, out of the way. Of course there was a rush mat cover to protect against the fierce sun or lashing rain. Two frames were set up in the space between girders, across which a ridge pole was laid with attached brackets right and left connected by wooden poles to support the rush matting. One rush mat was a little larger than your average tatami mat,[7] and in some cases considerably longer. Four of these provided roof cover over the open deck, so in the best conditions it served as the ceiling of a decent-sized room, protected from the sun and rain, rather like having a drawing room on deck. These fishing boats had a larger covered space on deck than most net fishing boats, and were really pleasant. If a rush mat was then spread out on the floor and covered with a rug, it was proper to kneel rather than sit cross-legged. The Kabuki actor Kōshirō told me an anecdote about a time when his master, the late Naritaya,

---

7. Approximately 90 cm x 180 cm

took him out fishing. At that time Kōshiro was still known as Somegorō, and although he always relied on Naritaya's instructions on stage, on this occasion Naritaya pushed him away and told him to do as he pleased, without teaching him anything. Even so, he still criticized Somegorō's seated position on the boat and scolded him harshly, "You idiot! What sort of way is that to sit?"[8] It's always like that when fishing for a higher class of fish like mullet, porgy, and sea bass.

And then, even if the fish did come, the sea bream class of fish was certainly spirited. Aficionados of this type of fishing call it "two-stage"[9] porgy fishing. It sometimes happens that the fish not only swallow the bait but make off with the pole, too, but that's rather rare. In the case of black porgy you show them the bait and move it around. Before long you can usually feel them nibble, so you slowly work the pole waiting for your chance. Then when the fish pulls the line tight, if the pole is on the righthand sweep you use your right hand to raise it, and quickly flick it up behind you, where the skipper is waiting to scoop the fish up in a landing net. Even if you catch a fish that isn't very big, it's gratifying to jerk it up and flip it over. The skipper scoops it up, removes the hook, and puts it in the seawater holding tank at the center of the boat. He then attaches fresh bait. When he announces, "The bait's ready, sir," you take the pole and start over again. Even if the customer is dressed in a fine linen kimono, he can still maintain his gentlemanly appearance while catching fish. Tea connoisseurs may keep some fine quality *gyokucha* on a tray at their side, and since this is two-stage porgy fishing, even if they are drinking tea when their prey nibbles, if they are well-practiced they can quietly put down their tea cup and then proceed to catch their fish. Those who like something a little stronger can enjoy a tipple while fishing in the ebbing tide. Many fishing trips are in summer, so *aomori* brandy[10] or *yanagikage* liquor[11] are

8. Naritaya was Ichikawa Danjurō IX, 1838–1903, and Somegorō was Matsumoto Kōshirō VII, 1870–1949. Both were very influential Kabuki actors of their time.
9. Sea bream are apparently very nervous and first have a tentative nibble. Only if it seems safe will they bite properly. If you try to reel them in on first nibble, they will take fright and flee.
10. A rice-based brandy from Okinawa.
11. A cocktail of the sweet rice wine *mirin* and the distilled rice liquor *shochu*,

popular, and all the necessary crockery and tableware for tea, liquor, and snacks is provided in a large box, although this is not quite as large as the average *okimizuya* cupboard used for storing utensils for the tea ceremony. Still, all these details make it truly pleasurable. And if the cypress-wood deck has been freshly scrubbed, it is perfectly clean. When the surface of the water is skimmed by a cool breeze, then seen from afar, even to a casual observer, a boat out at sea with one side of its matting cut away looks ever so refreshing—a slither of a boat, its shadow cutting through the wind, bobbing gently on the wide open tide, standing out against the blue sky like a single feather from a large bird fallen from the heavens.

Well, that's channel fishing. There is another type of fishing, however, when the fish fail to take the bait in the channel and are lurking somewhere in the shadows, so that's where you go to catch them. There was a popular Edo ditty that went, "Birds are to the trees, as fish are to the *kakari*, as people are to shadowy passions."[12] The *kakari* takes its name from some kind of obstruction (*hikkakari*) that obscures the fish moving slowly in the water, making it difficult to catch them with a net or even to cast a hook. Fish tend to hide behind such a *kakari*, so casting the hook close to them is called *kakari mae* fishing. If you don't catch any fish in open water, you try here—everyone does. Some people even like to go especially to old waterway posts, wrecked boats, or the structures for cultivating oysters and seaweed, where they try various tricks, quite aware that they might lose their tackle. In any case, fishing for porgy was indeed such a luxurious pastime as to be dubbed "fishing fit for a lord."

Well, the fun of fishing is all very well, but of course the root of the pastime is the matter of catching fish, so if you don't catch much your sphere of enjoyment is also reduced. There was one day when our friend failed to catch a single fish. When novices do not catch any fish, they are prone to griping about it to the boatman, but the man I am talking of was not so thoughtless as to say such things, and returned home in the same good humor as always. The following day was also

popular in the Edo period as a summer beverage.
12. This was a *yoshikono*, a type of popular song in the Edo-period, often witty or romantic, with a meaningless refrain to mark the rhythm.

scheduled for fishing, and so the man again went out with Kichi. Fish being fish, generally if there is bait they are apt to take it, but that is not always the case. On occasion they take exception to something about the water or the wind or anything else, for that matter, and then for whatever reason they won't take the bait for anything. It couldn't be helped. Not a single catch for two days. Having caught absolutely nothing, not even one fish, Kichi was downcast. You never know what will happen in a neap tide, but for a skipper not to have caught anything two days running on a good tide was a serious matter and unlikely to be overlooked by his customer. Also, for this customer the fishing made the man and he refrained from complaining, which just made Kichi feel even worse. It simply could not be helped. He had really wanted send him home with something to show for the day, yet despite having considered various places in the tidal currents and having tried this and that, they had not caught anything at all. Being a moonless spring tide, it really should have been ideal fishing. Having failed to catch anything despite his best efforts, even Kichi ended up feeling worn out.

"Sir, we've caught nothing in two days. I'm so sorry."

The customer laughed, "Come now, what do you mean by apologizing? This is no occupation for such foolishness! Ha ha ha! Not at all. Well, all that's left is to go back, so shall we be on our way?"

"Let's just try one more spot, then go back."

"But it'll be sunset soon, won't it?"

The approach of dawn and nightfall were times when the fish tended to come out, even if they had hitherto kept away. Kichi's gut instinct told him to try now, but the customer was against it.

"We're out porgy fishing and you want to try one more place at this late hour? How vulgar! Let's call it a day."

"Sorry, sir, but just one more spot."

Kichi had quite forgotten his place and now steered his boat in the direction he himself wanted to go.

Stubbornly reluctant to admit defeat, he maneuvered his boat to a location they had not yet tried and cautiously took his time over deciding the right place. Eventually he said, "Sir, prepare a pole and cast it directly before the bow."

It seemed they faced a prodigious *kakari* on all sides ahead. The customer reluctantly assented and did as he was told, casting well despite being undeniably halfhearted about it. But this time, just as he was wondering whether or not to put down the pole, he felt something—goodness knows whether it was a fish or piece of litter, but it was big. Whatever it was, far from waiting for the second bite, as soon as he felt it the line suddenly went taught with a sharp tug on the pole, so the customer gripped the butt of the pole, adjusted it slightly, and immediately began raising it. But this movement had no effect, since whatever was on the other end of the line possessed inhuman strength. The pole was a standard two-part quality item, but there was now a low groan from the base of the joint and the line snapped. They had not even managed to see what had taken it, yet it was another black mark against Kichi. What was more, he could not help noticing that the rod had been damaged, and his heart sank. This sort of thing was not unprecedented, and the customer remained patient to the end. Still without scolding, he turned to Kichi and commented with a smile, "Time to go back, isn't it?" He said it lightly, but naturally implied in that was the order, "Go back now!" All Kichi could do was to obediently pull away from the bank and start rowing.

"What a silly gamble that was," he said to himself, tapping his head and laughing sheepishly. His riposte nicely rounded off the day's play, and they both chuckled.

All the pleasure boats on the sea had gone; not a single one remained. Kichi pulled hard on the oars. It was late, and he was rowing against the tide as they headed for Edo. After a while the shore lay in darkness, the lights of Edo shimmering in the distance. Kichi was getting on in years but he was skilled, and he worked his body hard as he rowed. The rush matting had already been removed, and the boat moved smoothly along. The customer had nothing to do, and sat decorously gazing vacantly at the water. Gradually the light glinting off the surface ripples faded, and the hazy sky tinged red then muted to a dim inky gray. At this hour the sky and water do not so much become one as the light of the sky seems to penetrate into the sea with no sense of reflection, so you can barely distinguish between the water stretching out vastly blue in the gloom and the slightly brighter hue above it. The customer idly contemplated the lights of Edo growing steadily closer, trying to place where they were. Rowing against the tide, Kichi had moved the boat out of the current to where the water resistance was weaker. Now glancing to the east, where the current was not yet in total darkness but had turned a dark gray, the customer noticed something emerge briefly from the water. He watched more closely as the object again emerged, this time remaining visible a little longer before sinking back down. It looked like some kind of reed or grass—but if that was what it was, surely it would float level on the water. At any rate, some thin sticklike object, however strange that may sound, was bobbing in and out of the water. The customer had no need to know what it was, but since he did not understand it, he called out casually, "Kichi, there's something odd over there."

Kichi followed the customer's line of vision, and caught sight of the thin object as it emerged and then sank back down again. Having already seen it a number of times, the customer said, "I wonder what it is. It looked like a fishing pole sticking up out of the sea."

"Hmmm—it did, at that."

"But how could a fishing pole stick up out of the sea like that?"

"But sir, it didn't look like an ordinary bit of bamboo, so it might be a fishing pole."

Kichi still wanted the customer to have something to show for the day, and so he turned the boat around and headed for the spot where they had seen the strange object.

"What are you doing? Just because we saw something!"

"But it's strange and I don't know what it is, so just for my own edification."

"Ha ha ha! For your edification, you say. Ha ha ha!"

Kichi paid him no heed. Just as he steered the boat over, the long thin object reared up out of the water right in front of him as if to strike him. Kichi's face was drenched with spray as he reached out and grabbed it with one hand. He saw that it was indeed a fishing pole, and something on the end was pulling as if to make off with it. Trying to dislodge it, Kichi kept his grip on it firm as he took a closer look.

"Sir, it is a fishing pole. It's bamboo, a good 'un."

"Is that so?" replied the customer. "Oh, if it isn't a floater!"

A "floater" was the fishing term for a drowned corpse, and the customer's exclamation effectively amounted to an order, "Let go of it!"

Kichi, however, retorted, "But it's a good pole!" Peering at it in the fading light, he added "It's golden bamboo, unjointed." Unjointed meant that the pole was made of a single length of bamboo, rather than several pieces fitted together. Being of course the best for fishing, golden bamboo is also called fish-pole bamboo. Most poles were made from good golden bamboo attached to a piece of another type, usually short-spiked bamboo. An unjointed pole was, of course, made of one type only. This was not necessarily a good thing, but it was certainly rare to find an unjointed pole in such good, usable condition.

"I can't believe I'm hearing this!" The customer turned a deaf ear.

But perhaps Kichi still had in mind that his customer's own pole had been lost earlier, for he was intent on getting this pole. Taking care not to snap it, he pulled hard. By so doing, he was bound to bring the "mid-way" floater to the surface. There were three states of drowned bodies: while some floated on the surface and others sank to the bottom, those who remained floating in between were referred to as "mid-way." As Kichi pulled, the body surfaced right before where the customer was seated.

"Don't bother with such useless things! I said you should leave it," exclaimed the customer, but since it had surfaced right before him he could not help but notice that it was indeed a good pole. A sign of a quality pole was the well-proportioned spacing between the bamboo node rings. One glance was enough for this samurai to know that the pole now within his reach was truly a good one, and so he too grasped hold of it.

Noting that his customer had hold of it, Kichi was now bound to leave it to him. "I'm letting go," he warned, and then released his grip. Now that the pole was being held about a foot from its base, its entire form appeared cleanly above the water. It was as if a famous sword had been unsheathed to reveal its full beauty.

It had not appeared to be anything special, but as soon as

the customer took hold of it, a deep affection for it welled up inside him. He thrust at it two or three times to free it, but it was tight in the unyielding grip of the person in the water. In the fading light the floater's appearance was unclear, but they could see that he was corpulent, with long, thin eyebrows and extremely thick earlobes, and that he must be nigh on sixty, with his balding head. He appeared to be clothed in a pale blue-green unpatterned cotton crepe kimono, the undershirt with a linen collar, and while they could not clearly see his sash, his body shifted around, affording them a glimpse of his white tabi socks, which made quite an impression on them. He was clearly of the samurai class, the type of man who would wear a sword, even if it was wooden, and who would carry at least one *inro* at his hip.

"What shall we do?" the customer blurted out in a small voice. Just then there was a gust of evening wind, and he felt a chill run through his body. It would be a waste to give the pole up, but if he wanted to take it he would have to free it from its waterbound owner, who had given his life with it firmly in his grasp.

Noting his indecision, Kichi spoke up once again. "Well, sir, I can't see that he'll be doing any fishing at the River of Three Crossings,[13] so where's the harm in taking it?"

So the customer tried once again to push the body away, but it held on fast. It was just as if the pole's owner was adamant not to let go of it even in death, for he was gripping it so tightly that the customer could not free it. Yet he could hardly take a knife to it. A node in the bamboo was in the grip of the owner's little finger, preventing him from freeing it. There was nothing else for it: he used his thumb to pry the finger off. It was hardly a worthy use of jujitsu, but the finger snapped and the former owner abruptly slipped beneath the tide, leaving his pole behind. Making light of it, the customer thoroughly washed the hand that had done battle, and wiped it with several sheets of tissue paper that he then tossed into the sea. The ghostly ball of white paper drifted off into the darkness and eventually out of sight.

"*Namu Amida butsu, Namu Amida butsu,*" prayed Kichi,

---

13. The River of Three Crossings awaits the dead, who must cross it on the seventh day. Depending on the severity of their sins, they may cross by bridge, by ford, or by wading through the serpent-infested waters.

now in a hurry to get home. "Who was he, I wonder. Someone fishing from the shore, perhaps?"

"Yes, but I've never seen him before. I can't believe he's the type to frequent places like Honjo, Fukagawa, Manabegashi, or Mannen. More like Mukōjima, or even further upstream."

"Oh, I see. That's very perceptive of you."

"Oh, come now! It must have been a case of the palsy. Imagine squatting down in an awkward position on the shore to cast your line, and then, just at the moment you catch a big fish the palsy hits. If you fall in there and then, well, that's it, isn't it? That's why since way back it's been said that people susceptible to palsy should only go fishing on flat ground. Not that there's anywhere that's good for it, though. Ha ha ha!"

"I suppose not."

And so, the day drew to a close.

When they got to the usual landing place, the customer took the pole and was taking his leave when Kichi asked him, "Sir, what about tomorrow?"

"Well, we were due to go out tomorrow, but I don't mind taking a break."

"No, I'll come and pick you up again tomorrow—unless it's raining cats and dogs, that is."

"Really?" responded the customer as they parted.

THE NEXT DAY the customer awoke to see it was pouring with rain.

"Oh! With this darned rain, the fishing could be bad for two or three days. Or maybe there'll even be a red tide."

He had arranged to meet Kichi, but he doubted whether the boatman would turn up in this downpour, and so for want of anything better to do he stayed at home reading. It was nearing noon by the time Kichi appeared. He went around to the garden door.

"Sir, it was a bit doubtful whether we could go out or not today, but I brought the boat along. If you did want to go out, it wouldn't do if I didn't come along, now, would it?"

"Really? Well, I'm glad you've come. I worked you hard for two or three days to no avail, but it was odd how we got that pole in the end, wasn't it?"

"Getting hold of a pole is a good omen for a fisherman, you know."

"Ha ha ha. But I don't want to go out in the rain, not until it stops."

"All right. So, sir, where is it?"

"It? I put it up there on the lintel. Look!"

Kichi went off to the kitchen and came back with a cloth and some water in a basin. After thoroughly washing the pole, they saw that it really was splendid. The pair studied it closely. They would have expected it to be heavy, having been so long in the water, but even at the time they had thought that it had soaked up remarkably little water, and it was just as light today, too. They could only think that some waterproofing technique had been used on it. The node rings were beyond compare. And while the line loop on the tip appeared to be the work of an amateur, it was pretty well done nevertheless. Also, on the thickest part on the handle, there was a small artifice. Artifice is perhaps too grand a word, but a small hole had been opened up into which something could possibly have been inserted, and had been stopped up again. There was no sign of a safety strap having been used, which was rather strange. Apart from that, there was nothing else out of place.

"It's an uncommonly good pole, isn't it? I've never seen a golden bamboo pole that's so light and in such good condition."

"That's true. Golden bamboo is usually heavy. Nobody wants a pole that's too heavy, so there's a technique of stunting the bamboo by cutting notches to damage it while it's still growing. If it's on just one side, it's called single right or single left training, if it's on both sides it's double training. So the matured bamboo weighs less due to the lack of nutrients, which makes it good for fishing poles."

"I've heard about that, too, but doesn't trained bamboo get all wizened and unappealing to look at? That's not the case with this one. I wonder what they did to get this finish, or is there a type of bamboo that is naturally like this?"

When a fisherman wants a good pole, he will go to a bamboo thicket and himself select a suitable cane, arrange to purchase it, and then nurture it to his heart's content. That's the usual way to go about it, and part of the process of becoming a veteran fisherman. The Tang-era poet Wen Ting-yun[14] was an incorrigible libertine utterly lacking in moral scruples, but he had a childlike enjoyment of fishing and even wrote a poem in which, thinking to obtain a fishing pole of his own, he sneaks into a grove owned by a man called Haishi in search of a good piece of bamboo. One line goes, "A diversionary route through the long overgrown reed thicket," so he enters surreptitiously parting the reeds and brambles on the narrow winding path. It goes on, "Ever searching for graceful nodes, discarding weaker roots," which means he went around inspecting this and that bamboo one by one. In the Tang era, fishing was extremely popular, to the extent that there was even a recreational fish farm called Sesshi Pond, a famous name even today, and there seem to have been many shops selling poles, yet still the acclaimed poet apparently wanted to devote himself to his passion to the point of crawling through the thickets to get a pole that pleased him. In a humorous verse by the satirical poet Nakarai Bokuyō,[15] Urashima[16] has a fishing pole of black bamboo with node rings that are neither sufficiently widely or narrowly spaced—but seeing as a black bamboo pole in itself is not very impressive, simply by saying things like it had as many as thirty-six nodes he appears to be greatly praising it. So when one's passion reaches such heights, it is entirely natural to devote oneself to finding a good pole.

The more Kichi and his customer looked at the pole, the more they gradually came to understand why the old man had been so reluctant to let go of it even in death.

"You never see this sort of bamboo around here, so it must have come from other parts. Even so, it's a good twelve feet long! It's no joke to carry something like that around with you. Perhaps he was a ronin with time on his hands. He must certainly have known a lot about fishing, so perhaps he did have a fit of palsy. In any case, it's a fine pole," said Kichi.

"By the way, earlier, when you were looking at the loop on

14. Wen Ting-yun (812–870), a popular lyricist famed for his frivolity and penchant for courtesans.
15. Nakarai Bokuyō (1607–1678), known for comic or satirical tanka-style poetry.
16. Urashima Tarō of popular legend, the fisherman who saved a turtle and was rewarded with a visit to the Palace of the Dragon under the sea. Usually depicted holding a fishing pole.

the end of the pole, I don't know what you were doing, but you took off a bit of line, didn't you? I saw you wind it up and put it in your pocket."

"Yes, it was in the way. And what's more, when I saw it I thought to myself that the fellow wasn't from these parts."

"Why's that?"

"Why? Well, you see, it was attached to a taper—that means it starts off thick and tapers off towards the end. It's a complicated method that you use when go to Kashū[17] or somewhere flyfishing for sweetfish. If the fly lands wrong on the surface you won't catch anything—if the line hits the water first before the fly, then the fish'll keep their distance. That's what this method's for. You have to snip a handful of hair from the tail of a white horse—a healthy one, not too old—and then put it in tofu lees and weight it down. That'll make it nicely transparent. Then you take sixteen hairs and twist them round all in the same direction—to the right if you're right-handed—it's hard at first, but when you get used to it you'll find it's easy. So that's the first round. On the next round you use fewer hairs, and twist them in the opposite direction—to the left if you started out to the right. Then you keep on reducing the number of hairs and changing the direction of the twist, until you get down to the end where you use a single hair. I heard about it from a customer who's from Kashū—they're really into details, those folks out west. It's a set tactic. This pole isn't meant for sweetfish since it's fitted with gut line, but it's well done, tapering off nicely. This guy was pretty serious about fishing, I reckon. He did this so as to be able to break off. He was fishing from the bank—it didn't matter where he cast off from, as long as a hook was attached then he would make a catch. Then, tending the pole, to bring things to a close before the pole snapped he would place it so that the line would break in the right place. It breaks where it's thinnest, so if you use the feel of the pole to calculate this, then you needn't fear for the pole. Wherever you are, if you need to free the pole, you can break the line without snapping the pole. Then all you have to do is just attach another hook. I could tell right away from the way that fellow had made a neat taper that he really took care of his pole. And the way he was clinging on to it—it was really like the

17. Kashū is another name for the Province of Kaga, or present-day Ishikawa.

pair of them had committed a love suicide! That in itself was enough to show how much he prized it, wasn't it?"

While Kichi had been talking, the rain had begun to clear up. They both had lunch, the customer in his room and Kichi in the kitchen, after which Kichi asked the customer, "How about going out?" and the customer responded, "Let's go!" And so, despite the late hour, they decided to go out in the boat. Naturally they took the pole with them, and while they were on the way, the customer himself neatly made another taper for the line.

It rained on and off as they fished, but unlike the previous day things went exceedingly well. They were reeling them in so fast that it grew late, and again dusk was falling by the time they finally called it a day. They removed the line from the loop and stored it away, then put the pole up behind the rush matting. As they drew closer to home, the flickering lights of Edo again came into view. The customer recalled how he had seen the pole sticking up out of the water and then broken a finger to retrieve it, and thought he might name it "The Pointer." Kichi had been rowing hard—so hard, in fact, that the oarlock had become quite dry. This made it harder to row, and so he took the dipper in front of him and scooped up some water, then twisting his body round, splashed it over the oarlock. This was quite a matter of course for an Edo skipper, although not for those in the provinces. Twisting your body round, taking aim from up high, and then dashing the water down just at the moment that the oarlock is facing straight up—this spirited pose, well executed, is a favorite in ukiyo-e pictures. As Kichi now twisted around and dashed down the water, then turned back to face the same way as he started, he happened to catch sight in the east of something that looked very much like a reed. It was the same sort of sight they had seen at about the same time at dusk yesterday. "What's that?" he asked, staring toward it. The customer was seated in the space by the prow and, at Kichi's prompting, also now turned his gaze in that direction. There in the gloom, a piece of bamboo was bobbing up and down in the water, just the same as the day before. "Goodness! What the—" he thought, unable to comprehend what he was seeing. Kichi, too, was astonished and glanced at the customer, wondering whether he had seen it. The customer looked back at him. As they sat there baffled, a warmish easterly sea breeze sprang up. But Kichi quickly put on a brave front.

"What's this? It can't be the same thing as yesterday! We've got that pole here. Isn't that right, sir? The pole's here, isn't it?" By this he meant that they could feel safe in the knowledge that they had the pole, even if what they were seeing seemed eerily reminiscent, but even so he leaned across to check that the pole was indeed there. The customer, too, glanced up at where it should be. But it was too dark for them to ascertain whether or not the pole was there behind the rush mat. The customer looked at Kichi's bemused face, and Kichi returned his look. They each seemed to be trying to detect something of the other world in the other's eyes.

The pole was of course where they had left it. Nevertheless, the customer now took it and, praying *Namu Amida butsu, Namu Amida butsu*, he restored it to the sea.

The Inō Residence, Or,
The Competition with a Ghost

稲生家＝化物コンクール
(Inōke=bakemono concours)

By Inagaki Taruho (1972)　　　稲垣足穂
English translation by Jeffrey Angles

DURING THE SEVENTH month of the second year of Kan'en (1749), strange things happened every night at the home of an adolescent samurai named Inō Heitarō, who lived beneath the castle in Miyoshi Gomangoku controlled by a branch of the Asano clan. These supernatural appearances continued from the first of the month all the way to the thirtieth.[1] The record describing these events does not appear to be fiction. I understand that both Hirata Atsutane and, more recently in the Meiji period, Inoue Enryō, discussed it in their work, but I

---

1. All notes by translator unless otherwise specified.

   This story takes place in the northeastern part of modern Hiroshima Prefecture. It is based upon a well-known narrative called *An Account of Inō and the Spirit* (Inō mononoke roku) written in the eighteenth century. Taruho wrote several different adaptations of this story, including the version translated here. Another frequently anthologized version of this story crafted by Taruho is *Sanmono Gorōzaemon Now Takes His Leave* (Sanmono Gorōzaemon tadaima taisan tsukamatsuru). The same eighteenth-century story has influenced a number of other modern writers, including Izumi Kyōka, who refers to it in *Grass Labyrinth* (Kusa meikyū), Iwaya Sazanami, author of *Heitarō's Ghost Diary* (Heitarō kemono nikki), and Origuchi Shinobu, author of the humorous play *An Account of Inō and the Spirit* (Inō mononoke roku).

have not yet been able to read what they wrote.[2] In retelling his story, I am simply trying to share with my readers a group of ghosts that function as moving "objets d'art."

At the time this story takes place, the young lad Heitarō had already lost both of his parents and was living with his younger brother Katsuya as well as one samurai retainer named Gonpei.

The First Night

THAT EVENING, I had gone to cool off at the riverbank with my next door-neighbor Mitsui Gonpachi when a cloud began to form over Mount Higuma. The cloud was so dark it looked as if black ink had spilled across the sky. There was a flash of lightning, and suddenly a terrible summer storm overtook us. The rain looked like it would go on forever.

By two o'clock in the morning, the wind had blown out all the lamps, but suddenly the *shōji* lit up as brilliantly as if they were on fire.[3] I jumped out of bed, but everything went pitch black again. I tried to pull back one of the *shōji*, but it would not budge. I planted one of my feet against the base of a pillar and pulled at it with both hands, but the wooden lattice snapped and flew off the sliding door.

Next, I felt someone grab at my shoulders and obi and try to pull me backward.[4] I grabbed at the pillar and lintel with both hands and held on with all my might. Something seemed to have grabbed hold of me and was pulling at me with its fingertips. The creature was as thick as a log and covered with coarse, wild hair. The room went black for a few moments, and when the light finally returned, I saw a huge eye shining from the wall on the other side of the room.

I called out over and over, "Gonpei! My sword, my sword!" but there was no response. I pulled forward with a cry of effort, and as I did so, both sleeves of my kimono ripped off and my

---

2. Hirata Atsutane (1776–1843) was a prominent scholar of national learning (*kokugaku*), and Inoue Enryō (1858–1919) was a scholar of Buddhist philosophy and religion.
3. See note on page 121.
4. An *obi* is the cloth sash worn with a kimono.

obi came loose. The obi flew off, yanked off by whatever it was pulling at me from behind.

I grabbed at my sword, but it was pitch black again, and I could not see where to aim. A light began to shine under the floor. I tried ramming my sword between the tatami mats, and all of the mats flew up into the air at once—all except for the one on which my younger brother was sleeping. That one remained as it was. I realized Gonpei had lost consciousness. He seemed to have fallen over the tatami. The scattered tatami had piled themselves in one corner of the room all by themselves.

At that point, my neighbor Gonpachi came over. When he arrived, he said, "Just a few moments ago, I heard you calling for your sword over and over. I tried coming over, but there was a young priestly acolyte passing in front of your gate. I saw him put some water in a bowl, lift it like he was presenting an offering, and walk by. As I walked by him, my whole body went numb, and I couldn't speak. I crouched there for a few moments until I recovered, then came over as soon as I could."

I gave Gonpei some water to drink and rested a moment before putting the tatami back into place. My place was not the only one in the neighborhood that was attacked that night.

The Second Night

THE NEXT MORNING, as soon as the neighbors opened their gates, Gonpei rushed over and proudly recounted the previous night's adventures. In this way, word of the incident circulated through the neighborhood. My relatives came over, and so did Gonpachi. I decided my younger brother should stay at our uncle's house. I insisted I would not back down until I had ascertained the true nature of the ghost. I would stay put. Gonpei was more hesitant, saying, "I'll work for you during the day, but as for my duties at night...." I decided it would be fine for him to sleep elsewhere come nighttime.

Nothing strange happened during that day, but when evening fell, five or six of my friends came over to stay with me. As the hour approached midnight, the flame in the lamps began to flicker and grow taller bit by bit until they practically reached the ceiling. The corners of the tatami began to lift into the air. At first they lifted only three or five *sun* at a time, but their movement became increasingly dramatic.[5] One of the guests said, "I forgot something I need to do." This set off a chain of departures, and before long, everyone had beaten a hasty retreat home.

The tatami stopped lifting into the air, so I left my neighbor Gonpachi in charge, crawled into the mosquito net, and lay down. Before long, I realized a strange, raw smell was filling the space around me, and water began to bubble into the room. The water filled my eyes and nose. The whole room became so full that everything swayed back and forth in it, but then the water disappeared as if it had never been there at all.

The Third Night

EARLY THAT EVENING, I was drinking saké with five or six of the men from the neighborhood when our swords had disappeared. We found them together in a pile on top of the mosquito netting in the back room—something that made everyone go pale. The tobacco trays and small tables we had set around us began to dance, and the corners of the tatami began to lift and slam back down.

As midnight approached, we heard a deep grumbling sound. The house began to rattle, and soon the whole place was rattling fast and furious. One of my guests stood up, and within moments, the entire group was fleeing the room. When they stepped down into the garden, they found the house next door was not shaking.

Thinking I should look around to make sure my own house was not collapsing, I picked up a lantern and went into the bedroom, but as soon as I did, the lantern in my hand transformed into a stone pillar. Fire exploded from the bottom and began to spread. It looked like everything, including the stone lantern itself, would catch on fire. In a few moments, however, everything returned to the way it had been before.

I laid down, but I saw some green, slippery things descending from the ceiling. It was a bunch of calabashes—they were descending as if someone were lowering a vine of them from

---

5. A *sun* is a unit of measurement approximately 3 cm in length. Ten sun make up one *shaku*.

the ceiling. I figured I would go to sleep anyway. The next time I woke up, my whole body was covered with sweat, and something was on top my chest. From the light filtering in through the *shōji*, I could see it was a huge severed head of a woman. It was pale, and long trails of blood streamed from the place where it had been separated from its body. Still, it seemed to be smiling as it sat on top of me.

I rushed to the corner of the mosquito netting, thinking that as soon as the chance presented itself, I would hurl myself on the head and get rid of it. As soon as I tried to dispose of it, however, it flew right back to my chest. I tried kicking it outside the netting, but it passed through the netting as if it was not even there. It was only around the time the crows started cawing outside that the head finally disappeared.

The Fourth Night

WORD HAD SPREAD far and wide of my adventures, and many curious onlookers had gathered in front of my gate. As twilight fell, the women and children grew so nervous they would go in groups to use the toilet. People did not stop coming and going from the house until around ten o'clock. By that time, many of the people that had come to see me had gone home. One of the remaining few had no sooner said, "Looks like nothing is going to happen tonight," when the house began to rattle as if a great typhoon were blowing by. A few moments later, one of my guests said, "It looks like the rumblings have stopped," and got up to go. Most of the others quickly followed.

After that, the water in the water jugs froze, the lids on the pots refused to open, and the bellows refused to blow any air, no matter how much I tried. The tissue paper sitting on my shelves began to scatter, one sheet at a time, fluttering around the room like butterflies. When they fell upon the tatami, we were surprised to find morning had come.

The Fifth Night

AS NIGHT FELL, a group of around five to seven people gathered in front of the gate with their traveling bags and their bedding so they could listen to the rumblings of the house;

however, it began to rain around six o'clock, so most of them went home. My older brother Shinpachi came over to check on me, but when he did, his wooden clogs flew through a small hole over the lintel and began to walk all over the reception room.[6] I mentioned, "Strange things like this seem to happen when guests come over, so it's probably best for you to leave." With this, I sent my brother off.

Gonpachi came over just as my brother was leaving. We were talking when a stone the size of a few bushels of rice rolled in. Peeling its eyes back like a like a crab, it stared at Gonpachi then started coming right for him. I stopped him as he tried to grab his sword.

The next morning when it grew light, we found the stone from the previous night in the kitchen. Upon closer inspection, we found that it was one of the stones placed in the neighborhood streets to block traffic. Gonpachi told me, "Last night, I seemed to be coming down with a touch of fever, and I didn't feel especially good. Tonight, I'd like to take a night off and recuperate."

That evening too lots of butterflies flitted around the place. The rattling of the house had already become commonplace.

The Sixth Night

LAST NIGHT so many people had gathered in front of my gate that vendors came to sell frozen sweets, so an official notice saying "no spectators allowed" was circulated through the neighborhoods near me. Around midnight, Shinpachi accompanied some public officials to the house. We were talking when we heard something that sounded like a pair of flapping wings. Right then, an unsheathed blade flashed past us, slicing through the edge of Shinpachi's sleeve and landing with a thud

6. **Author's note:** Heitarō's older brother Shinpachi was adopted into the family. Heitarō's father was in his forties and still did not have any children so he took Shinpachi, the second son of his retainer Nakayama Genpachi, into his household. Three or four years later, Heitarō was born, and when he was about twelve, his younger brother Katsuya was born. Both of his adoptive parents died soon after that, leaving Shinpachi as the head of the household. Shinpachi, however, came down with a disease that made him have seizures and so went to recuperate at the home of his birth parents.

in the *karagami* behind him.[7] When he pulled it out, he saw it was a short sword he had lent to one of his retainers, but the sheath was missing.

As we were looking for the sheath, we heard a strange voice say, "tontokokoni." The voice was so raspy it sounded like wooden boxes scraping against one another, but there was no question, it was saying "tontokokoni." In fact, it said it three or four times. The voice seemed to come from a framed picture hanging on the wall. We removed the picture from the wall to see what was going on, and the sheath clattered to the floor.[8]

Gonpei had not shown his face for these three days, claiming he was sick. He also said he could not find anyone to take his place, and so there was nothing I could do—I was left alone that evening. I was taking a bath and resting a bit when Horiba Gon'emon and my uncle Kawada Moemon showed up. They were in the middle of a conversation when something whitish and round floated out of the kitchen. It was large enough that it would have filled their arms if they had tried to grab it. Also, a pair of wooden clogs flew out at them so forcefully that they went right through the *fusuma*.[9] As the whitish thing floated toward them, something sprinkled from it, scattering all over the place. The two visitors let out an exclamation of surprise and jumped out of the way. When the mysterious object fell to the ground, it was nothing but an old straw sack full of salt.

The Seventh Night

I WAS OUT making the rounds to the homes of my brother Shinpachi, Kawada Moemon, and several other people for the Tanabata holidays, but everyone raised a fuss and kept asking me what was going on.[10] I decided not to stay out. It was hot. There was one young woman who had been a regular visitor to

---

7. A *karagami* is a sliding door covered with patterned paper in the Chinese style.

8. "*Tontokokoni*" is written in katakana, as if the narrator cannot quite make out what the voice is saying. When the characters in the story find the blade, the reader realizes that the words must have meant "for sure (*tonto*), here (*koko ni*)."

9. A *fusuma* is a solid, wooden sliding door, often covered with paper.

10. Tanabata, sometimes called the "Star Festival" in English, is held on the seventh day of the seventh month. Legend had it that the stars *Orihime*

my house since before this all started, and she paid me a visit when evening came. She was about ready to go home when a washtub came rolling out. She screamed and rushed toward the front door, but the washtub chased after her, and she fled from the house, stumbling in panic.

A sudden storm arose that evening. By the time night fell, however, the sky had cleared, leaving a clear, cool view of the waves of the Milky Way—the same flow the stars were traversing that night for their annual meeting.

I was about to go into the kitchen, but there, in the entrance to the room, was a huge white sleeve filling the entire doorway. Emerging from it was a gigantic hand like a giant wooden pestle, faded in color. The fingers were each as a thick as a fist, and from their ends emerged another set of other pestle-like hands with its own fingers. From those, too, came a third set of hands, which were about the size of ordinary human hands. From these grew other pestle-hands that became progressively smaller and stuck out in every direction like spines on a cactus. The countless hands swarmed with movement. I let out a yell as I grabbed at the hands, but they disappeared within my grip. When I stepped back slightly, they burst forth again in countless numbers.

Before long, the bell sounded the midnight hour. I went inside the mosquito netting when suddenly I saw the heads of several priests appear. The heads were skewered on stakes like *dengaku* on bamboo sticks, and their eyes were round and glinted in the pale light.[11] Using the skewers as legs, they hopped around the room.

As I lay in bed, the pestle-hands occasionally grazed my face with their cold and unpleasantly soft touch. I pushed them away, but they would disappear for a moment only to reappear again. Finally, dawn rolled around, and the heads and the hands gradually faded away.

(Vega) and *Hikoboshi* (Altair) were lovers, kept separate by the expanse of the river of the Milky Way. They could only cross the river once a year to meet each other, and that meeting took place on the night of the Tanabata festival.

11. *Dengaku* is a food made of blocks of *konnyaku* covered with miso paste. It is usually served on bamboo skewers.

The Eighth Night

EVERY ONCE IN a while, the tatami mats would fly into the air, so I had a difficult time getting any rest. A summer storm raged outside, but when night fell, the sky grew clear. Six or seven people gathered at the house after ten o'clock. They suggested that I go to bed, so I went inside my mosquito netting. Meanwhile, they continued to chat to their hearts' content.

A little after midnight, as the moon was hiding behind the hills on the horizon, a gloomy pall fell over everything, and I began to feel a sense of pathos as if autumn had come. Right then, the tatami began to rise up into the air again. We all tried to hold them down, but the situation just got worse. As the mats clattered up and down, they blew the candles out and raised a cloud of dust so thick no one could keep their eyes open. Before long, the entire house had been transformed into a disheveled mess. One of the men shouted that he could not take it any more and dashed out of the house. With a chorus of "Me too! Me too!" the others followed, leaving only Gonpachi and me, all alone.

The rattling continued in the back of the house. When we went to take a look, we found all the tatami fastened to the ceiling with ropes. Before we had the chance to go get a ladder—*wham!*—all the mats fell from the ceiling at once. The color drained from our faces. We took a deep breath and retired into the bedroom when we heard more sounds. This time, a large staff like the kind that belongs to a priest was hopping around the living room.

The Ninth Night

IN THE MORNING, a broom made of palm fronds emerged from the closet and moved around the room, carefully sweeping the reception room. The rumbling of the house was even more intense than usual.

Early in the evening, Gonpachi stuck his head in the door. He told me, "Ever since the night I saw the young acolyte, I've had a fever on and off, and I haven't been able to eat properly."

I instructed him, "You don't have to come every night. Take care of yourself, and be sure to take some medicine." With this advice, I sent him home.

That night, the rumblings of the house were punctuated by long intervals. At one point, I heard the far-off sound of a *shakuhachi*, but before long, a *komusō* priest entered the room.[12] Then another entered, then another, until the living room was a solid wall of *komusō* priests. Before long, all of them started lying down around me where I lay in bed. Eventually, they started disappearing one by one until they were all gone, leaving me alone to sleep peacefully for the first time in many nights.[13]

---

12. A *shakuhachi* is a bamboo flute that is held vertically and has a windier, more plaintive sound than a Western transverse flute. A *komusō* is an itinerant Buddhist monk who covers his head with a basket and plays the *shakuhachi* as he wanders and begs for food.

13. Author's note: It has already been ten years ago, but I once had a dream in which I was walking road along the edge of a lonely moat with a woman I did not know. She was dressed in a kimono, and off to our side, there was a series of houses that formed a long, thin row. My companion made a faint smile as she pointed to an antiquated two-story building and said, "This is it. This is where we did it." What she was trying to say was, "Those times were really hard for us. That's why we finally committed suicide together there." When I told one of my guests about this dream, he nodded and said, "That's right out of the world of kabuki."

When I told the writer Shibusawa Tatsuhiko about the *komusō* in Heitarō's story, he showed great interest. Without question, there is something about this story that fits Shibusawa's sensibilities. In chapter 115 of the fourteenth-century collection *Essays in Idleness*, there is a passage about a duel that takes place between shakuhachi-playing "*boroboro*" priests on a riverbank. When compared to *boroboro* priests, *komusō* have a somewhat more suspicious air about them, and they seem more ghostly. Whether or not one goes to the Pure Land or falls to the depths of hell all hinges on the tone produced by their *shakuhachi*. The inside of their bamboo flutes are typically coated in red lacquer, but I have heard that there were *komusō* who coated the inside of theirs with lead.

Myōkōji Temple in Narutaki used to be associated with the Fuke sect of Buddhism, which believes that the *shakuhachi* represents one form of meditation. At the temple, there is a grave dedicated to *komusō* priests. It is my understanding that instead of placing flowers on the grave, there is a tradition of keeping the velvety moss sprinkled with water. The purpose of that, I suspect, is not to help the moss absorb the sunlight, but to help it absorb the moonlight.

It was the ninth evening of the seventh month that the *komusō* entered into Heitarō's living room, so that must have been around the same time the red, crescent moon was setting behind the mountains. When I think

The Tenth Night

A MAN BY the name of Ueda Jibuemon came to the house. He said, "I think this must be the doings of a fox or a *tanuki*, or perhaps even an old cat with two tails.[14] Let's try setting a trap for it." With that, he went home.

I was sitting on his veranda looking at the moon when an acquaintance by the name of Sadahachi dropped by. We were having a conversation when Sadahachi's head began to swell and split in two. Three creatures that looked like baby monkeys crawled out. No sooner had they scampered onto my lap than the three of them merged into a single, large baby which started to grab at me. I tried to get hold of it, but it disappeared without a trace.

The Eleventh Night

UEDA JIBUEMON CAME to the house with a trap operated by a catch. He baited the trap with a mouse that had been dipped in hot oil, then he went home.

That night, the house occasionally rumbled, and the tatami lifted into the air. After midnight when I went to relieve myself, I checked the trap and saw it had not caught a thing.

The Twelfth Night

WHEN IT GREW light in the morning, I checked again and saw the bait was gone. There was no way of getting it out of the trap without setting off the bamboo catch, no matter how nimble one might be. How had the bait been removed? The string that had held the bait in mid-air had also disappeared without a trace.

It was much later when I discovered the mouse hanging from the eaves. Why had the spirit undone the string holding the bait? This question seemed to exasperate Jibuemon, who said, "Whatever its reason for undoing the string, it seems

back on my dream from so many years ago, I feel as if there must have been a thin sliver of moon hanging in the upper branches of the willow trees lining the moat.

14. See note on page 56.

clear this is a rather elderly fox. I'm going to take a look at the footprints, then I'll think about what kind of trap would work best." He left for a little while, then when he returned, he scattered rice bran over the boards between the veranda and the kitchen.

That evening, during the early hours of the night, the rumbling of the house grew especially intense, and Jibuemon and I heard what sounded like the battle cries of a large number of people coming from nowhere. Jibuemon said, "That'll stop even a *tengu*," and he left the house confidently.[15]

The Thirteenth Night

JIBUEMON KNOCKED ON the front gate just as dawn was coloring the clouds in the eastern sky. When we examined the rice bran, we saw several sets of paw prints. They looked like they belonged to a dog or fox and were of different sizes, both big and small. Also mixed in among them were human footprints a full *shaku* in size.[16] "Judging from this, I doubt we can catch them in a trap. The only thing left to do is have someone perform a prayer to exorcise wild foxes! I'll ask the priests at Saikōji Temple." And with this, he set out.

When the priest heard his request, he said, "Ordinarily that would not be a difficult request, but right now, we are in the middle of the O-bon holidays, and we don't have the time to perform an exorcism.[17] Let me tell you what... The image of Yakushi Nyorai at this temple has been known to work wonders.[18] In fact, even the stand and incense burner we keep in front of it are said to have special powers. I'll lend you the holy painting and the two items. Take them to Master Heitarō's home. Set them up in his living room and pray before them with a pure and devoted mind."

---

15. See note on page 16.
16. A *shaku* is a unit of linear measurement equivalent to a little less than a third of a meter.
17. O-bon, sometimes called the "Festival of the Dead" in English, is a festival held during the middle of the year. People traditionally believed that the spirits of deceased ancestors return to earth at that time, and families celebrate and perform ceremonies to honor deceased relatives.
18. Yakushi Nyorai is a Buddhist deity associated with medicine and healing.

Jibuemon promised, "We'll come to get them this evening," then he made a quick stop at my home to tell me the news.

That evening, Jibuemon sent a young man by the name of Nagakura to my home. In the letter he sent with him, Jibuemon wrote, "Nagakura has lived in the mountains and fields since he was a boy. He is much stronger than an ordinary person, and he is well known for his ability to hunt animals with firearms. He expressed a strong desire to come help you, so I am sending him to you now."

I welcomed him. "I'm glad to have you, but to tell the truth, someone is supposed to go from here this evening to Saikōji to get a scroll painted with Yakushi Nyorai, but I gave my attendant some time off, so I am a bit of a bind. This is a big favor to ask, but would you mind going to the temple to borrow the painting for me?"

"No problem, but why don't we have a cup of tea first and chat for a while? Perhaps something will happen in the meantime. If it does, I'll go to the temple then. I've never seen a ghost, so I'd be disappointed if the scroll chased it away before I got the chance to see one. Let's hold off for a bit."

The two of us sat to have some tea. We finished dinner, and Nagakura told me about how he had singlehandedly brought down all sorts of animals, including full-grown wolves and wounded, raging boars. Before we knew it, it was after ten o'clock. The house began to rattle and shake, and the tatami started leaping up into the air.

"I've heard lots of stories. I thought most of them were either lies or tall tales, but my goodness! I suppose there are things in the world that we can't understand! Okay, I guess I'm off to Saikōji." And with that, Nagakura left.

It was the thirteenth night of the month, so outside it was as bright as day.[19] Along the way, however, the sky clouded over, and it became so dark Nagakura could not tell front from back. A fellow by the name of Nakamura Gentarō happened to come his way, carrying a lantern in his hand. He asked Nagakura where he was going, and Nagakura explained. Gentarō responded, "I'm almost home, so I'll lend you my lantern."

Nagakura borrowed it gratefully and continued on his way.

---

19. In premodern times, Japan used a lunar calendar, so the thirteenth day of the month falls in the middle of the lunar cycle, when a full moon was out.

A short time later, he came to the home of Tsuda Ichirōzaemon, which was on a corner lot next to a dense thicket. All of the sudden, something leapt out of the thicket. It was black and seemed to be shaped like the sheath used to store an umbrella. As it flew through the darkness, it glittered for a moment like a flash of lightning, then crashed down on Nagakura's head and wrapped itself around his neck. Along with it came something that glowed like a red-hot rock.

Tsuda Ichirōzaemon was in his living room enjoying the cool of evening when he heard a shout in front of his house. He looked out the lattice of the window to see someone collapsed on the ground. He ordered one of his men to go out, give Nagakura some water, and resuscitate him. When Nagakura came to, the clouds had cleared, and the moonlight made it once again as bright as day. The lantern he had borrowed from Gentarō was nowhere to be seen.

He thanked Tsuda's retainer and stood up. When he reached my gate, he simply said, "It's too late. I'll go to the temple tomorrow. I'll explain everything in the morning." With that, he went home.

The next day, he went to Gentarō and explained how it had come about that he lost the lantern. Upon hearing this, Gentarō responded, "That's very strange. Last night, there wasn't a cloud in the sky, and I didn't go out at all."

The Fourteenth Night

NAGAKURA CAME TO the house and told me what had happened, then set out for the temple. When he arrived, Saikōji was still caught up in the business of the O-bon holidays, but he gave a complete account of everything that had transpired. The priest was astonished. "I will offer some prayers and give you a protective talisman. Also, I will entrust you with the painting of the Yakushi Nyorai and the other ritual objects. Give them your single-minded devotion while they are in your possession." With this, he lent him the holy objects.

Nagakura reported all of this to me, but when he asked me to let him spend the night, I refused. As evening approached, I stopped by Shinpachi's place on the way to my family's ancestral gravesite. When darkness fell, I went home. Thinking

I would go to bed early, I put the painting in the alcove, set up the stand, placed the incense burner on top of that, and clasped my hands together in prayer. Afterwards, I sat for a while on the veranda looking at the moon and enjoying the cool air of evening.

At ten o'clock, I was about to get in my mosquito netting when the *karagami* to the room with the Buddhist altar began to slide lightly open. The doors of the altar itself also swung open, flapping right and left. Meanwhile, the stand and the incense burner floated three *shaku* into the air. It floated toward the altar as if an invisible person were carrying it. The ritual implements floated inside the altar, and the doors shut just like before.

The Fifteenth Night

IN THE EVENING, the tatami started lifting up and down again. A light rain had been falling since morning, leaving the air hot and humid so I had decided to take an early bath. I was reflecting that under normal circumstances, I would be celebrating *chūgen* and eagerly looking forward to dancing in the streets when Tsuda Ichirōzaemon, Kogane Bango, and Uchida Genji arrived.[20] "We thought you might be lonely, so we came by with a little saké," they said, producing a bottle. Thanking them, I got out some pickled vegetables from the afternoon and a dish of raw mackerel and vegetables in vinegar. We talked until after ten o'clock when my visitors said, "Tonight, leave things to the three of us." All of us climbed into the mosquito netting.

In the middle of the night, Bango said, "I'll put on a new pot of tea. That will wake us up so we can keep going." He put some fresh tea leaves in the teapot, and the conversation turned to a new topic. Right then, they heard shouting behind them, as if a big group of people were moving something heavy and were calling out the rhythm as they walked forward. The voices went from the courtyard round to the kitchen, and then there was a big thud.

This roused Ichitarō from his sleepiness, and he looked

---

20. *Chūgen* takes place midway through the lunar year, on the fifteenth day of the seventh month.

around to see what might have caused the sound. Something on the wooden kitchen floor caught his eye. I also woke up, and suggested that someone go take a look to see what it was. All three of my guests, however, were huddled together, so I lit a lamp and went by myself. What I found was a wooden bucket full of pickles from the storage shed. The storage shed should have been locked, but someone had brought out the eggplants, which had only been in the brine to pickle for a couple of days, as if suggesting that my guests have a snack. At first, no one dared take a bite. I was the only one who took an eggplant and had a little tea before retiring to the mosquito netting.

Next, the stand and incense burner began to float around the nets. All three guests hid inside. At some point, the incense burner left the stand and flew inside the netting. It tipped, and ashes scattered over all three of them. Uchida let out a cry and hid his face. I am not sure if he had been sick to his stomach before, but he vomited, splashing yellow liquid all over the other two. A moment later, when he got up and went outside the mosquito netting to clean up, he found the stand and incense burner had all been put away inside the Buddhist altar. I lead the three of them to the well, gave them a drink of water, then sent them home.

The Sixteenth Night

IT WAS *yabuiri*.[21] I went to visit my uncle Kawada Moemon. After we finished eating and drinking our saké, my uncle said, "If something were to happen to you, the rest of the family might accuse me of not taking good enough care of you. That would put me in a real bind. I think you should go stay with one of the relatives for a while and see how things go...."

I insisted, "I'm still not sure whether it's a fox or a *tanuki* haunting my place. If I abandon ship now and go stay somewhere else, people would call me a coward."

When the sun set, I went home with one of the other people who had been at my uncle's. As we sat on the veranda, letting the breeze cool down the house, I started to nod off. The young man who had accompanied me was about to light a fire and

---

21. *Yabuiri* is the day on the sixteenth following O-bon when employers would give their servants a day off so they could go see their families.

put on a fresh pot of tea to overcome the effects of the liquor when the ceiling began to creak. The ceiling was dropping. As it slowly dropped lower and lower, my guest let out a scream and flew out of the room into the garden. His voice roused me from my slumber, and I saw how low the ceiling had fallen. Still, I didn't bother to do anything and just continued to lie there.

When morning came, the young man went around saying, "Last night, it was my turn to run into Inō's ghost." Because of that, no one dared come by once night fell.

The Seventeenth Night

AROUND NOON, UEDA Jibuemon brought a talisman to drive away wild foxes. "I had requested this at Saikōji. Today, they finally finished the exorcism ritual and gave me this." He hung the charm in the living room and went home. When evening rolled around, he popped in again. "I doubt anything will happen tonight. The talisman ought to protect you." He came onto the veranda with me. We chatted and gazed up at the sky, waiting for the moon to rise.

When the moon finally appeared over the horizon, it began to shine, white and hazy, through the leaves of the trees in the garden. Among the trees was an oak, which was rather difficult to make out in the darkness. As we gazed at the moonlight, an exact replica of the moon just like the one in the sky appeared in front of the tree. The numbers of shining orbs increased in number, dancing through the air and forming different patterns of interlocking, overlapping circles.

Jibuemon asked, "What on earth's that?" Meanwhile, the interlocking discs spun ever closer to where we sat on the veranda. The dizzying whirl threatened to envelop us completely, so my guest edged back, ready to flee. I urged him to stay and talk a little longer, but he was ready to go right away. The overlapping discs, however, closed in from the direction of the kitchen, holding him back. Among them were some circles about the size of a small bucket, and these whirled about like smoke. Jibuemon stared at the spinning discs, thinking they must be the work of a wild fox. That is when he noticed a set of eyes and nose in each of the discs. No sooner would one face form before it would change and a new face would emerge, taking its place – glaring faces, smiling faces, all sorts of faces... Unable to get out through the kitchen, Jibuemon dashed into the garden. As he rushed out the gate to safety, the faces all burst into laughter. I also broke into laughter as he ran away. Still chuckling, I lay down for the night. Nothing else happened that evening.

The Eighteenth Night

THE NEXT MORNING, Jibuemon returned. "They're not afraid of the talisman. That means they can't be foxes or *tanuki.*" Gonpachi came by as we were mulling it over.

"All these comical things keep happening, one after another. I doubt there's any way you can win."

I was about to retort that of course there was no way we could win if we lost our nerve, but I got the better of myself and just said, "You still look pale. The best thing for you is to get back your strength completely. I've told you that before, haven't I? Just come back when you're completely recovered. Don't worry about me. I'll be fine."

I went to look at the talisman from Saikōji and found that someone had written something on it in watery ink. I did not remember seeing the extra writing last night. When I contacted the temple, the priest came right away. "That's Sanskrit! Your ghost is not some ordinary spook!" He left in a state of astonishment. Neither of us knew what the writing said, but someone at the temple must have committed an error or forgotten a word or two when they created the talisman.

That day, the utensils began to dance into the air before sunset. The bowls and other eating utensils rattled and flew out of the kitchen. They looked like they were going to run into the lintel and smash themselves, but the moment before they dashed themselves to smithereens, they dropped below the lintel and fell into the center of the reception room. If I touched them in midair, they would fall to the ground and break, but if I left them alone, nothing would get broken as they rattled around the room. Likewise, the lanterns would not spill a drop as they danced through the room, provided I did not lay a hand on them.

Early in the evening, three guests stopped by. After ten o'clock, when our conversation was beginning to peter out, my guests felt something lay a hand on their backs. A set of arms had zigzagged out of the kitchen, bending back and forth several times like a streak of lightning before laying its hands on them then retreating once again. The guests screamed, jumped off the veranda into the garden, opened the door into the alley, and ran away. Even after I went to bed, the arms continued to jerk back and forth in the tatami room, unfolding and folding again like a carpenter's ruler....

The next time I woke up, an enormous face of a hideous old hag had appeared, covering the entire surface of the ceiling. It extended its long tongue through the mosquito netting and licked me from my chest to my face. I did my best not to respond, and by the time dawn was breaking, the old hag had disappeared.

The Nineteenth Night

AROUND TEN IN the morning, there was a knock at the gate that roused me from my sleep. It was a fellow by the name of Mukai Jirōzaemon. "Well, the sun was up, but the gate was shut, so I thought I'd try seeing if everything was all right. It's late in the day, you know...."

"I appreciate it. Let me tell you what happened last night...." I ushered him in and told him what had happened.

When I finished, he said, "I see. I bet it's a fox or a *tanuki* like Jibuemon said, but since it was able to get the bait out of the trap the other day, it must be a rare kind of rascal—the kind of spook that comes along only once in a thousand years. You know, there's someone I should introduce you to. His name is Jūbei, and he lives in a little settlement on the edge of town. He's an expert in trapping things. Unfortunately, I've got some urgent business to attend to today, so I've got to go elsewhere, but I'll be sure to call on you again tomorrow."

I went back to sleep and remained in bed until it was nearly one. I got up and ate, then waited for night to fall. By ten o'clock, nothing had happened. I continued to wait. By midnight, still nothing had happened, and so I began to relax a little. No sooner had I done so, however, than the ceiling began to drop gradually. It continued to drop, a little at a time, until it was touching the top of my head. I refused to budge, and my head broke through the ceiling. The lantern also broke a hole in the ceiling, illuminating everything in the attic. There were lots of cobwebs and mouse droppings, and the whole place was pitch black from the old, blackened straw thatch on the roof. The ceiling continued to drop until it reached my lap, but I stayed firmly put. Eventually, it began to rise again to its original position. When I looked up, I saw there were no holes where my body or the lantern had broken through the boards.

What I did see, however, was a large beehive. Right before my eyes, it grew in size and multiplied so there were several hives. Bubbles emerged from the holes, like bubbles from the holes bored by crabs on the seashore, and a yellow liquid began to drip out. I pretended to ignore the hives, and soon they had disappeared, leaving the ceiling as before.

In the back of my house, there was a mortar for hulling rice. Since early in the evening, I had heard a rustling sound as if someone was hulling rice in it. I came up with a clever idea—I put a bunch of unhulled rice in the mortar and climbed into my mosquito netting. The next morning, I went to look, but unfortunately, I found the rice in the same state as when I had left it.

The Twentieth Night

MUKAI JIRŌZAEMON CAME to the house with Kawada Jūbei, who went about setting up a trap. Jūbei was around sixty. He told us he had hunted with a gun when he was younger, but he had learned the art of trapping a few years ago. While he was in Osaka, he happened to meet a hunter who bought and sold furs, and the hunter showed him an exceedingly large *tanuki* pelt.

The hunter had said, "This one's really amazing. This was no doubt one heck of an old *tanuki*." He let out a big laugh. "I hardly deserve such a prize. Now, this one here's a young *tanuki*. There're different kinds of *tanuki*, you know. Ordinarily they're about this big. This kind is pretty rare. Then there're *tanuki* that take on human form. You've got to be really something to catch 'em. They're awfully smart. Of course, they're not this big when they're born. If people and wild dogs don't get 'em, they naturally grow older and wiser. Then they start changing shape, and that's when they cause real trouble. This one's skin is real thick, and the fur is coarse, so it's not a very good pelt. In order to catch one like this, you need a special kind of trap. The trap I use isn't one lots of folks know about. It's a *fumiotoshi*—the *tanuki* steps on it then falls."

Jūbei had said to the hunter, "That's the first I've ever heard of such a trap. How do you set it up? Please, can't you tell me?"

"I got the knack of it only by doing it over the course of years. But I tell you, even the smartest foxes and *tanuki* hardly ever get away. There was a time when I was younger and some *tanuki* showed up at the three shrines at Tenma in the middle of the night. I snuck out there in the middle of the night and laid one of my *fumiotoshi* traps, and got myself a big *tanuki*. Its tail was split in two, and it was over four *shaku* from its neck to the tip of its tail. I killed it right away. The next day, when I showed it to the people in the area, they were ecstatic. They said it must have been the culprit behind all those weird things that happened at Tenma. They say old *tanuki* and foxes collaborate sometimes and transform into all sorts of different things. That's why it's so hard to catch 'em. I doubt they'll be able to get away from this trap, though."

Jūbei explained, "In the countryside where I'm from, the only thing we use to get wild animals is a gun. There seems to be lots of foxes and *tanuki* around, but if they sense a muzzle is pointing at them, they'll disappear, leaving us high and dry. Please, won't you teach me how to set up one of your *fumiotoshi* traps?"

That was how Jūbei became an expert in trapping. He had spent the last several years catching numerous foxes and *tanuki* with his skills. Once at a temple named Hōgenji, the Daihannya-kyō started to float in the air.[22] This strange event happened over and over again. Hearing the rumors that people had stopped coming to pray at the temple and that even stranger things had started to happen there, Jūbei decided to

---

22. Hōgenji Temple, founded in 1633, is the modern-day city of Miyoshi in Hiroshima prefecture, close to where this story takes place. The *Daihannya-kyō* is a collection of Buddhist teachings that is considered especially important to esoteric Buddhist sects, such as Tendai and Shingon Buddhism.

set a trap. He caught a *tanuki* that was who knows how old. He killed it, without even bothering to tell the temple beforehand. Nothing strange happened after that, and the temple prospered.

Another time, strange things were happening to a fellow by the name of Matsuo Tōsuke. Once day, he was in the living room taking a nap. When one of the servants went to call him, the servant found two people sleeping there—both of whom looked exactly like Tōsuke. The servant got frightened, ran into the next room, and called out Tōsuke's name. When he woke, however, there was nothing out of the ordinary. Similar things recurred after that; for instance, Tōsuke might be inside the house in back, but then someone would see him outside too. Something also seemed to be happening to Tōsuke, who felt some sort of disturbance at work within his personality. His relatives and other people tried prayers, talismans, and all sorts of things, but nothing did any good.

When Jūbei heard about this, he remembered what had happened at Tenma and came, offering to set a trap. That did the trick. He caught a rough, old *tanuki* covered in speckles with the hair thinning on its back. After that, Tōsuke had no further problems, and his family was as pleased as punch. Jūbei went on to further exploits catching foxes and *tanuki* with his skills.

When I told him what had happened at my house, Jūbei said, "It sounds like this is the work of an elderly cat or *tanuki*. Foxes don't usually do the kind of stuff you're describing. What they will do, though, is stay beside old cats or *tanuki* and watch as they cause all kinds of mischief. Cats sometimes forget themselves, and in the process of doing their ghostly business, they'll slip and let themselves appear in some transformed state. That's when you catch 'em in a trap and kill 'em. They think they're off scot-free, what with a fox's power there and all, but that's what makes them so vulnerable. In those moments, the cat's the only one you'll get. The fox just stays there by its side, smiling and looking on.

"There's nothing in the world cleverer than a fox. That's why most of the time you just get cats or *tanuki* in the traps. When you set a spring trap, the most you can hope to get is a wild fox, but those aren't the rascals that cause mischief like you're describing. Even when you do get a wild fox, it's always a young one. The old ones are too smart to nab.

"You've had all sorts of strange things happening here one after another. It would seem to me that you've got a whole bunch of different creatures doing their ghostly work. Still, it doesn't really matter how many of them there are. If you manage to get just one, the rest will scatter, and all the strange things will stop in a flash. But the more there are, the harder it is. I'll go ahead and set up the trap now." Jūbei took a survey of the hallway, then set the trap. "You stay hidden until I call you." I agreed, and he hid himself in the guest toilet. Jirōzaemon left after ten o'clock, and I lay down to catch a little sleep.

I slept until a little after midnight, when I heard groaning. I pricked up my ears and realized it was coming from the hallway by the guest toilet. When I went to look, the door to the toilet had been smashed, and Jūbei was lying by the trap half-conscious. I splashed some water on his face. When he came to, he had an expression like he had just woken from a dream.

He said, "A few moments ago, a cold chill ran up my spine so I thought whatever it was had come. I looked out, and a gigantic hand came out of the trap, grabbed me, and pulled me in. I tried to yell, but I couldn't make a sound.... I'm not sure what happened next.... This is no ordinary spook. It must be a *tengu* or some ferocious god who has come from the hills. What a frightening turn of events!" Leaving the trap just as it was, Jūbei went home, still trembling.

The Twenty-First Night

THE TRAP REMAINED properly set, and the door to the toilet remained broken, just as I had seen it last night. Before long, Mukai Jirōzaemon came, and I told him what that happened. He was stupefied, and said if Jūbei's traps were not up to the task of catching whatever it was in my house, I was really stuck. We tried calling Jūbei, but learned he could not stand. When the ghost had grabbed him, one of his bones had broken. He sent someone else to the house to take the trap home. Rumor had it took a long time for Jūbei to heal.

Jirōzaemon felt ill at ease so he went home. No one came by

the house that night. It was quiet, so I was thinking of retiring for the evening when I found a mouse hole in the corner of the living room. Something seemed to be moving inside. As I fixed my eyes upon it, I saw it was the tiny severed head of a woman. It was turned upside down and stretched to about four or five *sun* in length. Its hair, however, was extremely long and writhed around the head, forming an eerie halo. When it turned and revealed its neck, the place where it had been severed from the body glistened red like the insides of a pomegranate. The teeth had been dyed black, and the lips formed a broad grin as it flew toward me....[23]

Thinking what a strange sight this was, I straightened up to get a better look. As I did so, many similar little heads emerged from the base of the pillar and started flying in every direction, their hair forming long trails behind them. As they flew through the air laughing, they knocked against each other, making a sound like javelins jostling together. The heads closed in upon me, but I swatted at them with my fan. My movement sent them flying away, but I was unable to make direct contact. It was like I was swatting at a circling flock of birds, unable to hit any of them. They came at me from every direction, so I stood up and tried to chase them into a corner, but they just disappeared, only to reappear a moment later.... It was only as dawn approached that the severed heads gradually flew back to the base of the pillar and disappeared for good.

The Twenty-Second Night

KAGEYAMA SHŌDAYŪ CAME in the evening. "My older brother has a sword that has been passed down from our ancestors. The blade is well known for being able to put an end to fox-possessions, epidemics, fevers, and all sorts of other things. Why don't you send a request to my brother Hikonosuke and have the sword brought here?" He went home, leaving me with this suggestion.

I took a nap and a bath after that. Around ten o'clock Shōdayū showed up again. "I brought my brother's special sword."

---

23. In the Edo period, many women dyed their teeth black after they were married.

"What a pleasant surprise! I hadn't expected that he would even let me see it, but here you've gone and brought it!"

We put the blade in the alcove for the time being. As we were speaking, the severed heads from last night reappeared. "Look, it's here!" One of the heads flew straight at Shōdayū as he pulled the sword from the box. He swung and severed it right in two. Still, it did not stop—the newly cleaved halves flew right at him.

He swung again, and when the blade struck this time, sparks flew. It let out a loud crack and broke in two. The handle was made out of a light, white wood, and so the blade also separated from the handle. The pieces scattered everywhere. When we looked again, we saw that what we had thought to be a severed head was really a stone mortar from the kitchen. The other heads laughed out loud and disappeared into the base of the pillar, leaving no sign they had ever been there.

Shōdayū was pale as he picked up the broken blade. "I took the blade without telling my brother I was going to lend it to you. I can't possibly go on living now that this has happened."

"No, you came to help me out. You were thinking about my troubles. You were being kind to me—that's the only reason you brought it to me without talking to your brother first. Those are the incontrovertible facts. Tomorrow, I'll go to your brother's and apologize in your place. Tonight, just go home and don't worry about it."

But I had hardly finished saying these words before Shōdayū whipped out the sword at his side and thrust it into his own belly. His eyes turned toward the ceiling. Taken completely off guard, I shouted, "Have you gone mad?!" There was no response as Shōdayū pulled out the sword and rammed it into his throat. The tip of his blade emerged three *sun* from the back of his neck.

I was bewildered but realized I had to deal with this before morning. I pulled the blood-stained tatami into the storage room and covered the body with a quilt. It made no sense for someone to commit *seppuku* like that. He did not write a final testament—more importantly, it was not even necessary for him to kill himself in the first place.

I thought about how awful it would be if people began to suspect me of killing him. I was filled with regret. I had been right there by Shōdayū's side but still I could not stop him—that alone was enough to make me a laughingstock. I had a hard time guessing whether or not the authorities would come to arrest me. I also felt sorry for Shōdayū's brother. I had not meant to cause any trouble. My heart burned with chagrin. Shōdayū had died without leaving any explanation for his brother; meanwhile, I was the one left to live, exposed to shame.

Feeling that my time was up, I wrote a final testament and took my short sword in hand. I had reached that point when I finally started to reconsider—it was not the right time for me to die. When dawn came, I would explain what had happened to Shinpachi, and we would come up with a plan. Also, I had been through so much since the hauntings had begun that I did not want to leave the world without having seen the true form of the specters causing me all this trouble.

Before long, the clouds in the east began to change color, and the cawing of the crows indicated dawn had come. I decided to go back to the storage room, take the quilt from the body, and have another look, but when I got there, everything was gone. The broken blade was gone. The bloodstains were gone. The only thing left were the two tatami mats I had dragged out there. That was when it dawned on me the ghosts had been up to their tricks again.... Even so, the voice of the fake "Shōdayū" remained in my ears, leaving me feeling uneasy.

The Twenty-Third Night

I FELT COMPELLED to go to the Kageyama residence. Shōdayū was there. "Yesterday after I visited your place and heard about what was happening, I kept thinking about it, and the whole thing just seemed stranger and stranger to me. I told my family about the haunting, and they kept on asking for more and more details. They followed me all the way to the washroom wanting to know more. What a fuss they raised!"

That meant the Shōdayū who came the previous afternoon was undoubtedly the real one. The "Shōdayū" that came in the evening then disappeared had looked like just like him, but it must have been a ghost in disguise.

Shōdayū continued, "I thought you weren't going out because of all of this haunting business, but here you are. Are you here because of the sword?"

I considered telling him everything, but the particulars were so complicated that I just said, "No, that wasn't really why I came." I took my leave and went home.

Hiranoya Ichiemon came by as evening was approaching. I had decided to put all my swords—big and small—into an empty chest and lock the lid tightly, and I thought it would be a good idea if my guests put theirs in as well. That afternoon, every last blade went into the box.

Matsuura Ichidayū and Kageyama Hikonosuke showed up after dark. A fellow by the name of Chūhachi, who often came and went, stopped by as well. When I asked them to put their blades inside the chest, Ichidayū did right away, but Hikonosuke said he would, then kept on talking for a few moments. A few moments later when he went to get his sword, which he had left in the next room, he found his scabbard was empty.

They looked for the blade but could not find it. As they grew weary of looking, someone lit a pipe for a smoke when suddenly, a sound like thunder came from the kitchen. Something was rolling toward them. Ichiemon grew deathly pale and jumped down into the garden. The others were too embarrassed to run and stayed put, staring at the thing rolling at them from the kitchen. It was a large bucket. I carried it to the bathroom when another sound came from the kitchen. This time, an earthenware mortar and pestle came tumbling out by themselves and started rolling round and round the room. I said, "At this rate, who can tell what might happen tonight...?" Hearing this, Chūhachi prompted Ichidayū to stand up, and the two left together.

Hikonosuke stayed behind. I asked him about his missing sword, but there still was no sign of it. "I can't go in the morning without it. As morning approaches, I think I'll ask for some time off. I can go the following day."

"That's a good idea."

Hikonosuke went to open a door to the garden, but as he did, his unsheathed sword dropped from the lintel and dangled in midair, right before his eyes. This surprised him so much he squatted there cowering, glued to the spot. I dashed over, put the blade in the scabbard, and gave it to him. Hiko-nosuke stood up, and with his two swords at his side, started out the door. As he did so, the ceiling erupted with the laughter of many people. Hikinosuke ducked in fear again, so I helped him get up and walk to the door. I had no sooner closed it behind him than he sped away at top speed.

After that, I decided to lock my dagger in the chest as well. Later, when things were flying out of all the locked areas in the house, the things I had locked in the chest were the only ones that stayed put.

The Twenty-Fourth Night

THAT MORNING, HIRANOYA Ichiemon showed up. I asked, "Why'd you run away last night?"

He answered, "I felt like I was dreaming. It was only after I started walking home when I felt like I finally woke up. Tell me—what happened after I left? What was that thing that came rolling out at us?"

"A bucket from the bathroom."

"I thought it was some horrible, huge drum coming to roll over us."

Mitsui Gonpachi came over, as did Shiba Jinzaemon. In the conversation that ensued, someone said, "You know, Nanbu Jibudayū has learned the art of ringing a bowstring to chase away evil spirits.[24] I hear he's acquired quite a reputation with it. Let's go ask if he can help you out."

"Not even the prayers from Saikōji worked. I hardly think the ghost would be afraid of something like that."

"They say a ringing bowstring has something mysterious and awe-inspiring about it. Sometimes people even use bowstrings to cure the ill instead of medicine...."

"In any case, let's give it a try. I'd appreciate it if you'd go find him for me."

Later, once it had grown quiet, a very beautiful young woman showed up at the house claiming to be a messenger from the home of Nakamura Zaemon. She held out some

24. Japanese believed that making one's bowstring vibrate at a high pitch could drive demons and other supernatural forces away. This art is called *meigen* in Japanese.

sweet rice cakes she had brought. I did not remember ever seeing her before. I was extremely pleased to meet such a lovely woman and found myself momentarily distracted. When I returned to my senses, I exchanged a couple of pleasantries with her, then sent her on her way. A moment later, I stepped out the door after her, but she had vanished without a trace. Later, I learned the stacked lacquered boxes in which the Nakamura household kept their sweet rice cakes had gone missing.

Before long, it was ten o'clock. My stomach had been upset for the last few days, and I had been running to the toilet over and over, but I guessed it was just something going around, so I did not do anything about it. That night, I had to go to the toilet two or three times. I would sleep a little, wake up, rush to the toilet, then repeat the cycle.

I was going to relieve myself again when I heard a fire in the kitchen. The whole room was lit up with flame. I dashed in. Fire was spilling from the stove, and the wooden floor was covered in flames. I yanked up the floorboards and doused them with water, but I had not even finished when the room returned to darkness. I lit a candle and saw the floorboards were not scorched. I had thrown water into the stove so the water was running out, full of ashes, but I did not bother to clean up the mess right away. I was uncomfortable because of the diarrhea so I let everything go for the time being.

The Twenty-Fifth Night

I WAS CLEANING the kitchen when Gonpachi came in. "It's too bad you just didn't ignore the fire."

"No way, I couldn't just sit by and do nothing. What if it'd been a real fire? I'd be filled with a hundred times more regret. Say, let me know if Nanbu Jibudayū shows up."

Toward sunset, Shiba Jinzaemon came to the house with Nanbu Jibudayū, who was carrying his bow. He placed it in the alcove, and the visitors stopped to rest. Gonpachi came into the room and asked, "Will the fox appear to us in his true form when the bowstring interrupts his magic?"

Jibudayū explained, "No, it won't. Not much happens—the fox just tries to escape. The person with the bow chases it out of hiding and gets rid of it. There're probably foxes or *ta-*

nuki nearby, but they typically don't appear right at the place they're haunting."

As night fell, Jibudayū took out his bow and began the preparations for the exorcism. Jinzaemon turned to Gonpachi and said, "It's possible something might appear at the front or back of the house. You go home, get the spear hanging by your bedside, then come round to the front. In the meantime, I'll stand guard at the back. Don't leave your post, whatever you do!"

Gonpachi responded, "Yes, sir," and stepped outside.

Around ten o'clock, when the first of the night watches had ended, Jibudayū performed a rite of purification and took the bow in hand. Right then, a long object whistled through the air, entering the house from outside. It grazed the lock of hair on the side of Jinzaemon's head and hit Jibudayū's bowstring dead on. It snapped the bowstring in two, then clattered to the ground. It was a spear.

Gonpachi came running around. "I went home and got the spear, then went round to the front, just like you said. That's when I saw someone on the roof. He looked like a big Buddhist priest. I knew something was going on and stopped in my tracks. He nimbly jumped down from the roof and flung me against the fence in front of the house, but by that point, he had become invisible. When I tried to get away, it was like there was someone right in front of me holding onto me. I braced my feet against the ground and tried to pull away, but my invisible foe was incredibly strong. Then I gave a big pull and went flying back into the wall."

I said, "I figured something like that had happened. Forget all about the evil spirit. It looks like it's best just to let it do whatever the heck it pleases. Let's forget all about the vibrating bowstrings and all."

Everyone took that as an opportunity to leave, but as they were getting ready to go, a chuckle came from the ceiling. The ghostly laughter just sent them on their way all the faster. I sent Gonpachi home, bow and spear in hand.

Early the next morning on the twenty-sixth, I stopped by Gonpachi's place after visiting the graveyard. He said, "It seems like my fever's gotten worse." I advised him to get some rest then went home.

Gonpachi was a well-known wrestler—everyone knew him

by his family name Mitsui—but the haunting at my house shook him to the core. The more he fretted about what had happened, the higher his fever became. He grew terribly sick, and early in the ninth month, he passed away. Although he was not yet even forty, he was a great big man. He was as strong as they come, but once he had a dose of the ghost's noxious vapors, he just suppressed his illness, thinking it was just a temporary thing. Perhaps that was the reason he eventually succumbed. What a terrible turn of events!

The Twenty-Sixth Night

AFTER I CAME home from Gonpachi's, Nanbu Kakunoshin and Kageyama Shōdayū stopped by. I told them what had happened last night. "If they just hadn't got into that wrestling match, things wouldn't have turned out so badly...."

Shōdayū said, "We've been wanting all this time to get rid of the ghost—that's probably why it is raising such a fuss. Tonight, we'll just stay and talk and ignore the ghost." Kakunoshin said he would do the same, and the two of them left. They returned at twilight with their friend Maki Zenroku. It was the twenty-sixth, the day when everyone stays up until moonrise to pray, so the whole world seemed more awake and bustling than usual.[25]

At Kakunoshin's house was a persimmon tree known as the "frost topped." It had been given this name because the fruit was astringent until the ninth or tenth month, and would only reach the peak of flavor in the eleventh month of the lunar calendar—the month known as the "month of frost." What's more, that month, the upper layers of its bark would grow whitish as if it were really covered by frost. That was when the flavor was at its best. It was only late in the seventh month, so the young fruit was not at its best, but still it was quite edible. It would be another few weeks before the fruit even started turning astringent. Kakunoshin had brought some fruit, thinking everyone could eat it to help keep awake. I put it in a bowl to enjoy later. A couple of hours later, when I went to get it, there

---

25. There was a popular belief that on the twenty-sixth night of the first and seventh months of the year, Amida Buddha, Bodhisattva Kannon, and Bodhisattva Seishi would appear in the moonlight.

were only seeds left. We were commenting that the ghost must have eaten it when we heard what sounded like a thunderclap in the kitchen. Remembering what they had said earlier about not dealing with the ghost directly, Kakunoshin and Shōdayū acted like nothing special was going on.

Candlestick in hand, they went to look in the kitchen. There, their eyes fell on a mortar made from a tree that a windstorm had knocked down some years ago. Since it came from a large tree, it was much larger than an ordinary mortar. I usually kept this mortar in the storage room. They started grumbling about what a pain it was to have such a big thing in such a small space. Hearing this, Maki Zenroku stood up, opened the back door, picked up the mortar, and tossed it outside. The boldness of his actions seemed to take the wind out of the ghost's sails, and the sounds in the room quieted down. Inspired by his courage, Nanbu and Kageyama did not even bother to turn their heads to look when the tatami began to jump into the air; instead, they just kept talking. Around two o'clock, we heard a creaking sound from the ceiling, and the persimmons, which had earlier had been reduced to nothing but seeds, spilled out everywhere, having regained their original form. One of the men picked a persimmon off the floor and broke it open, only to find a bunch of bugs inside instead of seeds. As they crawled out, he scoffed, saying he had no need for seeds anyway, and stuffed it in his mouth. Zenroku also grabbed one and put it in his mouth, spiders and cockroaches still crawling from where the seeds should have been.

The bells of the temples began to toll. As everyone was praying to the moon rising over the horizon, the men went home, the eastern clouds trailing behind them. Dawn was ready to break.

The Twenty-Seventh Night

WHEN I WOKE up around ten, I looked outside where Zenroku had thrown the mortar, but it was nowhere to be seen. The only sign anything had happened was a dent in the earth where it had landed. Next, I went to look in the storage room. The mortar was in its usual place, but on the rim was a telltale smudge of dirt.

Kageyama Kinzaemon came in the evening. I told him, "Whatever happens, pretend like it doesn't ruffle you at all. Do that and the ghost will lose interest in us. Tonight, I'll stay up with you so we can talk."

I did my best, but I grew so tired after ten o'clock that I kept nodding off. At one point, Kinzaemon glanced into the next room and saw a vague shape drifting there like a waft of smoke. Pretending he had not noticed, he walked nonchalantly to the threshold of the room, hoping to get a better peek. The apparition looked at first glance like it had a human face, but really, it had multiple faces arranged like the diamonds in a net. Some of the diamonds were horizontal, others were vertical, but they were lined up and stacked upon each other as they turned on their ends, then on their sides. All the while, the faces continued to multiply in ever greater profusion. Kinzaemon panicked and called for me to get up. When I woke, he was pale as a ghost and had crawled into the farthest reaches of the room.

I stared at the network of faces. They were even creepier than the overlapping circles of faces that had appeared several days ago. When the faces were vertical, they would open their mouths, and when they were horizontal, they would shut them. This seemed to be how they exhaled. Kinzaemon grabbed his sword from the box and unsheathed the blade. He swung at the faces, but the sword did not affect them at all—it was like trying to cut down smoke. Meanwhile, the faces all burst out laughing. Frightened by this turn of events, Kinzaemon jumped down into the garden, quickly spat out an apology, and ran away.

I closed the door and turned to face the network of faces. The faces, each shaped like a vertical or horizontal diamond, were piled on top of one another like the bubbles children blow in thick green tea. The faces disappeared and reappeared, practically filling the whole room.... No matter which way I looked—forward, backward, right, left—they were proliferating everywhere, completely overwhelming me. I tried to grab at them, but it was just like trying to grab a fistful of air.

Thinking that I would let dawn come and take care of this as well, I went inside the mosquito net and lay down. I was dozing off when a sound woke me. Something large was walking toward me. It was a toad. It hopped around the mosquito net, then hopped inside. That was when I noticed a vine attached to its chest. "Ha!" I thought to myself, "This fellow is a kudzu plant transformed into a toad." I grabbed hold of the vine tightly and went back to sleep. When dawn came, I was lying on my back, and sure enough, on top my chest was a kudzu plant.

The Twenty-Eighth Night

THE CALENDAR SAID it was an auspicious day, but I slept most of the afternoon away. At dusk, I took a bath then sat on the edge of the veranda to cool down. It was almost ten o'clock and still no one had come. I took a lantern inside the mosquito netting to read a novel. As I settled down to read, I glanced at the reception room and caught sight of a shadow on the wall. It was of someone behind a bookstand. As I pricked up my ears, I realized I could hear someone reading a book in a loud, clear voice. It was reading the book I had just picked up a few moments ago.

It disappeared before long, and I started to think about calling it a night. I stepped out of the mosquito netting. Before going to bed, I usually go to the toilet by the living room, but tonight, I went to the veranda in the back of the house, thinking I would step out into the road partly to escape the heat. When I lowered my feet onto the step where I ordinarily put on my clogs, the step was as cold as ice and unpleasantly soft. I tried to pull my feet back up, but my feet were stuck—I could not lift them. The sensation was like stepping into *torimochi*.[26] I looked down and saw my feet had sunk into something whitish. I was standing on a person's belly. It was soft and cold to the touch, like the stomach of a corpse.

I bent over to look and saw it did have arms and legs, but they were extremely short. A strange, quiet flickering sound was coming from the place where its face should have been. It did have eyes, and what I was hearing was the sound of them blinking. The unceasing flickering it made reminded me of a black fly buzzing through the air. The soles of my feet were stuck, as if I were standing in a patch of mud, so to get back onto the veranda, I put my hands on the edge, lifted myself,

26. *Torimochi* is a gummy substance derived from the sap of a tree and used to catch birds and insects.

and crawled onto the platform. The stickiness on the bottoms of my feet clung to the boards of the veranda, making walking difficult.

Back in the living room, I looked at my feet, but there was nothing unusual stuck to them. I carried a candlestick over to look at the stepping stone, but the only things worth noticing were my wooden clogs sitting there. Still, I could hear the flickering sound. The bottoms of my feet were no longer sticky, so I went to the toilet by the living room. Nothing strange happened, but the flickering sound continued all throughout the night, making it impossible for me to fall asleep. It was not until the cocks crowed in the morning that I was able finally to get some rest.

The Twenty-Ninth Night

I HAD FINISHED lunch when Nakamura Heizaemon came over. He asked me what the face I had seen last night looked like. I answered, "It was dark, so I couldn't see it too well. The only thing I could tell was that its eyes kept blinking over and over."

"Did it look like anyone we know?"

He had no sooner asked this question than something struck him on the back. He looked over his shoulder to see a dangling arm quietly withdrawing into one corner of the ceiling. He screamed and bent down, hiding his face in fear. I tried to help him up. He finally stood, he apologized for needing to leave. Right then, the paper cord holding his topknot together came loose, and his hair tumbled down around his shoulders. I told him, "You can't go home with your hair all messed up like that," but he did not listen and scuttled straight home. That was the first time anything supernatural had happened so early in the afternoon.

When I went into the living room, I found it was as black as night, even though it was still only around four in the afternoon. Gradually it grew lighter, then dark again. This kept happening over and over, faster and faster until my head was spinning. Eventually, however, this stopped, and the brightness level returned to normal. It was almost as if someone was above the ceiling playing tricks on me.

Before long, the sun set, and it was ten o'clock. I thought I would keep a small fire going while I slept, but there was no charcoal in the bin where I usually keep it. I took down the charcoal scuttle and went out back. In the entrance to the storage room was the huge face of an old lady filling the entire door. There was no way to get in. I approached the face, but it just stared quietly. Its eyes shifted and its nose twitched as if it was about to say something. I took the metal chopsticks used for stoking the fire from the charcoal scuttle and prodded the face with them. The face was soft, and the chopsticks went right through it. The face did not make any move to disappear. Instead, it seemed to get gummy and start to sag. I thought it would be best to get rid of it, so I stuck the two metal chopsticks right between the eyes, then went back to the veranda. That was when I saw that the entire tatami room was completely white, as if the entire place had been coated with glue. The whole place reeked with an indescribable smell, rather like cut grass or unripe fruit. I remembered that the night the *komusō* had made their way in, a similar smell had filled the place. Even though both scenes were the work of the same ghost, there was something much more ghostly about the room filled with glue.

I would just get stuck if I tried to go in, so there was no way to get to my bed. I was leaning against a pillar in the living room and nodding off when the house began to really rattle, and I heard the weeping of a woman and some other sounds coming from above the ceiling. There were so many other voices that I could not make out what was going on, but it sounded like they were trying to say something. There was no way I could get any sleep. To make matters worse, it was hot, and when the wind blew, the air was unpleasantly warm. All these things made it impossible to stay asleep for very long. Even if I did begin to nod off, the tatami would rise into the air and crash back down. Finally, dawn broke, and I was able to get some shuteye. I slept until nearly eleven o'clock.

Wondering what had become of the old woman, I went to the storage room. The metal chopsticks were suspended in front of the entrance, in the very same place I had stuck them between her eyes. They were not impaling anything; they hung in midair as if dangling from invisible strings. In curious amazement, I stuck out my hand toward them, and they fell to the ground. I picked them up, but there was nothing out of the ordinary about them.

I took out some charcoal and made some tea, wondering what would happen that day. I was thinking about what recourse I could take to get the ghost to show his true identity when an eerie wind blew across me. There were countless particles of something floating through the air, and they began to sparkle like starlight, leaving trails that looked a profusion of fireflies. I felt rather moved by the sad beauty of this scene, and a sense of loneliness came over me—and all over such a trifling little thing![27]

---

27. **Author's note:** I have a vivid memory of a film by Georges Méliès in which a gigantic face fills a Western-style wardrobe. Also, I once had a dream rather like the scene with the sticky room in Heitarō's story. There is a fellow I call B-*chan* who sometimes appears here and there in my autobiographical works. That fellow went and formed something he called the "derrière club." He once suggested that I join, but I wasn't really too sure what he was talking about, and I didn't bother to find out and just let the invitation slide. It seems that a number of my friends—upperclassmen I knew from elementary school and who lived in B's neighborhood in Honchō—joined the club. In any case, B's parents were kimono merchants, and above their shop was a second story with small latticed window. The window faced onto the street and let light into the second story. I had a dream in which I was trying to go up their stairs to the second story, but the dimly lit stairway was slippery and damp so my feet kept on sliding, and I could not make it up the stairs. B-*chan* never appeared in the dream, just the slimy, phlegm-colored jelly that seemed to coat everything in the old building. The creamy slime had no smell, but I suspected that it had something to do with shit.

I also had another dream about a tent that looked like the kind erected over observers at a school sports event. Inside were a group of ladies with bonnets and men with silk hats. They were seated at a table eating. The food on their white plates was in the shape of a short cylinder with something that looked like a puckered rectum at one end, rather like what you might see through the windows of a henhouse. In other words, it looked like they were eating the backsides of chickens, except that the bits of flesh were fatter, more flaccid, and bluish gray. I realized the people in the dream were a family of *kappa* water-goblins, and as I think about it right now, I realize that they were competing to eat the rectums of human beings.

The Thirtieth Night

IT HAD BEEN a month since the haunting had begun. I couldn't help but wonder how long the ghost would keep this up, and I marveled at how persistent it was; however, I decided I would also persist and finally catch him.

The sky suddenly clouded over, and a summer shower began. Gusts of wind blew across the veranda at the back of the house, wetting the *shōji*, so I leaned the wooden doors from the closet against them. The reason the specter had been appearing in the living room for several days now partly had to do with my lack of preparedness. If I was going to see him in his true form, then I would also have to get to work. Thinking it might be a good idea to keep my short sword by my side, I took it out of the box and kept it with me constantly even as I ate.

After sunset, the rain stopped, and the stars came out in the sky. It was already ten o'clock as I brought in the wooden doors. When I opened the *shōji*, they still felt damp to the touch. I slid the *shōji* shut and came inside. Before I could sit down, the *shōji* at my back suddenly clattered open. An enormous hand stretched toward me. Thinking "Here's my chance!" I launched a sudden attack, swinging at it with my sword. The hand pulled back, and the *shōji* slid shut with a loud *whap*!

I started to chase after it when I heard a loud voice shout, "Wait! Hold it right there!" The voice lifted as it spoke the final word, dramatically punctuating the command.

This turn of events piqued my curiosity. I held my sword at bay, and a moment later, the *shōji* slid open. The man before me was a full *shaku* taller than the lintel of the doorway. His shoulders were broad and stiff, but he was so plump there was hardly a single angle anywhere on his body. He walked into the room, calm and composed. He appeared to be only about forty, and he was dressed well. He was wearing a pale blue *kamishimo* over a pink kimono, and he carried two swords at his side.[28] He strode quietly into the room and sat down facing me. Still standing, I pulled out my short sword and tried to swing

28. A *kamishimo* is a kind of ceremonial overcoat with large, protruding shoulders. It is worn on the outside of a kimono.

at him, but he simply slid back into the wall, still seated, as if there was a cable connected to him that drew him backward.

Although I could only see his silhouette on the wall, he spoke to me with laughter in his voice. "There is no need to come to blows. I've come because I have something to tell you. Put away your sword and calm down."

I reconsidered. If this was the situation, I had no choice but to try to figure out his weak spot. I put my short sword back in its scabbard and sat down. Still seated, he slid out of the wall as if someone were pushing from behind.

"Well, well, you're a young one, but you certainly deserve some respect!"

"Who are you?"

"My name is Sanmoto Gorōzaemon. It's not Yamamoto, although it's written with the same characters. It's pronounced San-moto."

"That's not a human name. There's no way you could be a human being. Are you a fox? A *tanuki*?"

"I'm nothing as vulgar as a fox or *tanuki*!"

"If not, then are you a *tengu*? Come on, tell me what you really are!"

"I told you—in Japan, I'm known as Sanmoto Gorōzaemon. Like you said, I'm not a human being, but I'm not a *tengu* either. So what am I then? You'll have to guess. I first came to Japan during the Genpei Wars. I am the same kind of spirit as Shinno Akugorō."[29]

A sarcastic smile formed on his lips as he stared at me. Four *shaku* to the left was a brazier. All by itself, the lid lifted into the air and floated into the next room. Next, pieces of charcoal started dancing from the charcoal bin into the air one after another, gathering and forming a small mound like one might place under a metal teapot. The mound continued to grow until it was the size of human head. Two horns formed on top of that, and in between them, little intermittent puffs of smoke emerged. Then, the places that looked like horns, or perhaps handles, started to shrink and round themselves out until they

---

29. The Genpei Wars, fought between the Taira and Minamoto clans, took place over the course of most of the twelfth century. Little is known about Shinno Akugorō, the other ghost that Sanmoto Gorōzaemon mentions.

became like the little clumps in a *karako* haircut.[30] The steam was rising in big puffs from the two little bumps when boiling water began to overflow from them, flowing onto the tatami mats. The spilled water began to wriggle back and forth, and as I stared at it, I saw it had turned into earthworms. The pot-like thing boiling the water was really a big clump of worms, and now the worms were spilling forth and wriggling across the tatami toward me.

There is nothing in the world that I really dislike—other than earthworms, that is. Earthworms disgust me so much that the mere sight of one makes me feel like I am going to pass out. Just finding one in front of me on a grassy path is enough to stop me dead in my tracks, and I cannot go any further. My worst nightmare was unfolding right in front of me. The earthworms that had boiled out were crawling my way. I recoiled in horror. My heart began to pound, and I felt like I was suffocating. I realized it made no sense for the earthworms to be there. I tried to convince myself everything was all right, but that was no easy task.

They gradually squirmed toward me, crawling onto my lap and working their way up my body to my shoulders. I had to fight not to lose consciousness. I was trying to regain control when the lid to the brazier flew up into the air again and returned to its original place. I didn't see the earthworms crawl back, but suddenly they were gone.

Laughter filled the air. Sanmoto unfolded his fan and fanned himself as he said, "You're quite the tough man, aren't you? But it's because you're so courageous that you've encountered these hardships. This year, you were destined to enter a time in your life of many hardships. That's not just because you're sixteen. Hardship befalls everyone. My job is to frighten people with hardship coming their way and make them feel a little fear. It's nothing personal. Don't blame me!" As he spoke, an enormous, pale, glowing face appeared on the opposite wall. It glared in my direction with protruding eyes that looked

---

30. Here, the narrator likens the lumps to the clumps of hair in the so-called "Chinese child's" (*karako*) style. In Edo-period Japan, parents would sometimes follow the Chinese custom of cutting their children's hair extremely short, leaving only little tufts in the front or on the sides.

like those of a dragonfly. At moments, it began to fade away, but at others, it seemed to grow thicker and more solid.

Sanmoto Gorōzaemon continued, "I first ran into you at Mount Higuma.[31] I followed you and waited for the time when you were destined to encounter hardship, thinking I'd scare you then. Once it came, I tried to frighten you, but you didn't get scared. As a result, I ended up staying, even though I hadn't planned to. In fact, your bravery made me throw all the more effort into my work. However, word got around and people came from elsewhere wanting to find out about me, but they weren't the ones destined to encounter hardship, so I just got rid of them. You see, if someone persists and tries to see me, they are inviting hardship their way. Let me clarify: I do not create hardships for people. Those people seek out hardship on their own accord.

"I must go now. The time has come for me to go down south to Kyūshū. I will be traveling across the islands of Japan, so you should not be troubled by any other strange, ghostly events. Your time of hardship has passed, so Shinno Akugorō should not be coming your way, either."

As he spoke, he took out a mallet. "Here, I'll leave this with you. If any ghosts come to bother you, all you have to do is face north, call out 'Sanmoto Gorōzaemon, come!' and strike a pillar with this mallet. I'll come right away to help you. Thank you for letting me stay so long. I had not meant to spend so much time here!"

He bowed, and I lowered my head in return. Right then, the upper half of a man—from his waist up only—appeared at Sanmoto's side. He was wearing a hat like those worn by nobles in ancient times. I guessed this was a local, tutelary deity, and although he had not been summoned, it was his responsibility to send off Sanmoto.

Sanmoto said, "Come see me off." He stood up, and I followed him onto the veranda. He stepped down into the garden, and gave a slight bow once again. I sat and bowed, but deep within my heart, I was struggling with the desire to cut him down. Even if that desire had won me over, I could not have acted upon it. I could not move. I felt as if large, invisible

---

31. Mount Higuma is located in the city of Miyoshi, in modern Hiroshima prefecture.

hands were holding me down. I wanted to put my hand on my short sword, but my hands were stuck to the veranda as if someone was holding them there.

Finally, I felt the invisible hands loosen their grip, and I stood up. The house and garden were filled with his retinue. There were palanquins and servants carrying spears, long swords, and lacquered traveling boxes at the ends of poles. There were men carrying umbrellas with long handles and lifting palanquins. There were petty servants as well. The palanquins were of the ordinary type, but the figures in the retinue all had outlandish appearances. Their *kamishimo* and *hakama* were of all sorts of styles, and their faces were weird and ghostly.[32] They formed a bizarre entourage as they stood there waiting.

I wondered how on earth Sanmoto, as big as he was, would fit into one of those small palanquins, but as soon as he stuck his foot in, he slipped inside without the slightest trouble. It was almost as if his body collapsed to allow him to go inside. The head of the procession began the march forward, but with each step, the retinue floated higher into the air—although their first step with their left foot was in the garden, the second step with their right landed them on top of the garden wall. The figure stretched to all shapes and sizes—some of the figures stretched out, becoming long and tall like the figures in a *toba-e*, while others were whittled away to an unnatural thinness.[33] They flew in unison into in the air, rather like silhouettes projected by a revolving lantern. I was able to keep track of their dark forms in the starlight for a few moments longer, but then they entered a cloud. And with that, they disappeared completely, just like a sound swept away by the wind.

* * *

THE PART IN the story about going to Mount Higuma refers to a trip Heitarō made on the first day of the seventh month of the second year of Kan'en—about one month before the story begins. It was the middle of the summer. Heitarō and his

---

32. A *hakama* is a pleated pair of loose men's leggings that resembles a skirt in shape.

33. *Toba-e* were humorous cartoons drawn during the Edo period.

neighbor Mitsui Gonpachi were playing "one hundred tales," when they drew lots to see who would climb Mount Higuma.[34] Heitarō got the losing lot, and so he set out to the flat area of Senjōjiki on top the mountain.

The top of the mountain was overgrown with large trees. Not even woodcutters went there to gather wood. In one corner of the flat area was a place known as the "Mound of Lord Miyoshi," an old burial mound said to have belonged to Miyoshi Wakasa. Rumor had it that all you had to do was touch the stone marker and a ghost would come to haunt you. People were afraid even to approach it.

It was dark and raining the evening Heitarō set out. He walked from a ditch by Saikōji, crossed in front of the Ōtoshi Daimyōjin shrine, and climbed up to the flat area on top the mountain. It took him a little while to find the old mound, but he tied up the wooden sign they had there with the name burned into it, and then he went back home again. Gonpachi was there to meet him at the foot of the mountain, but there was no sign of any ghost. They had a good laugh together then went their separate ways.

Since the Sanskrit on the protective talisman from Saikōji was written by the ghost himself, many people came to see it. It remained in good shape for several years, but over time, it grew soiled and smudged from all the wear. The mallet entrusted to Heitarō was kept in Myōeiji Temple, but on the eight day of the sixth month of the second year of Kyōwa (1802), the head of the temple was transferred to another temple, and so the mallet was taken to Kokuzenji in Hiroshima. It was most likely preserved there, but who knows what became of it during the atomic blast that destroyed Hiroshima.... After this story took place, the young Heitarō changed his name to Inō Budayū and lived an incredibly quiet life.

So who or what was Sanmoto Gorōzaemon? I am reminded of the story of Hassan Khan as described in the writings of the

34. "One hundred tales" (*hyaku monogatari*) was a popular pastime in the Edo period. People would gather and tell ghost stories, one after another, saying that after one hundred stories, a ghost would appear. Sometimes the group would start with a number of lit candles but would extinguish one with each story, so that as the stories ended, the room was plunged into darkness. This pastime was especially popular during the summer, since ghost stories bring a chill welcome in warm weather.

Oriental scholars Vincent Smith and John Oman, visitors to Calcutta in the late nineteenth century.[35] The supernatural force this sorcerer was called upon so often was none other than a *djinn*—that class of spiritual beings to which Brahma himself belongs.[36]

---

35. Hassan Khan was a Muslim mystic known for performing miraculous feats of magic in mid-nineteenth-century Kolkata. One description of his powers can be found in John Campbell Oman's book *The Mystics, Ascetics, and Saints of India*. The novelist Tanizaki Jun'ichirō also read Oman's book and, in 1917, published a story called "The Sorcery of Hassan Khan" (Hassan Kan no yōjutsu).

36. Hinduism identifies Brahma the Creator as a *deva*. *Djinns* (or "genies" as they are usually known in English) are a category of spirits described in Arabic literature, but Taruho seems to have conflated *devas* and *djinns*, much like John Campbell Oman himself, who did the same thing in his book describing Hassan Khan.

Through the Wooden Gate

その木戸を通って (Sono kido o tōtte)

Yamamoto Shūgorō (1959)　　　　　　山本周五郎
English translation by Mark Gibeau

One

SEISHIRŌ WAS ABSORBED in the document before him when the assistant from the councilor's office came in and announced that Lord Tahara would like to see Mr. Hiramatsu. Seishirō continued to pore over the accounts, giving no sign that he had heard, so the young samurai walked over to his desk and repeated the message.

"Oh, you mean me?" Seishirō said, looking up. "I thought you said Hiramatsu.... Ah, yes," he said, chagrined, "That would be me, wouldn't it. I see. Tell him I'll be right there."

He continued to the end of the page, set down his brush and went to see Gon'emon Tahara. Head of the middle councilors, Lord Tahara was dictating to his secretary, Matsuyama. He broke off when Seishirō entered and, dismissing the secretary, gestured for him to sit. Seishirō sat.

"You once told me that all your old 'attachments' in Edo had been taken care of, didn't you?" Tahara demanded.

"Yes, that's right."

"And you remember what I said when we started negotiating the betrothal with the Kajima family?"

"Yes, I remember."

"I know your reputation. That's why I made a special point of asking. I asked if you had any lingering relationships with women in Edo. I said you had better be honest about it if there were. Right?"

Seishirō nodded. He paled almost imperceptibly as a vague sense of anxiety and uncertainty stole across his face. But just as suddenly the fear vanished and he nodded decisively with a renewed confidence. "It is precisely as you say. That is correct."

Lord Tahara grimaced, one side of his mouth twisting downward in a movement that exaggerated his already deeply wrinkled skin, making it look as though he were pulling a strange face.

"Then might I ask what your relationship is with the girl who is staying at your house?"

"A girl? At my house?" Seishirō swallowed hard. "But there is no girl at my house."

"Of course there is. I wouldn't ask otherwise."

"It must be a mistake," the words stumbled out of Seishirō's mouth. "As you must know, my work on the audit has kept me confined to the castle for the past three days. I can't say what has happened in the meantime, but up until three days ago...."

"There is a girl at your house." Tahara said quietly, putting the matter to rest. "And what is more, Lord Kajima's daughter has seen her."

Seishirō gaped. "Lady Tomoe?"

"Yesterday," Tahara began, his mouth again twisting into a wry grimace, "Lady Tomoe took it into her head to stop by for a visit. Apparently she thought you were off-duty and she brought you some peonies she had arranged. When Yoshizuka said you were at the castle she told him to bring her a vase and went inside to adjust the flowers before departing. That's when she saw the girl. She asked Yoshizuka about her but apparently he got so nervous he could barely speak. Eventually he stammered out some story about how the girl had come to see you but she wouldn't give her name or say where she was from. Naturally, Yoshizuka claimed that he had never seen her before."

Seishirō gulped audibly and his eyes darted about in his confusion. "It must be some kind of mistake," he said uncertainly. "I don't know any such woman. Once I'm finished at the castle—"

"I have received protests, vehement protests, from the Kajima family." Tahara Gon'emon interrupted. "If you have some kind of relationship with that girl you need to understand that it will mean the end of the betrothal."

"There is nothing, nothing of the sort! It's simply a mistake, of course. Once my work here is finished I'll find out exactly who she is, what she is doing there and why. I'll report back immediately."

"That will be all," Tahara said.

The audit took until the end of the following day. This day and a half seemed to pass with maddening slowness, yet it also felt altogether too short. Seishirō burned to discover the truth, but at the same time, he wanted nothing more than to delay the moment when he would be forced to confront the truth. These two opposing forces battled within him as he worked.

To be sure, I haven't exactly been a model of virtue, he thought. Indeed, if he were to be frank with himself, he might admit to belonging to that segment of society commonly referred to as "playboys."

But I'm not a true *rake. When I misbehave I at least have the decency to recognize the fact, I vow never to do it again. Nobody would believe me, but even when I break with a woman, I'm not cold-hearted or cowardly about it. I do what I can for her, and when we part the break is a clean one.*

Is that really *true? Are you absolutely certain of this? In every single case?* Seishirō sat lost in his thoughts for a moment before answering his own question. *It's true*, he told himself, a decidedly uncertain note creeping into his voice.

But if it's true, why is there a girl at your house? Who is she? What does she want? What does she have to do with you? He could almost hear Tahara Gon'emon's accusations ringing in his ears.

"Mr. Hiramatsu," a young samurai from the finance office had come in. "Are you finished with this volume?"

"Hira—ah, you mean me. That's right, umm," he said, giving his head a shake as though he had just been drowsing. "No, I'm not finished with that one yet, I'll be done soon."

The samurai, whose name was Nogami, asked in a hushed voice, "Is there anything wrong, sir?"

Seishirō gave a quick smile in response.

"Well, I am relieved to hear it," Nogami said. "Lord Murata instructed me to tell you that, once you are finished at the castle, they will be waiting for you at the Umenoi in the Ishigaki district."

It was the custom to hold a banquet each year to celebrate the completion of the annual audit. This was Seishirō's third year as an auditor, and he recalled the previous year's banquet, also held at the Umenoi, where he had garnered high praise for his display of Edo sophistication. This year there was a new Superintendant of Finances, an old man called Murata Rokubei. Murata was famous for his eccentricity, and Seishirō was definitely not in the mood for him today. He turned the invitation down flat.

"What do you mean, 'no'?" Nogami repeated. "Why not?"

"What does it matter?" Seishirō answered, unconsciously raising his voice. "Do I have to explain myself to you now, then?"

Nogami Heima gaped, and muttering vague apologies, fled from the room.

Seishirō was head of the ten auditors, and it was not until five o'clock that everything was finally finished and he was able to make his report to the director of the audit, Assistant Councilor Kōnoshin Sawada. Upon completing his report Seishirō headed straight for his home in Sekibata.

Two

THE SITUATION WAS precisely as Tahara had described: there was a girl at his house. Before meeting with her he called his steward in for an explanation.

"It was a little before noon three days ago," Yoshizuka began. "Uchimura was stationed at the entrance hall, and he came in to tell me that a young lady had arrived. She was asking to meet with the master of the household. It took me quite by surprise."

Each of the three attendants and all the various servants and runners in the house belonged to the castle. Only Yoshizuka Sukejūrō and his wife Mura had accompanied Seishirō from Edo. Seishirō's father, Kageyu Iwai, was chamberlain to the lord of the Shinano *han*. The Yoshizuka family had served the Iwai house for generations, so when it was decided that Seishirō would go back home from Edo, his father selected Yoshizuka to go with him. As they were familiar with Seishirō's habits of old, it was understandable that news of a female visitor should come as a bit of a nasty shock.

"I went out and met her. She was a complete stranger, I had never seen her before. I told her you were engaged with your duties at the castle and wouldn't be back for two or three days," Yoshizuka continued. "I asked if she would like me to pass on a message and asked for her name and so on, but she didn't reply—she just stood there."

The way her hair was arranged and the way she carried herself indicated that she was from a samurai family. Yet her robes were torn and covered in mud, her hair was disheveled, dried mud spattered her hands, feet and face, and she wore common straw sandals.

"Again and again I asked the reason for her visit, her name and so on, but all she would say was that she wished to meet with Lord Hiramatsu Seishirō. Then she started to sway and she collapsed on the spot."

"At the entrance hall?"

"Yes, at the entrance hall." Yoshizuka said.

Yoshizuka had no choice but to carry her to the inner rooms where his wife, Mura, looked after her. Her collapse seemed to be the result of a combination of hunger and exhaustion. They waited for her to recover, made her take a bath and gave her some of Mura's robes to wear. They asked if she would like to eat, and her weak, silent nod was enough to show the pitiful extent of her hunger. Mura suggested they let her rest a while, and once she had recovered a bit, they could try to find out what was going on. Yoshizuka thought this reasonable and left the girl in her care.

"She was very obedient—she followed Mura's every instruction without complaint. After eating she lay down and slept soundly for about four hours. When she awoke, Mura had her wash up and sat her down in front of a mirror. The girl obeyed all of her instructions but attempted nothing on her own. The whole time she was fixing the girl's hair Mura kept plying her with questions."

But aside from "meeting Seishirō," it seemed that the girl remembered nothing. She had no idea where she was from. She couldn't even remember her own name. Naturally she had no idea why she wanted to meet Seishirō either.

"What an odd story. Something about this doesn't smell right," Seishirō said. "Something definitely stinks here. There is something else going on behind the scenes—I'm sure of it."

Yoshizuka Sukejūrō did not speak.

"So...," Seishirō began. "When Lady Tomoe came, she said she saw the girl. Where was she?"

"She was walking in the garden, I believe." Yoshizuka replied. "Given the way things were I couldn't simply chase her away. I thought we might learn something when you returned."

Seishirō held up his hand, cutting him off. "That's fine, that's fine. I don't care about that, but unless we are very careful this whole thing might get out of control."

"In any case," Yoshizuka said, "will you meet with her now?"

Seishirō considered for a moment before nodding. "All right, let's go. Show her into the parlor."

About half an hour after Yoshizuka announced that the girl was ready. Seishirō got up and went to meet her. Before entering the parlor, however, he stepped into an adjoining room and opened one of the sliding doors a fraction of an inch so he could peer inside. He had never seen her before. He was certain now.

Either this is someone's idea of a joke, or it's a trap.

Thinking he would be damned if he fell for that kind of trick, he entered the room with a vague sense of nervous excitement. The girl appeared to be about seventeen or eighteen years old. Her round, plump face was set off by a slightly upturned nose and a small double chin. Her rounded shoulders made her petite frame appear even smaller still. She wore a simple, finely-patterned gray robe tied with a black sash wound tightly about her waist—no doubt borrowed from Mura, he thought. A flattened silver hairpin and a lacquered comb had been set in her hair. The girl sat motionless with eyes downcast as Seishirō observed her.

"I am Hiramatsu Seishirō," he began. "What can I do for you?"

The girl lifted her head to look up at Seishirō. He returned the gaze coldly. Her small eyes clouded over and her lips began to tremble before, hands twisting nervously atop her lap, she let her head sink softly down once more.

"I don't know you," Seishirō said. "Do you know me?"

Without lifting her eyes, the girl shook her head slowly.

"I don't know you and you admit that you don't know me," Seishirō pursued. "So why have come here?"

Three

EYES DOWNCAST AND in little more than a whisper the girl said she didn't know. Seishirō stared hard at her. *Your little charade isn't going to work,* he thought scornfully. *I'm not a simpleton to be deceived by your tricks. You picked the wrong man.* He imagined she would probably burst into tears next. But the girl did not cry.

"I don't understand it myself," she said deliberately. "I don't remember anything other than the name 'Hiramatsu Seishirō'. I don't know where I'm from, I don't know my name and I don't even know why I'm here. I feel as though I'm dreaming or have been possessed by a spirit."

"In that case, there's nothing I can do," Seishirō said coolly. "I'm sorry, but I have a prior engagement that I must attend to. Please excuse me," he said, leaving the room.

Yoshizuka came and asked how the interview went. "I'm not sure," Seishirō replied. "I know that there something going on here, but I can't figure out what it is," he said. "Regardless, it's best not to get involved. Please send her away immediately, and I will go to Tahara." He immediately set off for the Tahara house at Takezaka and met with Gon'emon.

"It is just as I said," Seishirō announced triumphantly. "I've never seen the girl before and she doesn't know me, either. There is absolutely no connection between us whatsoever."

"That's good, if it's true," Tahara looked at him skeptically. "But you say the girl doesn't know you?"

"Yes. She admits as much herself."

"But isn't that odd? What sort of business would a girl you have never met have with a man she doesn't know?"

"That's precisely it. She doesn't know that either."

Seishirō explained the circumstances, and because it was

such an improbable story, Tahara Gon'emon was not easily convinced. Seishirō mentioned his suspicions that it might be a trick or a trap. He was, after all, Iwai Kageyu's third son. Despite having lived in Edo until the age of twenty-five, it was he who had been selected to head the newly reestablished Hiramatsu house. The Hiramatsu house was one of the more highly esteemed in the han. It once received an annual stipend of over nine hundred *koku*[1] and had come with the rank of elder councilor. Even now the restored Hiramatsu house received four hundred and fifty *koku*, or half the old stipend. In terms of rank he was just below elder councilor, and should a vacancy appear among the elder councilors, he would be restored to the old rank.

"And what's more, I am betrothed to the daughter of the Castle Steward. So not everyone thinks kindly of me," he said. "It might be that someone has heard rumors of my behavior in Edo and is trying to disrupt the betrothal."

"Don't be stupid!" Tahara interrupted. "A true samurai could never behave in such a despicable manner. You ought to be ashamed of yourself for even thinking such a thing!"

These provincials will stick together, Seishirō thought.

"I apologize. It was a shameful thing to say. Furthermore, I have ordered the girl to be sent away immediately, and I beg that you will take that into consideration."

"I will make a note of it," Tahara said, nodding.

Tahara Gon'emon was a close friend of his father's from many years back. Thus it was that, on his father's request, Seishirō received the appointment of auditor when he returned from Edo. It was also largely a result of Tahara's efforts that the castle steward, Kajima Daigaku, had been persuaded to accept the match between his daughter and Seishirō. Seishirō was very fond of the Lady Tomoe—so fond, in fact, that he still would have been desperate to marry her even had she been the daughter of an ordinary foot soldier. Seishirō naturally felt a great debt of obligation and gratitude toward middle councilor Tahara, but this latest incident had caused those feelings to harden somewhat. Tahara had acted very coldly during his earlier interview in the castle, and now Tahara had told Seishirō that he "ought to be ashamed of himself."

1.   See note on page 54.

Seishirō felt he had done all he could to be agreeable, and had been slapped in the face for his trouble. He could not help feeling more than a little put out by the whole incident.

"I suppose he thinks everyone from the country is a saint or a sage," he muttered irritably when he was outside. "If it's not someone playing a trick on me then why? If I were in Edo I'd show them a thing or two. But out here in the country, nothing these bumpkins do makes any sense."

Seishirō spat on the ground, and suddenly realised that he was hungry. *All right, off to the Umenoi then. The banquet will just be getting lively now*, he thought. *I'll get good and drunk!* Thus resolved, Seishirō hurried off to the Ishigaki district. Seishirō sang, danced and drank to excess. As though he suspected an enemy of lurking among the party, Seishirō seemed almost defiant as he ran wild and eventually drank himself into a stupor. In the end two of the finance officials had to help carry him home, but Seishirō himself remembered virtually nothing.

It was raining when he awoke the following morning. He had been given the day off in recognition of his hard work over the past several days, and as a result, nobody had come to wake him. He considered taking advantage of this opportunity to doze off again, but as he drank a glass of water to rid himself of the last remnants of the previous night's debauch, he suddenly looked up and his eyes narrowed.

"Of course!" He muttered. "That's what I should've done. Then I would've been able to discover what's really going on." With that he jumped up, and still in his nightclothes, went to his steward's chambers.

Yoshizuka Sukejūrō was drinking a cup of tea.

"What did you do with the girl?" Seishirō asked suddenly. "Did you send her away?"

Yoshizuka set down his cup. "Well, you see," he began slowly, "her robes were torn and needed mending so we couldn't, not yet—"

"Good, good. That's fine," Seishirō said. "It's better this way. I've had an idea. I want you to send her away this evening. Then I'll get to the bottom of all this."

His steward gazed skeptically at him as Seishirō turned and, muttering indistinctly, returned to his bedroom and went back to sleep. He woke a little before midday, ate his noon meal and returned once more to his bed. He was exhausted from the labor of the past five days, but he also wanted to consider carefully what to do next. However, since these problems were easily solved, he drifted off to sleep again and it was a little after three when Yoshizuka woke him. The rain was falling harder now and Yoshizuka wore a glum expression on his face. He told Seishirō that the girl really did not have any place to go and he couldn't bring himself to send her away. If Seishirō would permit it, he said, he and his wife would be happy to look after her for a little while.

"No. That's precisely what they want us to do," Seishirō said, shaking his head. "If we do that Tahara will get suspicious and the betrothal with Lady Kajima will be called off. Don't worry, just do as I say."

Yoshizuka looked at Seishirō, the sour expression on his face making his opinion of Seishirō quite clear, and told him his raincoat and hat were ready.

Seishirō donned his rain gear and the bamboo rain hat, tied up the hems of his robes to keep them out of the mud and went out to stand by an intersection about a block from his home. It was late in the third month, so he was not particularly cold. He carried only the one short sword and he wore the scabbard loosely so that it wouldn't protrude from his cloak. Watching his house from the corners of his eyes, he saw the girl emerge from the gate.

"Good thing it's raining," he muttered. "With it coming down like this she won't keep the charade up for very long. Now, let it begin!"

The girl wore a raincoat and cloth leggings over her straw sandals—no doubt presents from Yoshizuka and his wife. A small bundle was slung diagonally across her back and she held an oiled paper umbrella over her head. She looked around for a moment and then headed straight in Seishirō's direction. Seishirō retreated into the intersection and waited for her to pass by. He let the distance between them grow to about fifty feet before he turned to follow the girl.

She turned left at the main street and passed through the town. Heading straight for the main highway, she picked her way down the paths separating rice paddies. She neither hurried nor stopped. Not once did she turn back to look behind her, nor did she look to the right or the left. She maintained a constant pace and walked straight on, as though drawn by some invisible force. By the time they crossed the Ikura River bridge and passed the Shimada Shinden district, the sky around them had begun to deepen into evening.

"Hey now, what are you up to?" Seishirō muttered to himself. "Are you going to keep up with the act or are you going to meet your confederates?"

The heavy rain, falling continuously since morning, meant there were few travelers on the roads. From time to time a farmer led his horse past, but the girl walked on as though she hadn't seen him and continued down the darkening, rainy path. Seishirō cocked his head as a thought occurred to him. *Has she figured out that I'm following her?* He considered this briefly before dismissing the idea. If she had caught on, he reckoned he would be able to tell by her posture and movements. But if she hadn't realized he was following that might mean she had been telling the truth when she said she didn't remember anything. He scratched absently where the strap of his hat rubbed against his cheek.

"Well, let's not be hasty," he said to himself. "Let's watch a little longer."

Four

ABOUT FOUR MILES from the city and just as they were about to reach the main highway, the girl left the path and went into a small shrine dedicated to the bodhisattva Kannon. Surrounded only by five or six spindly pine trees and what appeared to be memorial markers carved on three small slabs of stone, the shrine was so small that it apparently didn't merit a caretaker. Even so, it would serve to shelter her from the rain. As Seishirō continued past he saw the girl standing under the roof, folding her umbrella. He walked on for another two blocks before turning around and heading back. In order to avoid detection by the girl he crept around from the side to hide behind the shrine, thus sheltering himself under the overhanging roof.

"It sure is coming down," he muttered, shivering. "How much

longer is this rain going to keep up? This is getting ridiculous!"
He had been grateful for the rain earlier, but so far nothing had
happened, and now that it was growing dark the temperature
had also started to drop. He was soaked to the skin now, and
his earlier enthusiasm had begun to fade somewhat. Wondering what the girl was up to, he tiptoed around the corner
of the shrine and made his way toward the front. He removed
his sedge hat, and sticking his head around the corner, peeked
inside. The girl sat atop the veranda, elbows planted atop her
knees and her face buried in her hands. Peering inside he saw
she was shaking and heard a faint cry: "Mother!" Her tear-filled
voice was pitifully weak and echoed with despair.

*Could all this be an act too? Could anyone take a charade this
far?* Seishirō asked himself as a sharp pang of pity shot through
his chest.

"Mother!" The girl sobbed. "Mother!"

Seishirō put on his hat and tied the strap. Just then he heard
men's voices from the road. In the rain and gathering darkness
he saw the figures of two men. They had stopped and were
looking this way. Seishirō quickly slid back behind the shrine
as the two men approached from the road.

Her accomplices? Seishirō thought.

He listened carefully as the men spoke with the girl. They
both sounded drunk, and from the manner of their speech,
he thought that they were probably teamsters or palanquin
bearers.

"What's wrong, miss?" one of them said. "What're you doing
out here at this time of night? Sitting around, all dressed for
traveling.... You waiting for someone, then?

"Huh? What's that?" The other said. "Speak up now, we can't
understand a word you're saying. What's that now?"

Snatches of the conversation made their way back to
Seishirō. He heard things like "Did you run away from home?"
and "It ain't safe out here for a girl all alone," and "We can show
you to a good inn." He couldn't make out anything the girl was
saying but it sounded as though she had succumbed to the
words of the two men, so Seishirō stepped out to the front of
the shrine. The men were covered from head to foot in rain
gear. One was holding the girl's hand and the other was opening her umbrella.

"Hey you, stop! She's with me!" Seishirō called out. "Who the hell are you two?"

The two men jumped. "Don't surprise us like that!" The man holding the umbrella said, stuttering somewhat. "And what's it to you anyway?"

"I am that girl's companion."

"Don't make me laugh," the man holding the girl's hand shouted back at him. "If you're with her, what's she doing here all alone? You come out now, bold as day. I think you're trying to make off with her, aren't you!"

"That's right," the man with the umbrella said. "I bet that's just how it is. Say, miss, do you know that man?"

Her eyes fixed firmly on the ground by her side, the girl shook her head slightly.

"It's me!" Seishirō called out to her. "It's Hiramatsu Seishirō. Don't you remember me?"

"Enough! The lady says she don't know you," the man with the umbrella interrupted. "We're palanquin bearers from the city—I'm Genji and he's Rokusa. We've made a bit of a name for ourselves on the highway, so if you make any trouble you'll pay for it."

"Is that so? Palanquin bearers?" Seishirō said, removing his hat. "In that case you ought to recognize me. I am Hiramatsu Seishirō of Sekihata."

The two men fell silent. Even in the faint glimmer of the twilight they should be able to make out Seishirō's face. The man called Rokusa was the first to react, dropping the girl's hand whispering, "It's Lord Hiramatsu."

"Hey, Genji! This is bad!" Rokusa said in a stricken voice, waving his hand at his partner. "It's Lord Hiramatsu of Sekihata—we've made a terrible mistake!"

"You know him?"

"He is an honored customer," Rokusa said with another frantic wave. Then, facing Seishirō, he dropped to his knees and bent so low that his nose almost touched the ground. "I most humbly apologize, my lord. Dressed as you were, I did not recognize you. Had we known it was you we never would have spoken so rudely. Hey, Genji! Hurry up and apologize!"

"There's no need. It's enough that you recognize me," Seishirō said, nodding. "It would be criminal to force apologies from men who have 'made a name for themselves on the highway'."

"I beg you, please, forgive us," Rokusa said, his hands flat on the ground and his head pressed against them. "You can see how it is—please find it in your heart to forgive us."

"But I wonder," Genji said, still suspicious. "Why did Lord Hiramatsu's companion say she doesn't know him?"

"As for that, I cannot say," Seishirō replied. "There is something of a mystery surrounding this girl and it's too complicated to get into now. But I believe I can prove I am not trying to kidnap her." Seishirō walked over to the girl.

"Why did you say you don't know me?" Seishirō asked. "Did you forget who I am?"

The girl kept her eyes fixed on the ground and did not reply.

"Do you really not know—"

"I," the girl began softly, "I heard that my presence was causing problems for Lord Hiramatsu, so...." She spoke haltingly, in a low, thin voice. Yoshizuka must have told her. He must have said that her being there was complicating the marriage negotiations with the Kajima family. That must have been why she denied knowing him. Seishirō lifted his face and took a deep breath.

"That can wait," he said, his voice shaking with suppressed emotion. "Come back with me, I beg you. Come back." The girl said nothing.

"You should do as the gentleman says," Rokusa told the girl. "It's raining and if you go wandering about like this who knows what could happen!"

Five

A WEEK PASSED, and Seishirō was summoned to Tahara Gon'emon's house. Though the district where Tahara lived was known as "Bamboo Hills" there was, in fact, nothing so steep as to merit the name of a hill. There was only a mildly sloping path of red clay that turned into a muddy quagmire with the slightest rain. Such was the case now, and the path was churned up by the earlier rains. Seishirō arrived at the Tahara household covered in sweat and spattered all over with mud.

Just as he had expected, Tahara Gon'emon wanted to talk to him about the girl. Seishirō explained the situation and added that, since it was what Yoshizuka and his wife wished, he had decided to let them look after her. Tahara listened irritably without comment, staring out at the garden.

"So that's your story?" He asked coldly when Seishirō had finished.

"I have merely related the facts," Seishirō replied.

"Rumors are spreading everywhere. They are even talking about it in Honjuku. How do you plan to explain this to the Kajima family?"

"This is a private matter and, as such, has absolutely nothing to do with the Kajima family. Accordingly I do not see the need to explain or justify my actions," he said. "The girl doesn't know where her home is, where she was going or even her own name."

"So you have said."

"If you had seen her sheltering from the rain in the shrine as night fell," Seishirō continued in a rush, "with no idea where she was going to spend night, weeping with despair, calling out for her mother—I dare say you would have found it impossible to ignore her too."

"The Kajima family has sent protests," Tahara said, still looking out at the garden. "If there really is nothing at all between you and the girl, then why upset such important negotiations on her account? I will say it one last time: you should send the girl away immediately."

Seishirō stiffened, and lifting his chin slightly, said, "I cannot send the girl away."

"You are resolved in this?"

"I don't really understand why, but I can't do it. In any event, I'm the only person she can rely on right now. She has nobody else to turn to."

Tahara Gon'emon sat silently for a moment. "In that case we will break off the betrothal with the Kajima family."

"I don't see how it can be helped," Seishirō said. "If they cannot be persuaded to understand the situation then there is nothing for it. We must each act as we see fit."

"I understand. That will be all."

Seishirō left the Tahara household. He was not entirely

convinced that he had done the right thing. On the one hand, from an outsider's point of view, it probably was not acceptable for him, as one betrothed, to keep a girl of unknown family in his house. But this was not a normal case. There were very special circumstances in this case, and the Kajima family had utterly refused to try to understand those circumstances. They cared only about gossip and their own reputation. It was their behavior and not his, Seishirō thought, that was reprehensible.

"And so what if she is the castle steward's daughter?" Seishirō muttered fiercely. "It would be worse by far to have people say that I only succeeded because of my wife's connections. I'm better off without her." He screwed his face up in a scowl and shook his head hard, as though trying to erase the vivid image of Tomoe, clever and lovely, that rose up before his eyes.

Mura took to calling the girl "Fusa" after her own daughter, who had long since been married off to an Edo family. As her daughter had a very mild disposition and had enjoyed perfect happiness since her marriage, Mura hoped that by giving Fusa her daughter's name, she might gain some of her good fortune as well. Yoshizuka Sukejūrō and his wife also had a son, Kihei. He was married and had already given them one grandchild, but he served as a page in Edo, and this left Sukejūrō and Mura alone in the countryside. Thus they were happy to look after the girl. Mura in particular seemed sensitive to the girl's plight, and in addition to seeing to all of her daily needs, she tried everything she could think of to bring the girl's memory back. She had Fusa examined by one doctor after another and even brought her to Mt. Shino so that she could purify herself by standing under the Kongen Waterfall. But in the end all of her efforts came to nothing.

"You hear about things like people getting spirited away or possessed by a *tengu* demon and so on," Yoshizuka said one day. "I remember, just a few years ago, hearing a story about a man who went from Edo to Kanazawa in just one night. Even he didn't know how it happened. He was just walking along and then before he knew it he was in Kanazawa, some two hundred miles away. When he asked the people what the date was, sure enough, only a single night had passed."

"Mm," Seishirō nodded. "I've heard those stories, too, though there's no way to tell if they are true or not."

"There's another story about a man from Osaka who somehow ended up in Nagasaki. And another of a person who was sitting in a room one moment and went missing the next, and didn't come back for years and years. There are lots of stories like that. Sometimes I think the girl might have met with a similar misfortune."

"I can't believe that those kinds of things really happen, but...I wonder if her accent would give us a hint."

"She seems to speak with an Edo accent," Yoshizuka said, his head tilted to one side in thought. "But most samurai families have picked up some amount of Edo speech. Since her original accent is mixed up with Edo speech, it would be very hard to figure out where she's from by her accent alone."

"Well, then, all we can do is wait for her memory to come back on its own."

"Then again," Yoshizuka said, as though trying to probe his master's feelings. "Her memory might never come back." Seishirō didn't reply.

Seishirō saw Tomoe three times on the street before autumn. Though he had meant for the break to be complete, he retained a strong sense of affection toward her, and so when he nodded to her in greeting, he felt his face flush a bright red. Each of the three times they passed Tomoe looked particularly dazzling in her resplendent gowns, accompanied by servants and ladies-in-waiting. And each time she ignored his greeting and walked by without so much as a glance in his direction. Each time his face flushed deeper still at the insult and embarrassment, and he broke into a sweat.

"Well, now it's done," he told himself after the third meeting. "Yes, now the thing is done. Now I am completely finished with her."

It was around this time that Fusa started looking after him. From Seishirō's point of view, it was certainly nicer to have the younger Fusa taking care of him instead of the older, motherly Mura. Fusa was quick about her tasks and always seemed to know what he liked and disliked. Thinking on this much later, he realized that Yoshizuka and his wife must have taught her his preferences, but at the time she seemed willing to sacrifice almost everything in order to serve him. Seishirō felt himself deeply moved as he realized just how much she relied on him. These feelings, once stirred, grew stronger day by day.

"Lady Fusa must have had a very refined upbringing," Yoshizuka said. "She has a mild disposition, graceful bearing and her calligraphy is truly something to behold. It's quite out of the ordinary."

Six

IT WAS THEN that Seishirō first noticed that everyone in the household, and not just Yoshizuka and his wife, had taken to calling the girl Lady Fusa.

"If only we had some clear proof of her background," Yoshizuka continued, "she could marry into the noblest of families without shame. It seems such a pity."

Seishirō saw through his steward's words and realized what he was getting at.

"So," he said, "You think I should marry Fusa, is that it?"

"I wonder...would that work?" Yoshizuka made a show of pondering the question. "You are of a highly esteemed house and we don't know anything of Fusa's background, so even if you wanted to marry her I doubt the senior vassals would permit it."

"The senior vassals—" Seishirō's eyes flashed, making the contempt and hostility he felt for them perfectly clear. "Hmph," he gave a cold laugh. "You can say we're an esteemed house, but the Hiramatsu house was abolished, and what am I? Just someone who's been adopted into it, that's all. No, I don't think that we are so important that they will make a fuss over who I choose for my bride."

Thus Seishirō's feelings toward Fusa, spurred on by his resentment toward Tahara Gon'emon and Tomoe, started to grow. Of course if he hadn't liked Fusa to begin with that would have been the end of it. There was no telling when she would recall her past and no way of predicting how the situation would change when that happened. It was a bit of a risk for Seishirō to consider someone in such an unstable position as a potential wife. But Seishirō was no coward, and he decided to confront Tahara Gon'emon directly.

Don't let yourself be surprised, and don't lose your composure, he told himself as he marched in, intending on a frontal assault. He told Tahara that they had named the girl "Fusa," and announced defiantly that he intended to take her for his wife and would like the Tahara family to adopt her. He was prepared to be shouted down and have his requests refused even before he formed them. But Tahara did not shout, nor did he seem at all surprised at Seishirō's words. He was silent as Seishirō spoke, and when he was finished, he remained silent. Tahara's face wore a somewhat bewildered expression but nowhere could Seishirō see any hint of anger.

"This will be a little difficult," Tahara said quietly. "We have only just broken off the betrothal with the Kajima family, and in the twelfth month the lord of the domain will be returning. Your father, Lord Kageyu, will be accompanying him, so why don't we wait until then before making any decisions."

Seishirō felt a mild excitement run through him. "Of course. That is fine," he said, "but what do you think of the matter?"

"My opinion?" He said, glaring sternly at Seishirō. "And I suppose you would change your plans based on my opinions?"

Seishirō was at a loss for words. Tahara's reaction had been so different from what he had expected and he had almost seemed friendly towards him. Seishirō was so elated at this turn of events that he forgot himself. *I'm an idiot*, Seishirō thought, taking himself to task. *I sound just like a toady.*

"I misspoke," he said humbly, with a deep bow. "I will wait until my father arrives, as you suggest. Please forget my other words." He left the Tahara house feeling rather pleased with himself.

On the tenth day of the twelfth month the lord of the Shinano *han* returned, and Seishirō's father, the lord chamberlain, was among the retinue that accompanied him. After a long talk between Tahara and his father, it was decided that Seishirō's marriage to Fusa would be formally recognized and that the ceremony would take place in the new year, on the eighth day of the second month. Fusa was adopted into the Tahara house and the go-between would be middle councilor Sawahashi Hachirōbei.

Two days after the ceremony, Kageyu summoned Seishirō and angrily accused him of being the most stubborn and disloyal son he had ever known. It was then that Seishirō learned that the negotiations with the Kajima family had been entirely his father's doing and that Tahara had been nothing more than a messenger.

"You have no idea how useful having relatives in the Kajima family would have been for your future," his father said. "Maybe you think it's shameful to get ahead through your wife's relations, but that kind of naive thinking is going to make the restoration of the Hiramatsu house all that much more difficult!"

Seishirō said nothing. It wasn't his fault that things had come to such a head. He had wanted to marry Tomoe. He considered saying this but there was no point in trying to justify himself. He loved Fusa now and they were officially married, so there was nothing for him to do but to take his scolding quietly.

"I only agreed to let you marry Fusa because Tahara pushed for it so strongly," Kageyu said. "Think about that. You have a lot of work ahead of you if you don't want to become the laughingstock of the family."

Seishirō bowed silently.

Seishirō's life with Fusa was going well, and while his father had quarters in the castle, he would come for a visit once every ten days or so and on rare occasions he would stay the night. However, once every ten days soon became once every seven days and, in the summer, once every five days, then every three days. As the interval between his visits grew shorter and shorter, he also ended up spending the night more and more frequently. Though he never said as much, it was clear that he had taken a liking to Fusa. Whenever he visited, he never allowed her to leave his side. After dinner she poured his drinks as he regaled her with stories, and oftentimes he would be in such high spirits that he would forget even to sleep.

"Father, it is past eleven now," Seishirō said, past endurance. "We have an early day tomorrow, so let's finish for tonight and get some sleep."

"Don't stay up on my account," Kageyu said with a wave of his hand. "You go on ahead to bed. I'm going to drink a little longer, so I'll borrow Fusa."

Fusa was not an especially adept hostess. She was a little too tall, and faint gray shadows remained where her eyebrows had been shaved. Her plump chin stood out from her otherwise unremarkable face. Gentle and sedate, she moved and spoke with an almost sluggish manner. It must have been this quality that Sukejūrō was thinking of when he said she was "graceful." When one became accustomed to it, her languid movements and slow speech had a calming and relaxing effect on the people around her, creating a peaceful and congenial atmosphere. It was this special talent, Seishirō thought, that had captivated everyone in the household starting with Yoshizuka and his wife, then the servants and retainers, and finally his father. The obvious pleasure that shone on his father's face as he drank and talked with Fusa aroused a faint sense of pride in Seishirō, as though he were performing an unexpected act of filial piety.

Toward the end of the tenth month, the lord of the domain's procession departed for Edo, and Seishirō's father along with it. On the day before his departure, he came for a visit, and, thanking Fusa for her hospitality, he presented her with a surprisingly expensive gift. He called Seishirō over and told him to take good care of Fusa.

"She's wasted on a man like you," Kageyu said. "Next time I visit I expect to see a grandchild."

Seven

SEISHIRŌ'S FATHER ALREADY had a grandchild. Kōjirō, his eldest son, already had a three-year-old boy named Tsuruno-suke, so Seishirō interpreted his father's parting admonition more as a sign of his deep affection for Fusa than a demand that she produce a child.

In the eleventh month, Lady Tomoe was married. Her husband was the eldest son of the superintendent of the storehouses, Watanabe Kikuma. Soon after they were married her husband was given the position of middle page in Edo and the two of them left the castle. Not long thereafter, Tahara Gon'emon invited Seishirō and Fusa to his house for the first time, and it was from then that he began regular visits to the Hiramatsu house.

"Since I was responsible for breaking off the betrothal I

thought it best to refrain from visiting until Lady Tomoe was married," Tahara said when he invited them to his home. The relief on his face as he said this was visible, as though a heavy burden had been lifted from his shoulders. Seishirō suddenly recalled what his father had once told him.

"Father said that you recommended the match with Fusa. Is that true?"

"And why does that matter?"

"It's just that...," Seishirō paused, unsure of how to proceed. "Well, I always thought that you were angry with me."

Tahara gave him a faint smile, "If you had been foolish enough to send a girl like Fusa away, well, then I suppose I might've truly gotten angry."

"But surely you didn't know Fusa back then?"

"Ah, it doesn't matter. Go on, drink up," Tahara said.

The question was still bothering Seishirō, and when he got home he asked Yoshizuka and discovered that Tahara had visited and met Fusa when Seishirō was still at the castle. From that first meeting he had been completely taken with her. What is more, Yoshizuka said, from the way Tahara spoke about the match with Lady Tomoe, it seemed that he had been opposed to it from the very start. Tahara let slip that he thought Seishirō could do better than become the son-in-law of the Castle Steward.

Seishirō let out a groan. "So you mean to say that when he yelled at me, it was all an act? What a rotten old man!"

Though he called him a rotten old man, this further evidence of Fusa's popularity made Seishirō feel considerably better, and when Tahara came to visit he did his best to be hospitable.

Shortly after the new year, Mura announced that Fusa was pregnant, and Seishirō was content. But it was then, when he was thinking of how happy the news would make his father, that the first shadows intruded on what had been a perfectly happy life. One night toward the end of the first month he awoke to the sound of his bedchamber door sliding open. Fusa entered, dressed in her bedclothes. Since his wife had never come to his chambers before, he asked if anything was wrong. Fusa seemed not to hear him, however. She walked over to the wardrobe and came to a stop.

"Fusa," he repeated, "Is something wrong?"

Fusa stood rooted to the spot, and he heard her muttering softly to herself.

"You go out here from the bedroom, and this is the hallway...," Fusa gave a limp wave with her hand. Her head was tilted to the side as though she were concentrating, trying to remember something. "The hallway is here, there's a cedar door, and then...."

Seishirō froze. It was as though a cold hand had suddenly run down the length of his spine and he felt his skin prickle. He immediately rose and approached his wife. Fusa was remembering her past, and that "past" might steal her away from him. Thinking that she must not be allowed to remember, Seishirō placed his hand on her shoulder and whispered softly to her.

"Fusa," he said. "Wake up. You're having a dream."

Fusa turned slowly. Her face was transformed. Her visage blank and flat like the surface of a wall, she looked at him with a cold, distant expression—as though he were a complete stranger. Seishirō shuddered and felt his hair stand on end.

"Fusa," he grabbed his wife's shoulder and shook it. "Wake up, Fusa! It's me!"

Fusa's face suddenly relaxed, and he felt her whole body go limp. She leaned heavily against her husband's chest and let out a long sigh, as though relieved.

"What's wrong with me?"

"Look, you're freezing," Seishirō said, rubbing his wife's back. "You mustn't catch cold. Come to bed, we can sleep here together."

"What was I doing?"

"Nothing," Seishirō said as he made her lie down in his own bedding. He held her tightly to his chest and said, "You weren't doing anything. You were just dreaming, that's all."

She nodded in her husband's arms. Moments later he heard the quiet rhythmic sound of her breathing and she was asleep.

It must be the changes happening in her body. She's pregnant, and that's making her body react strangely, Seishirō thought. Nevertheless, he was unable to forget the events of that night. There was no question that she had been recalling her past. "Go out of the bedroom here, a cedar door in the hallway there." Fusa standing there, her head tilted to one side.

She had certainly been remembering the layout of the her previous house. And the way her face had transformed, her eyes cold as though she were looking at a stranger—she had been in her past. Of course Seishirō tried to dismiss this notion, but try though he might the sense of certainty remained.

"It will happen again," he muttered to himself. "And next time it might come back more clearly. She might remember everything."

For a while he was unable to escape these thoughts, whether at home or working in the castle. He often woke up in the middle of the night, and tiptoeing over to Fusa's chambers, he would peek inside to check on her. This continued for a whole month before he finally resolved to stop worrying about it.

"What does it matter?" He asked himself. "No matter what she remembers, we're already married and she's pregnant. Whatever she remembers now, what's done is done, and nothing can destroy our life together."

No matter what happens or who appears, I'll never give her up, he thought, puffing out his chest as though trying to reassure himself.

But nothing happened. Fusa did lose some weight in the summer heat, but by the autumn she had recovered completely. In the middle of the tenth month she gave birth to a baby girl. The baby was healthy and the mother was fine.

"But," Fusa said shyly, "your father will surely be disappointed when he learns that it is a girl."

Seishirō dismissed the notion with a shake of his head, and explained that his father already had one grandson in Edo. "He will probably be even happier to hear that it's a girl," he said.

They initially intended to wait until Seishirō's father returned to the provinces before informing him of the birth, but they learned that his master, the lord of Shinano, had been given the post of Magistrate of Temples and Shrines. As a result, his father would not be able to return that year, so they sent a belated letter with word of the birth half a month after the event.

Eight

THEY NAMED THE girl "Yuka" after Seishirō's mother.

"Such a pretty name," Fusa said happily, rubbing her nose against the baby's cheek as she lay in her bed. "Miss Yuka. Cute, pretty Miss Yuka. You must grow up nice and healthy!"

Seishirō gazed down at mother and child and felt his eyes swim with tears.

The days that followed passed peacefully. Fusa's convalescence was proceeding well, and she was producing more than enough milk for the baby. In the third month of the following year Yuka came down with the measles, but she came through the crisis unharmed. He received letter after letter from his father in Edo demanding to know how Yuka was doing, and his mother sent Fusa letter after letter filled with advice on how to raise a child. Tahara Gon'emon was a frequent visitor, and as he had no grandchildren of his own, he loved nothing more than walking around the garden, holding Yuka somewhat precariously in his arms.

On the fifteenth of the eighth month, Seishirō, Fusa and Yuka held a small moon-viewing party just for themselves. They spread a carpet in the garden and laid out the various moon-viewing decorations and accoutrements, along with trays of saké and delicacies. They placed small lanterns on either side and burned incense to keep the mosquitoes away. Both Seishirō and Fusa relaxed in their light summer robes. Yuka had only just begun to speak and was thoroughly enjoying the novelty of eating outdoors. She bounded from one lap to the other in high spirits, but when they stopped her from eating the decorative dumplings she burst into tears. Seishirō tried to placate her by saying they would make them tomorrow, but Yuka only sniffed at that, and with her nose high in the air, pronounced that, "Daydy is *antypantyful.*"

"What does 'antypantyful' mean?" he asked Fusa.

"I don't know," she replied with a gentle smile. "I imagine it's something Lord Tahara taught her, though I haven't any idea what it means."

Old people, Seishirō reflected, delighted in teaching children silly words without a thought for the trouble it caused. But he did not voice these thoughts.

The gardens at the Hiramatsu house were very large. In front of them stood a hillock of pine trees which, if climbed, afforded a clear view of the castle beyond. Cypress trees were planted here and there across the acre or so of lawn. Off to the right there was a grove of plum trees, and beyond that a wooden wall. The moon emerged from the leftmost edge of the pine trees, but since the night was cloudy, it was hidden almost as soon as it appeared. Yet even so the vivid contrast between the milky blue light of the clouds and the black of the pine trees provided a dramatic spectacle. As the moon rose, Yuka began to grow restless, and Fusa went inside to put her to bed.

Seishirō sat on the carpet, drinking, when he noticed that the chirping insects had suddenly fallen silent. Looking around, he saw that Fusa had returned. She held a saké bottle in her right hand and approached with her usual languid gait, but suddenly, just as she had reached Seishirō, she stopped. The moon slipped out from behind the clouds and her face was bathed in its light. Seishirō almost dropped his cup: it was the same face as before.

Her face had frozen, transformed. Eyes opened wide, she stared hard at a distant spot in the garden, as though she were looking for something. Seishirō watched silently. He could hear the blood pounding in his ears and his breath came in gasps. She started to walk. One step at a time, as though carefully picking out a path, Fusa headed toward the plum trees. Seishirō rose, and without troubling to put on his shoes, followed after her. She stopped after about twenty paces.

"This is the bamboo path," Fusa muttered. "And beyond that there is a wooden gate—"

"Yes, keep going," Seishirō whispered. "What's beyond the gate? What's outside?" Fusa stood rooted to the spot, her lips pressed tightly together.

"Fusa," he said in a low whisper, laying a hand gently on her shoulder. "Think now. Is that your house? Is it your garden? Where do you go when you pass through the wooden gate?"

Fusa stumbled and dropped the saké bottle she had been carrying. Seishirō caught her and supported her with both hands. She looked up at her husband in surprise and straightened.

"What's come over me?" Her face had returned to its natural expression, her eyes focused once more.

"You were trying to remember your past," he said. "Just stand there and close your eyes and listen. I'll describe it to you."

"No," Fusa shook her head. "I am happy with the way things are. I don't want to remember the past."

"But one day it will come back," Seishirō said gently. "This has already happened, though you don't remember it. And it will probably happen again. If your memory is going to come back, the sooner it happens the better. Now, go ahead and close your eyes."

Fusa closed her eyes.

"Just now," he said, lowering his voice to a whisper. "Just now you were walking down a bamboo path. You had been walking in the garden, I suppose. This is the bamboo path and beyond it there's a wooden gate."

Fusa held her breath, her eyelids pressed shut.

"You walk down the path and arrive at the wooden gate," Seishirō continued quietly. "You go through the gate. Now, what do you see on the other side of the gate?"

Seishirō waited, not daring even to breathe. Fusa stood silently for a moment and then shook her head.

"It's no good—I can't remember anything," she said, opening her eyes. "Did I actually say all of that?"

"You did."

"I don't remember any of it," she said with another shake of her head. "I can't even remember saying it."

"How do you feel? Do you feel ill?"

"No."

"Well, that's good, then," Seishirō patted his wife's shoulder gently. "Shall we look at the moon a little while longer? Oh, and you dropped the saké bottle, over there." Half-disappointed and half-relieved, Seishirō returned to the carpet.

Once again Seishirō's furtive monitoring of his wife's behavior drove him to a state of nervous exhaustion. Yet the year drew to a close without any further unusual occurrences.

Nine

IN THE THIRD month the annual settling of accounts began again, and Seishirō's presence was required at the castle for the last five days of the audit. A little before noon on the third day he was told that his steward had come to see him. Normally, all personal business was strictly prohibited during the final days of the audit, but Yoshizuka, claiming that it was an urgent matter, had received special permission. Thinking that perhaps Yuka had fallen ill, Seishirō hurried off to find Yoshizuka, his face pale and drawn, standing outside the west gate.

It's Fusa, Seishirō thought automatically. The strained expression on his steward's face was enough to tell him that something had happened to his wife. Yoshizuka stared miserably at the ground as he confirmed Seishirō's suspicions.

"What is it? Is she sick?"

"We can't find her," Yoshizuka said. "Last night she was out in the garden with Miss Yuka, and then it seems she just disappeared. We've searched everywhere for her but we haven't been able to find her."

So, Seishirō thought, *It's happened at last*. His first thought was that the event he had been expecting for so long had finally taken place.

"Wait here," he told Yoshizuka.

Seishirō went to the councilor's office and asked to speak with Tahara Gon'emon. The news came as a terrible shock to Tahara, and for several moments he seemed incapable of speech. When he recovered, however, he told Seishirō that he would take care of it, and Seishirō was refused permission to leave the castle. Seishirō informed Yoshizuka of this and then returned to his work. The audit itself was not terribly complicated. It was simply a matter of comparing the books with the results of the inspections, yet even so, it served to keep his mind busy. Since Seishirō was too frightened to even consider what might have happened to his wife, he forced himself to concentrate on the job in front of him.

They'll let me know if they find her, Seishirō thought. But the audit ended and still no word had come from Tahara. Seishirō declined the invitation to the customary banquet in Ishigaki and went straight home.

They still hadn't found Fusa. Yuka, about whom he had been so worried, was fast asleep. She had been playing with Mura and the servants, and she hadn't even noticed that her mother was missing. Yoshizuka told him that, on the evening in question, Fusa had been playing with Yuka in the garden when Mura heard Yuka crying. When Mura went outside to see what was wrong, she found Yuka all alone. She asked Yuka where her mother had gone and Yuka pointed to the plum trees and said, "There." Mura walked all around the plum trees, but Fusa was gone. They searched the entire house and the grounds but the sun started to go down and they still hadn't found her. So they divided up, with Yoshizuka heading out for the main highway and the retainers starting up the mountain road.

The retainers inquired at the border checkpoint on the mountain road, but nobody matching Fusa's description had been seen. They searched the city and all its outlying districts. They checked with all of the stables and palanquin bearers and tried all of the inns. But there was so much traffic on the streets that it was impossible for anyone to be certain about anything.

Yoshizuka called on the local authorities, and between them they searched the highway for twenty-five miles in each direction, but they found no trace of Fusa. Tahara Gon'emon, it seemed, had arranged for an even wider-ranging search. But since Fusa had no money and since a woman's legs could only go so fast, it was unlikely that she could have gotten far. If they hadn't found her after three days of searching, there seemed little hope of finding her now, Yoshizuka said.

"There is one thing, however, that I haven't told you," Yoshizuka said after he finished his story.

Seishirō looked at the steward.

"The first time we met Lady Fusa, she hadn't really come to see you," he continued. "I had gone out and was just returning when I saw her just standing there outside the gate. She asked me who lived here, and I replied that it was Lord Hiramatsu Seishirō's residence. I asked her who she was looking for, and she stood there for a moment thinking, and then, probably because she had just heard the name, she said that she was looking for Lord Hiramatsu Seishirō."

She having lost her memory entirely, the first name she heard would no doubt leave a deep impression. She probably convinced herself that this name was the person she had been looking for. Seishirō turned away.

"Enough. I understand."

So had she remembered who she really intended to visit and gone to meeet them? He considered that for a second but then shook his head. *No*, he thought. *After living four years as husband and wife? With a three-year-old child? Impossible. She would never leave so abruptly, without so much as a note, just because her memory had returned. Fusa could never be so heartless.*

"Where's Yuka?"

"I believe she's in our chambers."

"Leave me now," Seishirō said.

When Yoshizuka had left, Seishirō stood up. Distracted, he kept his arms folded and his eyes closed.

"You left the same way you came, Fusa," he whispered. "Where are you now? What are you doing?"

He recalled Fusa as she had looked on that rainy night, sitting under the shrine, so desperate. His face twisted painfully and his chest heaved as a sob rose up in his throat, and he wept. Even as he walked out onto the veranda, he wept. Still weeping, he put on his sandals and stepped down into the garden. Seishirō stood at the edge of the lawn, and wiping his face, gazed down at the grove of plum trees.

"The bamboo path, and over there is the wooden gate...."

Yuka said she had gone over there. Had Fusa passed through the wooden gate? He thought he could almost see his wife standing there, next to the gate he knew did not exist. But she'll come back, he thought. This time she has a husband. She has Yuka. Of course she'll remember. She'll come back one day, through the wooden gate. Seishirō reached out with both arms.

"We're waiting for you. Come home, Fusa," Seishirō whispered to his wife. "We'll keep waiting till you return."

Behind him, he heard Yuka singing merrily.

其ノ四十四 ✤ 其ノ四十五 ✤ 其ノ四十六 ✤ 闇夜の怪三話

Three Eerie Tales of Dark Nights

by Sugiura Hinako
translated by Dan Luffey

①

②

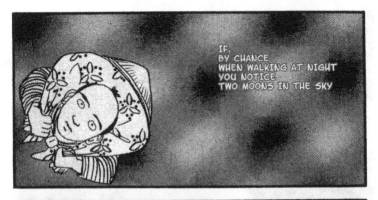

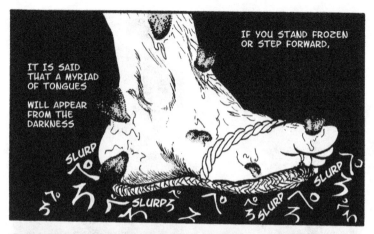

②　①

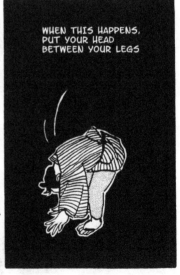

IF YOU DO NOTHING
THEY WILL GRADUALLY
BECOME HEAVIER

UNTIL YOU
ARE UNABLE
TO MOVE,
AND WILL BE
PULLED DOWN
TO THE
GROUND.

①

②

Jeffrey Angles
("The Inō Residence, Or,
The Competition with a Ghost")

JEFFREY ANGLES IS an associate professor at Western Michigan University, where he teaches Japanese literature and translation studies and directs the Japanese language program. He is the author of *Writing the Love of Boys: Desire between Men in Early Twentieth-Century Japanese Literature* (University of Minnesota Press, forthcoming), and the translator of three volumes of poetry by Tada Chimako, Itō Hiromi, and Arai Takako. He has won grants from the National Endowment for the Arts and the PEN Translation Fund to support his translation projects. When not residing in Japan, he lives in a house in Kalamazoo with an overgrown garden.

Stephen A. Carter
("The Futon Room")

US-BORN STEPHEN CARTER is a long-time resident of Nagoya, Japan, where he lives with his wife and a large friendly spider, finds it fascinating how the new Japan is replacing the old, and doesn't drink nearly as much beer as he'd like.

Dorothy Gambrell

DOROTHY GAMBRELL, WHO localized Three Eerie Tales of Dark Nights, has neither a career nor hobbies. She has spent the last ten years self-publishing cartoons at catandgirl.com.

Mark Gibeau
("Through the Wooden Gate")

I AM A lecturer in Japanese language, literature and culture at The Australian National University in... Australia. My interest in Japanese literature was first sparked by the Abe Kōbō story "The Magic Chalk" in Van Gessel's wonderful anthology of short stories, *The Shōwa Anthology*—an interest that (much to my own surprise) ultimately led me to graduate school and a Ph.D. dissertation on Abe Kōbō. In addition to teaching, trying to improve my literary translation and slowly converting my dissertation into a book. I am interested in Okinawan literature and the work of Medoruma Shun in particular.

Higashi Masao 東雅夫
("Introduction: The Origins of Japanese Weird Fiction")

HIGASHI MASAO IS a noted anthologist, literary critic, and the editor of Japan's first magazine specializing in *kaidan* (strange tales) fiction, named *Yoo* (幽).

In 1982 he founded Japan's only magazine for research into strange and uncanny literature, *Fantastic Literature Magazine* (幻想文学, Gensō bungaku), published by Atelier Octa, serving as editor for twenty-one years until the magazine folded in 2003. It was an invaluable publication not only for its content, but also because it discovered and nurtured a host of new authors, researchers and critics in the field.

Recently he has concentrated on compiling anthologies, producing criticism of fantastic and horror literature, and researching the *kaidan* genre, active in a wide range of projects. As a critic he has suggested new styles and interpretations in the field, including the growing "Horror Japanesque" movement and the "palm-of-the-hand *kaidan*" consisting of uncanny stories told in no more than eight hundred characters. He is well-known as a researcher of the uniquely Japanese *hyaku monogatari* tradition, with numerous books and anthologies published.

He serves on the selections committees for various literary prizes in the kaidan genre, and since 2004 has written the Genyō (幻妖) book blog on uncanny and fantastic literature cooperatively with online bookseller bk1, at http://blog.bk1.jp/genyo/

Pamela Ikegami
("The Chrysanthemum Pledge")

PAMELA IKEGAMI, A native of Portsmouth, NH, teaches Japanese language and culture at the University of New Hampshire. She has a BA in Japanese and Asian Studies from the University of Colorado Boulder and an MA in Japanese from the University of Hawai'i at Manoa. She has also worked as a freelance translator since 1990. She loves to read scary Japanese stories, but can't bear to watch Japanese horror films.

Edward Lipsett
("The Face in the Hearth")

I HAVE BEEN in Japan now longer than I lived in America, where I was born. When I went back to the US a few years ago, I was dismayed to discover that the nation I grew up in is no longer there—I was as foreign as any native-born Japanese. I don't feel any different on the inside, though, and that's why translation is so interesting to me: I want to find ways of expressing the way things look from the other side to people who've only experienced a single culture. I spend most of my time translating technical documentation, wishing I could speak another language or two (probably Chinese and Korean, in that order) and wondering when I'll have time to read a good book next...

Dan Luffey
("Three Eerie Tales of Dark Nights")

DAN LUFFEY WAS born on May 27, 1987, in Pittsburgh, PA. He studied Japanese literature and translation under Professor Luke Roberts at UC Santa Barbara, and just recently finished his final year of undergraduate studies at Kyoto University. Dan is now working on a translation of Shiba Ryōtarō's *Moe Yo Ken* while preparing for graduate school and working hard to hone his skills as both a translator and an author.

Miri Nakamura
("Introduction")

MIRI NAKAMURA IS Assistant Professor of Japanese Literature and Language at Wesleyan University. She specializes
in Japanese fantastic fiction, and she is currently working on
a book on the rise of the uncanny in modern Japan. She has
translated several academic works, which can be found in *Ro-
bot Ghosts and Wired Dreams* (University of Minnesota Press,
2007) and *Pacific Rim Modernisms* (University of Toronto
Press, 2009).

Rossa O'Muireartaigh
("Three Old Tales of Terror")

ROSSA O'MUIREARTAIGH IS a freelance Japanese to English
translator. He has previously studied Asian philosophy at
Nagoya University in Japan. He has also lectured in Japanese
studies at Dublin City University, Ireland and in Japanese
translation at Newcastle University in England. He has written
various academic papers on translation, drama, and religious
studies. Married with one adorable daughter, he is currently
enjoying a change of scenery residing in Malta.

Nancy H. Ross
("Here Lies a Flute")

NANCY H. ROSS worked as a reporter and editor before coming to Japan in 1993. She was the winner of the Distinguished
Translation Award in the 4th Shizuoka International Translation Competition in 2003 and the 2008 Kurodahan Press
Translation Prize. Her other translations include *Mind Over
Muscle* and *A Bilingual Guide to the World Economy* for Kodansha International. She lives in Hiroshima prefecture with
her cat Koharu.

Ginny Tapley Takemori
("The Pointer")

GINNY TAPLEY TAKEMORI started out translating Spanish and Catalan, and went on to work as a literary agent specializing in foreign rights (with Ute Körner in Barcelona) and as an editor with Kodansha International in Tokyo, before returning to translation, this time from Japanese. She holds a BA (Hons) in Japanese from SOAS (London University) and is currently studying for an MA with the University of Sheffield. Now based in Tsukuba, Japan, she has long enjoyed roaming other worlds, and hopes to similarly touch the hearts and minds of readers with her own translations of fiction and nonfiction.

Robert Weinberg
("Preface: An Ordinary World, Interrupted")

ROBERT WEINBERG IS the author of sixteen novels, two short story collections, and sixteen non-fiction books. He has also edited over 150 anthologies. He is best known for his trilogy, the *Masquerade of the Red Death*, and his non-fiction book, *Horror of the Twentieth Century*. Bob is a two-time winner of the Bram Stoker Award; a two-time winner of the World Fantasy Award; and a winner of the Lifetime Achievement Award from the Horror Writers Association. www.robertweinberg. net

Colophon

About the cover: Minamoto no Yorimitsu Striking at the Ground Spider
Print by Yoshitoshi Tsukioka, courtesy of the John Stevenson Collection

> Court nobleman Minamoto no Yorimitsu (948–1021) and his faithful companion Watanabe no Tsuna are credited with ridding Kyoto of unusually numerous demons during the tenth century.

Yorimitsu, suffering from fever, imagined himself attacked by demons. Watanabe and his other chief retainers watched over his bedside, but fell asleep. The Spider Demon entered and began to bind Yorimitsu with a rope, and though weak with fever he summoned enough strength to draw his sword and strike it, causing it to flee. His retainers awoke and followed a trail of blood to a mound north of Kyoto, finding a huge spider which Watanabe killed. Yorimitsu recovered immediately.

Yoshitoshi Tsukioka (芳年月岡), aka Yoshitoshi Taiso (芳年大蘇) (1839-1892), is generally recognized as the last master of ukiyo-e woodblock printing, as well as one of its great innovators. His career spanned the Meiji Restoration, covering from the feudal era to modernizing Japan, and while Yoshitoshi was interested in new ideas from the West he was concerned with the erosion of traditional Japanese culture, including traditional woodblock printing.

His life is perhaps best summed up by John Stevenson, in his book *Yoshitoshi's One Hundred Aspects of the Moon* (Hotei Publishing, 2001):

Yoshitoshi's courage, vision and force of character gave uki-yo-e another generation of life, and illuminated it with one last burst of glory.

The cover is from his *New Forms of Thirty-Six Ghosts* (1889–1892), a series of 36 prints now recognized as one of his greatest achievements, together with the one hundred prints in his masterpiece, the *One Hundred Aspects of the Moon* (1885–1892) series.